Samuel Parris: The town minister whose desire to expose the sins of others hides his own guilty conscience. . . .

Israel Porter: One of the town's leading merchants, whose opposition to Samuel Parris will cost him and his family dearly. . . .

Goody (Goodwife) Putnam: Wife to Joseph, mother to Annie, the stillborn infant who would have been her son is a spark to the madness that engulfs Salem. . . .

Joseph Putnam: He hired Samuel Parris despite the overwhelming objections of his neighbors. When his half-brother's marriage threatens to ruin Joseph and his family, he strikes back fearlessly—and without mercy. . . .

Annie Putnam: Eleven-year-old daughter of Joseph and Ann, she is one of the first children to fall into hysterics—and accuse her elders of witchcraft. . . .

William Stoughton: Appointed to oversee the Witch Trials by the governor, his stern and unceasing brand of Puritanism ensured judgment would be swift and merciless. . . .

SALEM WITCH TRIALS

SALEM WITCH TRIALS

KATHRYN WESLEY

POCKET BOOKS

New York London Toronto Sydney Singapore

An *Original* Publication of POCKET BOOKS

 POCKET BOOKS, a division of Simon & Schuster, Inc.
1230 Avenue of the Americas, New York, NY 10020

ISBN: 0-7434-3143-X

First Pocket Books printing February 2003

10 9 8 7 6 5 4 3 2 1

POCKET and colophon are registered trademarks of
Simon & Schuster, Inc.

For information regarding special discounts for bulk purchases,
please contact Simon & Schuster Special Sales at 1-800-456-6798
or business@simonandschuster.com

Printed in the U.S.A.

SALEM WITCH TRIALS

⊙ONE

She had worn shackles before, but never like this. Never before had she felt such hatred.

And fear.

Tituba Indian slogged through the March slush, her hands bound, her legs in irons. Her body ached from the beatings she'd had. The air was frigid and smelled of unwashed bodies. People crowded around her, all of them familiar, people she had spoken to, hesitantly—a slave never spoke without permission—but who had always been cordial to her.

It seemed as if the entire village was here, but she knew that wasn't true. So many were inside the meeting hall, just up the rise. She didn't look at the men—they would give her no sympathy; they had barely known that she existed before all of this began—but

1

the women: the women knew her, worked beside her in the Parris's house.

She scanned the faces, but they were contorted beneath their white hoods. Their eyes were filled with loathing. The last time she had been in chains—in Barbados—she had been dragged through a crowd, but then, people had looked at her with interest. She had been a commodity then, something to be purchased.

Now she was something to be hated.

Two constables—rude, rough men—dragged her up the rise toward the meeting house. Its white-washed walls seemed more imposing than usual, and no smoke came from its small chimney. Its windows were dark. From inside, she could hear moans and wails, familiar voices carried on the wind.

And then, a whisper from beside her.

"Witch!"

She turned and saw Goodwife Glover, looking surprised at her own words. They had always gotten along. They were close to each other in age, and even though Tituba was a servant, Goody Glover had been kind to her.

"Goody Glover," Tituba said, knowing that her bruised and bloodied face might be unrecognizable, "it is me. Tituba."

One of the constables shoved her forward, and she stumbled in the mud. She wasn't supposed to talk to anyone or look at anyone. They were all afraid of the evil eye.

"Witch," Goody Glover said, her voice gaining intensity. "You signed the Devil's book."

How could Goody Glover believe that? She knew who Tituba was as well as anyone in this horrible village. Tituba hadn't asked to come here; she had been dragged along with the Parris family, to this cold and unforgiving place.

And now they were accusing her of terrible things.

As the constables pushed her forward the crowd parted, afraid to brush against her. That was not new; they'd always been afraid to touch her. She looked different, had an accent they'd never heard, had an unusual name. She'd seen things most of these people couldn't even imagine.

Most of them probably didn't know how it felt to be in chains.

Goody Glover kept pace with her.

"Witch!" she said. "Hell waits for you."

The last of the crowd parted, revealing the faded wood steps that led to the meeting house doors. The constables shoved her forward, and Tituba stumbled again, uncertain how she would get up those steps with her feet so tightly bound.

"Confess, witch!" Goody Glover said.

Tituba turned toward her. Surely there was something she could say to Goody Glover, something she could do to convince her that she really was innocent. All she had done was help her girls. That was all she had ever done.

Tituba started to speak, but at that moment the doors to the meeting house banged open. The moans and wails intensified, as if ghosts and beasties haunted the place. But Tituba knew better. She rec-

ognized those voices, knew what those cries were—
and they terrified her.

The constables yanked her forward, half dragging,
half carrying her up the stairs.

"Confess!" Goody Glover shouted behind her.

But Tituba could barely hear Goody Glover now.
Instead, her attention was on the building before
her—the wailing, the moaning, the cries of pain and
horror from within.

She didn't want to go in there. She had no idea
what awaited her, but she knew it couldn't be good.
She would have struggled, but she had learned long
ago that struggling while she was chained meant
nothing. No one would help her.

She was alone.

The constables gripped her arms tightly as they
dragged her toward the open doors and the darkness
beyond.

Samuel Parris had never seen his church in such disarray.

He sat near the communion table, his beautiful
daughter Betty prostrate on the floor, four other girls
beside her. All five were moaning, tearing their hair,
wailing and screaming. The congregation, the
Putnams and the Proctors in their pews near the
front, watched with rapt attention, as if this were a
show put on for their benefit.

But this was no show. Parris felt the tension in
the muscles of his back and his shoulders. He
couldn't even look at Betty or the other girls, so dis-

torted were they by the touch of evil all around them.

Tituba, a woman he had brought into his own home, stood across from him, shackles binding her wrists and feet. She looked strange in her plain clothing. The long skirt with its shapeless bodice had never suited her. She always looked as if she was dressed in someone else's clothes.

Her eyes were wide with fear, but he did not know whether she feared him, his God, or the children who were revealing her wickedness. When his gaze met hers, she turned her pleading face toward his.

"I am innocent!" Tituba shouted. "You must believe—"

Screaming drowned out her voice. The five girls had fallen into fits. They were slapping themselves, clutching their arms, and crying out. He couldn't tell who was shouting—Annie Putnam, Mercy Lewis, or his own precious Betty—but someone was.

"Biting! Biting! Stop the biting!"

And May Walcott—or was it Abigail Williams?—shouted, "'Tis the witch here!"

The entire congregation looked at Tituba, and she cringed.

"Shall you deny your own eyes?" Parris shouted, pointing at the girls. "Why are you hurting them?"

Tituba shook her head. "I do not hurt them."

How could she deny her actions, Parris thought, *when they were so plain?* She was using some kind of magic—some kind of conjuring, just as she had used it in his own home—to harm these poor girls.

"They are suffering," Parris said. "Look at them!"

Tituba closed her eyes.

"Look!" he shouted.

She turned and stared at them. For a moment, he thought he saw horror and confusion in her face. Did she not know her own power, then? Had the Devil taken her so strongly that she was unaware of what she did?

Perhaps, but Parris was not. The moment Tituba's gaze brushed the girls, their wails increased. Their fits grew worse, and they all shouted at once.

"Biting! Biting!"

"No! No!"

"Stop!"

" 'Tis the witch biting us!"

"Help us!"

Behind the girls he could see his congregation. He loathed the fascination on some faces, and he wanted to comfort some of the others. Toward the back, a woman bowed her head as if she couldn't bear to watch any more.

Tituba stopped looking at the girls and turned to him. He felt the weight of her strange eyes. Her lips were trembling, and if he had not known better, he would have thought she was terrified.

"I . . . I . . . I . . ." She spoke as if she had forgotten her English. And finally the word emerged. "Innocent."

She was not innocent. The girls, those five afflicted children—they were innocent.

Parris slapped his palms on the wooden tabletop

and stood. He would get her to confess. Maybe then this would end.

"Tibuta Indian," he said, putting all of his fury into his words. "Are you a witch?"

She froze in place, and he could see the confession in her eyes. He pointed at her. "Answer!"

And as he yelled, the girls screamed with him.

"She is!"

"My flesh! My flesh!"

He saw them out of the corner of his eye, their strange fits increasing. They scrambled to get away from the invisible demons that tormented them.

He could see Betty, his sweet nine-year-old Betty—

And he made himself look away, toward Tituba and her evil.

"The Lord Almighty shall strike you!" Parris shouted at Tituba.

She ducked as if his words had hurt her. He took a step closer to her and shouted, "Answer!"

She brought an arm over her head, protecting it. "Do not strike—"

"Are you a witch?" Parris demanded, towering over her, the girls banging against the wooden floor, their cries mingling with his.

"Yes!" Tituba finally shouted. "I am a witch."

He let out a breath. At last—the words he had been waiting for. Beside him, the congregation cried out in shock and fear. Some even recoiled. And the girls screamed even more. He had thought they might stop once someone confessed.

Tituba was gasping for air. She was still cowering before him, her evil plain now for all to see.

"You are a witch?" Parris asked. "Satan speaks to you?"

She seemed to cower even more. "Yes."

The crowd was shouting too, but he couldn't make out the words. Through the din, though, he could still hear the voice of his child, his Betty, moaning in pain.

"Is he speaking to you now?" Parris yelled, making his voice powerful. "In this very meeting house?"

Tituba looked terrifed, as if the Almighty might smite her where she stood. "Yes."

The women in the congregation screamed, and some of the men cried out in shock. Parris could feel their fear. It mirrored his own. He had never before faced such horrors as this.

The Devil was here, in his meeting house, where every Sabbath he led the villagers in prayer to God.

He could feel the evil presence. It seemed to dog him—and why not. Tituba had been in his house, afflicting his children.

"And what doth Satan say?" he asked.

Tituba froze, then raised her head. For a moment she seemed confused. Was she just listening to a voice he could not hear? Then she cast her evil eye on the children.

Their screams continued unabated. She was inflicting pain on them without touching them, doing the Devil's work.

She shook her head as if she could not stand what she saw.

8

Parris could not stand what he saw. She was lying to them. Lying to them all about her innocence. He could feel her confession slipping away—and confession, the Lord said, was good for the soul. It would be good for the village, good for the girls. It would save them all.

"Answer!" he cried, making his voice boom over the incredible noise in the meeting house. "What does the Devil instruct you? Tell me. The Lord Almighty shall strike you."

Tituba ducked away from him. His hand was upraised, as if he were going to strike her for his Lord.

"He tells me to hurt them!" she said. "To hurt the children!"

Parris felt his heart twist. Betty still writhed, something unseen torturing her and all the others.

"The blessed children?" Parris asked. The innocents, the most precious among them. He did not understand this.

Tituba continued to cringe. She was no longer speaking to him. But he needed her to. He wanted to know why Satan wanted their children.

"Why?" Parris shouted. "Why?"

But Tituba did not answer.

Two ☉

The horses were screaming.

May Walcott stopped just outside the barn, a battered metal bucket in her hands. Flames soared above her, lighting the night sky.

The heat was intense—she could feel it like a live thing before her—and it made the air hard to breathe. The stench of smoke was everywhere.

And the horses were screaming.

Her papa was organizing the villagers, setting up a bucket brigade. Her mama was throwing dirt on the flames with her bare hands. More people were arriving all the time. Goodman Corey and Goodman Tarbell were already fighting the flames, and in the distance, May could see her uncle, Thomas Putnam, his broad form recognizable on that big horse he always rode.

10

The fire crackled and spat. Sparks flared. May tossed the water—such a pitiful amount of water—on the flames that were eating the wood near the barn door. The water sizzled and then evaporated in a small hiss of steam.

The horses' screams sounded almost human. She could hear their pain and fear.

A beam fell, and more sparks rose like fireflies in the night air. May's eyes burned, and her face felt grimy. She grabbed her bucket to get more water and saw that her skirt was on fire.

The flames had already charred her hem and were working their way up the side of her skirt.

"Papa!" she screamed. He would help her. He would know what to do.

She slammed the bucket against the flames, but nothing happened.

"Papa!"

He was in front of the barn, directing more water at it, throwing dirt, doing everything he could. People were shouting all around her, instructions, orders, and she was getting hotter.

The flames had eaten into her petticoat, and she had no more water. Her leg felt hot.

She pounded at the fire with her hands, then recoiled at the pain.

"Papa, help!"

The barn's roof caved in, and one of the horse's screams cut off abruptly. But the others screamed again, even more panicked and frightened than before.

The tumbling roof made the entire structure look

as if it was going to come apart. More sparks flared toward May, and she flung herself into the dirt, rolling, rolling, rolling on the cold ground until her skirt stopped burning.

Her leg ached, her lungs burned, and her eyes stung. She couldn't see anyone anymore. The fire was too bright. More of the barn collapsed.

Then a timber fell beside her with such force that the ground shook. Her screams mingled with the horses'. She was going to die here in the filth, burned to death like her favorite mare.

She crawled away from the flames, then reached the edge of the woods. The air was cooler here, and the darkness soothed her eyes. She could still see— the fire was so bright it probably lit as far away as Salem Town—but the screaming was ceasing. Each horse's voice stilled, cut off in mid-thrum.

Beams were falling all around. Something exploded—a pitch-filled piece of wood, perhaps—and suddenly she was running, running, running into the woods.

Sweat ran down her face. She was cold and hot at once. Her legs felt curiously free in the shortened dress. But her lungs ached, and she needed air.

She stopped, wrapped her arms around a tree trunk, and hugged it. Her breath was coming in sobs. The horses were gone, and her papa was so close to those flames. She hoped he would be all right. Her mama had been far enough away, but she might go close, to see if Papa was all right and—

A twig snapped behind May. She stopped sobbing

and held her breath for one long moment, listening. Then she heard them: footsteps, running. Coming closer.

From the other direction. Not from the barn at all.

The tree trunk no longer felt safe, but she clung to it a moment longer, the bark scratching her skin. The farm was at the edge of the woods, and her papa had been warned so many times. She'd heard the men talking when she'd been in her bed, their voices rising through the cracks in the floorboards.

You need some kind of warning plan, Jonathan. Some way to get help quickly. If those savages strike Salem Village, they'll get you and yours first. . . .

A grunt, and then a call, masked as the hoot of an owl. She looked over her shoulder, but she couldn't see the house anymore. The fire still lit the night sky, but the orange brightness seemed very far away.

Her papa hadn't heard her scream when she'd been near him. He'd never hear her now.

She let go of the trunk and headed back toward the light, running as fast as she could. But she was already so tired, and she had so much smoke in her lungs that she couldn't get a good breath.

The footsteps were behind her, closer now, getting ever closer. Not just one person's footsteps, but many, chasing her. They could hear her running, those savages. They knew what she was thinking even before she thought it.

They had magic. Everyone said so. They could see in the dark and had the Devil's own hearing, and they would get her, they would get her.

The footsteps were closer. They were right behind her now. She could hear a man's soft grunt. She glanced back just long enough to see three men, their black hair long and braided, their clothing a parody of plain clothes. The men were tall and strong, and they carried knives.

They were almost upon her. They knew she was heading toward the barn. She would lead them to her family, to the village. And there would be no stopping them, because everyone would see only the fire and not the real danger. Her family, her friends, wouldn't know what was coming until it was upon them.

She couldn't lead these men home. At the last minute she veered away from the orange light and headed deeper into the woods.

Another warrior appeared from behind a tree. He grabbed her, put a knife to her throat. She couldn't move anymore. She would plead for herself, not tell them about her family. Maybe then everyone would survive, everyone but her . . .

The blade bit into her skin. She closed her eyes. So this was how she would die. Not in a fire's hot flames like the poor horses, but in the middle of the forest, a knife's cold blade slicing through her skin.

She waited.

And nothing happened.

She opened her eyes, blinked, felt the grime from the fire between her lashes. The flames reflected on the tree in front of her. In the distance, an owl hooted.

14

But she couldn't hear any breathing but her own. There were no footsteps, no laughter among victorious men.

Gingerly she put a hand up to the knife blade and found instead a branch against her throat.

Her fingers caressed it, cool and smooth and so deceptive. She whirled, looking, but the only footprints in the frosted ground were her own.

There were no Indians.

She had been alone all along.

THREE

Orange glowed against the night sky. Annie Putnam sat near the window, her hands clenched. Not once in her twelve years had she seen such an ominous sight.

In the bedroom, her mother cried out, and Annie closed her eyes. Her younger brother Nathaniel pressed against her, his body warm against the house's chill.

"If it's Indians, they'll kill everybody."

Annie opened her eyes and looked up at their maid, Mercy Lewis. She was a lot older than Annie, nearly seventeen, and she'd seen more of the world.

Still, Annie didn't want to think about Indians and dying. Not tonight.

"Isn't so," she said. "My father's there."

16

Nathaniel shivered. "Is Father going to be killed by Indians?"

"They killed my father." Mercy was staring at the orange light. There was a slight frown on her forehead, but her voice was calm, just as it always was when she told this story. "And my mother. And the children. Indians kill everybody, one by one."

Annie's mother screamed. Nathaniel jumped. Annie could feel her own heart pound. She didn't like this night. Mama had said this was normal, that the baby would come out of her stomach and into the world tonight, and Annie would have a new brother or sister.

But Annie thought this was a bad night to have anything happen. The sky was orange when it should have been black, and Mercy was talking about Indians again.

A door closed behind them, and Annie turned. Hanna Morse, the midwife who'd been tending Mama these past few weeks, came into the room. Her sleeves were pushed up, and her apron was askew. Her face was red as if she'd been standing too close to the hearth.

"It's time, Annie," the midwife said.

Annie gasped. She had hoped they would forget her. She didn't want to be grown up. She didn't want to be a young mother and learn what women knew. She still liked her dollies, would secretly pull the last one she'd been given—when she was six—out of the cupboard where Mama had put it years ago.

The midwife's mouth thinned as she looked at

Annie and the other two standing by the window. "What are you standing around for, useless things?"

None of them answered her. Nathaniel looked at the sky as if he wanted to ask about it.

But the midwife didn't seem to care about him. Instead, she glared at Mercy Lewis. "Maid, where are my boiled clothes?"

Mercy jumped as if she had forgotten them. Annie pressed her back against the window's casing, felt the cold night air blowing through the chinks in the wood.

But try as she might to disappear, she couldn't. The midwife's glare turned on her again. "Come on now, Annie. Don't just stand there staring, child. You're going to learn how to bring a baby into the world."

Then she grabbed Annie's hand and pulled her into the best room. It smelled bad, like sweat and blood. The fire was high in the hearth, but it didn't heat the whole room.

The midwife handed Annie a candle. "Hold it near," she said and pushed Annie toward the bed.

Her mama lay in it, her body sunk into the feather mattress, her belly swollen and taut. She wasn't wearing a hood, and her hair, normally so thick and pretty, was wet and scraggly around her face.

"Annie," her mama said, and reached for her, but as she did, her stomach rippled, and she tilted her head back, her teeth bared and her eyes closed. A scream flowed out of her.

Annie backed away.

"The candle, child!" the midwife said. "Move closer."

Annie didn't want to be closer. She didn't want to see. Nathaniel said he did, but Papa said that men didn't belong in birthing rooms. Nathaniel would never have to see this, never have to do this.

It wasn't fair. It wasn't—just as taking the dollies away when Annie still liked them wasn't fair either.

"Come on now." The midwife stood at the foot of the bed, between Mama's legs. Mama's nightdress had been pushed up, and Annie could see her private parts—parts that were supposed to be hidden.

But no one seemed to be saying anything. Instead, the midwife was talking to Mama, who still had her teeth clenched, her hands gripping the blanket as if she were going to rip it with her fingers.

"Push. Harder! Come on, Goody, push for the new baby."

"No more!" Mama said. "I can't! Why is this taking so long?"

Her voice sounded funny, and tears leaked from her eyes.

"Get thee closer, child. Can't see me own hands in the shadows."

The midwife was talking to her. Annie knew it, but couldn't move. Her mama was in pain, and her stomach looked funny. Everyone told her nakedness was a sin, yet the midwife and Mama acted as if this was normal.

Wax dripped on Annie's fingers, burning them.

"Annie!"

19

Annie looked at the midwife, who had moved even closer to Mama. Mama hadn't opened her eyes for what seemed like a long time now.

"Is she dying?" Annie asked.

Mama screamed, and Annie nearly let go of the candle. The midwife didn't look at her. Annie shrank back, but not before she saw something drip to the floor. She looked down and saw a small circle of blood on the wood near the midwife's feet.

"Annie! Bring the candle, for God's sake. Help me!"

Help me. The words echoed in her head, sounding almost like her own words. All the sound vanished, even though she could see Mama's mouth move as she cried out, and the midwife, her hands moving between Mama's legs.

"Help me," Annie said.

Mama was going to die. And then Annie would be the little mother, alone with all these tasks, having to give orders and run the household.

"Mama." She didn't want to lose her Mama. She couldn't. "I'm scared."

Help me. The candle slipped through her fingers and landed in the blood. The light went out, making the room seem even darker than it should.

She was so scared. She couldn't look anymore. She flung herself under the nearby table and put her hands over her ears to block out the horrible sounds. Then she rocked back and forth, the way she used to do when she was allowed to hold her dollies.

The silence faded, and she could hear again, even

though she didn't want to. The voices were muffled. She could still see the blood, the candle in it, the midwife's face, frowning, concerned. If she tried, she could even see Mama, but she didn't want to, didn't want to watch Mama die. . . .

"It's here, Goody Putnam," the midwife was saying. "It's here. Just another push. Come on now, another push and you'll see your beautiful little baby. Push!"

Mama made an odd choking cry. Annie saw her hand drop down, the fingers knotted, the bones visible through the thin skin.

"Yes, yes, I see it!" The midwife's voice rose. "Goody, here it is."

The sounds were awful. Sucking, wet sounds. Annie pressed her hands tighter over her ears, but the sounds wouldn't go away.

" 'Tis a boy. He's a big boy, Goody Putnam. Just as you were hoping."

And then Mama gasped. The room went quiet, even quieter than it had been before. Annie let her hands move away from her ears. She heard nothing. Not the midwife, not Mama.

Not the baby.

The midwife had something cradled in her arms. She had her back turned. Annie couldn't see her. But she could see Mama, propped up on her elbows, her face so pale and shiny that it hardly seemed like Mama's face at all.

"Come on, little boy." The midwife hovered over him. "Come on."

21

Mama's stomach was flat. She hadn't moved. She was watching with big eyes. Annie stared at her, at the blood still dripping onto the floor.

"Please . . ." the midwife said, but she said it the way people did when they knew there was no hope.

She turned toward Mama and shook her head.

"No," Mama cried, and Annie cringed. But not before she saw the crown of a head in the midwife's arms.

All that, and nothing. No baby. And Mama, falling backward on the bed, looking as if she could die herself.

"Fire! Fire in the Village! Fire!"

A crier, riding through the streets of Salem Town. Lizzy Porter clutched a hand to her stomach. Fire, even if it was miles away in Salem Village, was a horrible thing. It could spread or be caused by Indians. And even if it didn't spread, it always meant horrible, horrible loss.

She ran down the central hallway, her siblings beside her, her mother following, just as her father came in the front door. He stood proud and strong and unconcerned, as if the fire were happening in Boston instead of the nearby village.

"Where is it, Father?" Lizzy asked.

Father looked past her, at the younger children. They were wearing their bedclothes, but they clearly weren't sleepy. The crier had awakened them, even though he hadn't awakened her. She was sixteen now, old enough to help Mother with the last of the night's chores.

"Go back to bed, all of you," Father said to the children. Even though his voice was stern, there was fondness in it. They headed back down the hallway, but Lizzy didn't.

Her father watched as if he knew she would stay. Then he answered her question. "It is out in the Village. The Walcott farm."

"Are you going?" Lizzy's mother asked before Lizzy could ask the same question.

Father's face hardened. He made a show of locking the front door. "Not even if the fire were across the road."

His words made Lizzy gasp. Before she could stop herself she said, "That isn't Christian, Father."

Father's jaw moved as if he were clenching his teeth. Mother's eyes narrowed, the first stage of anger.

"Lizzy," she said, "he has not asked thee to speak. Go on to bed."

Lizzy's heart pounded. She knew better than to question her father. She could get in great trouble for it. Honoring thy father and mother was in the commandments, and failing to do so was a great sin.

She bowed her head and headed down the hallway toward the stairs. But her father caught her arm, his touch gentle.

"The Walcotts are kin to Thomas Putnam," her father said as if he wanted her understanding. "He would as soon have *me* in the flames as welcome my help extinguishing them."

Lizzy's mother fluttered near them as if she did not

want them speaking of this. Lizzy faced her father so that she couldn't see her mother's distress.

"But why?" Lizzy asked. "They are Puritans, like us."

This time, her father bowed his head and sighed. "These are complicated times, child."

She waited for him to say something else. Instead, he let go of her arm. The moment was past, and she still didn't understand her own parents' lack of Christian charity. But she dared not question it anymore

She picked up a candlestick and, holding it for light, headed up the stairs.

Samuel Parris hunched over his desk, a candle beside him. It offered the only real warmth. The heat from the fireplace across the room dissipated at this distance. Occasionally he had to blow on his hands to keep his fingers from cramping.

He dipped his quill pen into the inkwell and wrote in his neatest hand:

We are, beyond all others of this Earth, a people chosen specially by God; created by Him for a special mission: We are Puritans!

He was careful to blot the quill's tip so as not to smear the page. This was his record, like the merchant's ledger he had once kept back in the days when he thought he could be a successful businessman.

The loose sheets from Sunday's sermon were spread before him, words crossed out, the ink running across the pages. The sermon was not as strong as he had hoped—few were—but when he copied them into the book, he heard them not as he had spoken them but as he wanted to speak them, his voice rich and filled with God's power.

By that it is meant we are knit together in all ways, in pleasure and pain, feast and famine, as one body.

He could hear his wife's voice downstairs, murmuring with distress. Elizabeth's health was difficult at best, and he hoped nothing would plague her tonight. He had much work to finish.

He dipped the quill pen into the inkwell again, carefully using the blotter before continuing.

Private will is to be distrusted always, for it is original sin. It is the work of the Devil!

Loud, urgent knocking sounded below. Parris closed his eyes for but a moment. Such sounds did not bode well for his night's work, no matter what happened with Elizabeth or the children.

He listened for a moment, then heard nothing more. He let out a small sigh and continued to write.

We must always have before our eyes God's special determination for us: that we are one. We are connected parts of the same Puritan body.

Footsteps were coming up the stairs. He concentrated harder and hoped that no one was coming for him.

This is not only our salvation; it is God's mission for Puritans in this new—

Another knock, this one respectful, and then his wife, speaking softly. "Samuel."

Even though he had heard her approach, she still

startled him. His quill made a ragged jump across the page. He stared at it for a moment—a blot on the record—and knew there was nothing he could do about it.

The door opened. His wife, fragile yet attractive in her daily gown, wiped her hands on her apron. Her forehead was knotted in a frown.

"There is a fire," she said.

He had not expected this. A fire boded poorly for the village and the church. Theirs was not a rich parish, and taking on the burden of others, difficult at any time, would be nearly impossible now.

He set his pen in its holder and hurried to the window. The fire glowed against the blackened sky, distant from him, nearer the woods than the center of the village. But the orange light illuminated the buildings and the Ingersoll road anyway, as well as the meeting house not far from the parsonage.

"Might it be the Indians?"

He didn't answer her. He wasn't sure what they were facing, but the fear in his belly told him that something was on the horizon. He'd only been minister to this place a few short years, but he'd known something like this would come.

All ministers were tested, and in that test, they would gather their flock to them and use the calamity to spread the word of the Lord.

He uttered a soft prayer: "Is this it, God? Is this my test? I have been waiting. Let me show you I am ready."

The wind came through the poorly built walls. On

it he could smell smoke. The Scriptures told of the three young men, tested in fire, and they had walked from the flames unscathed.

Nothing was impossible for a man who believed in the Lord.

Parris was ready. He turned toward his wife, made sure he sounded calm so that he could ease her fears.

"Protect the children, Elizabeth," he said as he gathered his things. "And I must have my cloak."

She fetched it for him as he closed his sermon book and blew out the candle. The light from the hearth still gave the room a glow. But the room had an extra glow as well—the glow from the unnatural fire out the window.

He went down the stairs. The children were spread out below the hearth down there, finishing their daily tasks. He would miss their bedtime, as he had so often recently.

Elizabeth handed Parris his coat, then kissed his cheek. "Godspeed, husband," she said.

He squeezed her hand and let himself out into the night.

The air was brittle, even more chilled than it had seemed coming through the walls. He still wasn't used to New England's weather. He missed the warmth of Barbados, the climate in which he had been raised. He missed so much about that warm place.

But perhaps God was taking him to a better place on this night.

The orange of the fire guided his way across the

fields. A full moon added to the eeriness of the night. He was not used to such light in the darkness.

His breath formed before him, a white vapor. He shivered and drew his coat tighter around his shoulders.

The village was quiet—empty, although he could see candlelight in many of the windows. A crier had gone through; the other men would be going to the fire as well.

But he saw none of them.

Although he heard voices on the wind. Crying, moaning voices, voices in pain. In them he thought he heard a child's voice, one he recognized—Betty?

He turned, but his daughter was not with him. She was sitting in front of the hearth, finishing some mending for her mother. He had seen her before he left.

He shoved his hands into his pockets. The voices surrounded him. Perhaps he was hearing the sound of people fighting the flames. But he wasn't close enough. The orange glow still flickered in the distance, far from him.

A wail pierced the night, then another, and another. His heart pounded, and he licked his lips, feeling the moisture freeze on them. His wife had mentioned Indians, and it had made him nervous. Who else could start a fire?

Some kind of maliciousness was in the wind. He could feel it pressing against him. Something skittered across the ground, and he turned—

But nothing appeared on the moonlit field.

Nothing except his own shadow, eerily long in the moonlight.

He was not strong enough for this. His wife had been ill. The congregation fought among themselves, and he was not holding them together as he had hoped.

Now the fire. The testing, the will of the Lord facing him.

He fell to his knees almost before he realized he'd done it.

"My Lord," he whispered, "I have fear of this night."

His hands were pressed together, the skin cold. He could feel the frozen earth through the thin material of his breeches, the wind blowing against his long stockings, making him even colder.

He needed something, a sign that what he would do would be right.

"Touch me," he whispered.

And then he realized he could hear the voices no longer. There was silence on the wind and the smell of smoke.

Misfortune was often the sign of the Devil's work. And Parris was beginning to believe that the Devil had his finger in this part of Massachusetts. Why else would they be so beleaguered?

But the Psalm said that fire traveled before God and destroyed His enemies. Sometimes fire purged and cleansed.

Parris would go to the scene of this fire and judge it for what it was. When he saw whose hand was in it,

29

he would know what faced him—what faced them all in Salem Village.

And the Lord would give him strength to see it through.

By the time Parris reached the Walcott farm, the orange glow was gone from the night sky. The fire was smoldering now, even though a handful of people were still throwing dirt on the remains of the structure.

The fire had been intense. Charred beams fell across the smoldering earth, but there was little here that still resembled a barn. The stench of burned horseflesh hung in the air, mingling with the overpowering smell of smoke.

Parris stood in front of the barn. He'd been studying it for some time, looking for a sign. He did not see the hand of the Lord here, in such ruination, and in May Walcott's tale of Indians in the woods.

The girl had arrived shortly after he had, one side of her skirt burned away to the knee. She had brambles in her hair and was covered with dirt. She didn't seem to know that her ruined skirt showed an indecent stretch of leg.

She babbled incoherently about what she had seen, and Parris listened while he studied the ruins. This was a test, as he had first thought: a test of his leadership, a test of the village's strength.

There was much discord here, and the discord was drawing the Evil One. He had been trying to stem the tide—hence last week's sermon about unity among Puritans—but he seemed to be one man standing against an ocean.

Most of the villagers were gone now. Thomas Putnam remained with his kinsman. The womenfolk had gone inside, Deliverance Walcott to tend to her daughter, and the rest to prepare a meal for the remaining workers.

The moon was going down as well. Its odd light lengthened the shadows. He saw Walcott's and Putnam's shadows as the men stopped behind him.

"What if May is right about the Indians?" Walcott was saying. He sounded worried.

Of course he was, being so close to the woods. If the Indians came—*when* the Indians came— Walcott's property would suffer the first attack.

Parris rubbed his hands on his coat, feeling the smoky grease cover his clothing.

"She was faulty in her senses, Jonathan," Putnam said. "She admitted as much. There are many things that can burn a barn. Where is your pipe?"

Parris turned as Walcott slapped his pockets, searching. His eyes widened as he understood what Putnam meant. Then Walcott's expression changed. Apparently the suggestion made him angry.

"Do you suggest the barn burned through a mistake of my own?"

The discord made Parris's shoulders tense. Even among kinsmen there was disagreement.

Parris stepped in, as his job demanded.

"This was not an act of Indians." He could be certain of that. Indians did not stop with one barn and then chase a young girl through the woods. They destroyed many things in their desire to ruin an entire community. "I believe it was the Devil's specter that did this."

Both men turned toward him as if they did not realize he had been standing there. They looked shocked.

"Witchcraft?" Walcott asked. "But I am a good Christian. Why would I be plagued by—"

"Because on this night the hand of Satan has been laid on us all." The Lord had given Parris the ability to feel it. There was a darkness in Salem Village, a darkness that was growing worse. "This is just the beginning of it."

Putnam shivered, then looked at the barn. Walcott took a step closer as if he could see the roots of the magic. As they contemplated Parris's words, a woman ran toward them.

Parris watched her come, knowing that this did not bode well either. The women should have been inside the house, but this woman came from outside. As she drew closer, he recognized her: Hanna Morse, the midwife.

"Thomas Putnam!" she cried as she ran toward them. Putnam walked toward her. His expression did not change, but Parris felt his tension. Putnam's wife, Ann, was nearing the end of her confinement, and such things had never been easy for her.

Hanna Morse reached them. She was breathing hard as if she had run all the way from Putnam's house.

"You are needed at home, Goodman Putnam," she said, breathless. "The baby—'twas born still."

Parris closed his eyes for a moment. His greatest fear when Elizabeth suffered travail was her death. His second greatest fear was losing the child.

It seemed so common here in the cold north, even more common than in his family's home in Barbados. Perhaps this was another sign of the Devil's work.

"Never took a breath," Hanna was saying. "Poor thing. Not a single one."

Parris opened his eyes and gazed at Thomas Putnam. His face was rigid, as if the news meant nothing to him or as if he were trying to contain great emotion. Parris sometimes had trouble reading Putnam, the man on which so much of Parris's own job depended. He had trouble reading Putnam now.

" 'Twas a wicked travail, nearly five hours," Hanna said. "Goody Putnam struggled. She will survive, but I believe—"

"Was it a son?" Putnam's voice was harsh.

Parris took a step forward. Surely the man did not understand. The child was stillborn.

He was about to speak when the midwife said, "Goodman Putnam, the child—he was not alive."

Her words were careful. She clearly did not want to insult one of the most powerful men in the village, but she too seemed to think his reaction odd.

Putnam's chin went up slightly as if the words were going in. Parris finally understood. Putnam knew his wife was in travail when he came to the fire, and he had expected to hear news. So he'd planned to ask after the child first. The question came out, even though it had been inappropriate.

Walcott reached for Putnam, but Putnam moved away. The mask covering his face had cracked slightly, and Parris could see grief.

Parris glanced at the full moon, nearing the horizon. No wonder so many spoke of nights such as this as witches' nights. The Devil could see when he went abroad, and he saw much in Salem Village.

"Shall I tell your wife you are returning?" Hanna Morse asked.

Putnam did not answer her. Instead, he walked toward the remains of the barn. Parris felt his stomach clench. Putnam would want words of comfort, and Parris did not have them.

Walcott hovered near Putnam, obviously feeling the same way Parris did. Walcott said, "May Christ bless you, Thomas," and the words had the comfort that Parris felt lacking in his own soul.

But Putnam ignored his kinsman. Instead, he stopped beside Parris. Putnam looked at the midwife, then at the ruined barn, and his grief seemed to increase.

"You were right," he said to Parris. "It is just the beginning."

FOUR

nnie leaned against the table leg. She was cold. The warmth of the fire didn't reach her there. Her face felt swollen, and her bodice was soaked with tears.

The midwife was long gone, and Annie's mama hadn't moved on the bed. Once she moaned, and that was all. Annie clung to the table leg, staring at the pool of blood. The room still had a funny smell—not the scents of candlewax and woodsmoke that she always thought of as part of her parents' bedroom.

She didn't want to be here. She didn't want to be Mama's namesake. She didn't like the best room any more, or the things that happened there, and she certainly didn't want to have babies herself.

Babies came out in blood and pain, and then they died.

They died.

Her mama sat up on the bed and looked down at Annie as if she had heard Annie's sinful thoughts. Mama would understand. Mama had been so sad when she heard that the baby had died. She knew how Annie felt.

All Annie wanted to do was run to Mama and bury her face against Mama's shoulder. The last time she'd done that, Mama had said she was too old. Twelve years was old enough to wife in some places, Mama said, although Annie couldn't believe it.

Here, twelve was old enough to help with babies, and birth, and this.

This.

"Annie?" Mama whispered the word, as if she had no real energy for speech.

Annie looked up. Mama was watching her. Mama could see how upset she was—and this time, Mama would not say she was too old.

Annie crawled out from underneath the table, careful to stay away from the blood and the spilled candle.

"Bring it to me."

Annie blinked. Her mama didn't want *her*. Maybe Annie had misunderstood. Maybe—

"I want to hold him."

Him. Not Nathaniel, her younger brother, but the baby.

The dead baby.

Mama wanted to hold *him*, not her. Him.

Annie shook her head.

Mama's eyes narrowed, the way they did when she was about to get angry. "Annie."

Annie's mouth was dry. She didn't dare disobey, but she wasn't sure she could hold that—thing. That dead thing that was supposed to be her new brother.

She glanced at it, wrapped in white linen, and shivered. "Please, Mama, no. I don't want to."

"You tempt Satan when you disobey," her mother said. "Bring it."

Tempting Satan was the worst thing she could do. One wrong action, one mistake, and the Devil might take her soul.

Annie stood, using the table for balance, and stared at the tiny bundle. So still.

Come now, little boy. Come on. Please.

Mama was watching Annie as if waiting for the Devil to take her. Annie walked to the bundle. A sob hitched in her throat, but she kept it back.

Someday, she would have to do this: lie in a bed, suffer travail. And she might have a baby like this. Most women she knew did. She'd heard her mama whisper of it to the other women long before the babe was born. They all spoke of horrible fears, of death. . . .

Her mama stirred, and Annie knew she would get even angrier soon. There would be no hugs. Annie was too old for hugs. She bent over the linen and saw the wizened face inside, so like the faces of living babies that she'd seen at the meeting house. It was perfect—its little snub nose, its tiny bow-shaped mouth. But its skin was bluish, and its eyes were pressed shut.

Another sob shuddered through her. She didn't want to touch the bundle, but she did, startled at how cold it was. Babies weren't supposed to be cold. They were little wriggly bundles of warmth. She'd held so many of them when the goodwives of the village asked her, and dreamed of her own.

But not like this.

Please, Mama, not like this.

But Mama was still watching her, waiting not for Annie, it seemed, but for the bundle.

Annie gathered it, just as she would gather her dolly, and cradled it. It was stiff, unyielding as a board. Revulsion flared in her, and she gagged, somehow managing not to become sick.

She carried the cold, hard thing to her mama. Her mama's eyes were feverish, her hands reaching toward the bundle as if it were alive. Annie no longer wanted those hands to touch her. They didn't even look like Mama's hands, all grasping and tight. Mama had more dignity than that.

Annie brought it close, moving with caution, afraid to trip or lose her hold on the bundle, afraid that if she dropped it, it would shatter.

Then she reached her mama's hands, and they took that bundle, pulling it close to Mama's breast. Mama didn't even look at Annie. Her strange bright gaze was only for the bundle, pulling back the linens so that she could better see its tiny perfect face.

This time, the sob escaped Annie. But Mama didn't notice. Mama was gone from her—she was with the bundle, rubbing her hand over its head, cooing at it.

And Annie couldn't take any more. She wasn't going to be strong any longer, and she wasn't going to be anyone's little mother, not ever. She spun and ran from the room, going to her own bed—which had, at least, a measure of warmth.

Thomas Putnam paced in front of the roaring fire in Israel Porter's hearth. The center hall seemed warmer than it should have on this frosty winter dawn. Porter sat near the fire, and so did John Proctor and Giles Corey.

Putnam wasn't sure how he had come here. He hadn't had a plan until he dismounted from his horse. He didn't always get along with Porter, and he had no real use for Proctor or Corey. But they had been here when he arrived. He'd seen the smoke rising from the chimney, seen the light inside and the activity just before sunrise, and stopped.

Putnam had ridden home first, going to his wife. She would need him. She had become fragile since the death of their last child, and now this. He was afraid it would destroy her.

It nearly destroyed him.

He sat on his horse, the stench of the Walcott barn fire still on his clothing, and stared at his own house—a place that should have been a haven, a respite from all the trials with which God tested the living.

But God had brought the trials inside Putnam's house, and he could not face them, not so soon after learning of them. Putnam would have to be the strength, and he had little left. He wasn't sure he could see another dead infant's face, or watch his wife hide in her bed in tears.

So he rode, thinking of Reverend Parris's words, and knowing that the man was right. The Devil had come to Massachusetts, finding His unholy delights in Salem Village. And somehow, he, Thomas Putnam, would have to find a way to stop Him.

The men had listened to him tell of the barn, and now he had gotten to repeating Hanna Morse's message. The babe, born still.

Born still.

He faced the men. Proctor was whittling, unable to look up at Putnam. Israel Porter watched with guarded eyes. Corey had his hands folded over his belly, his expression neutral.

"This death still cuts as sharp as the first," Putnam said. "You know this. You have lost children."

Their expressions did not change. Porter looked at Proctor as if the other man could guide him. Procter said nothing. His whittling continued. Little shavings of wood fell on Goody Porter's clean floor.

"We are sorry for your loss," Porter said, and he sounded sincerely saddened. They did understand. They all did. Men bore a tougher burden of grief, for they headed their households and had not the luxury of losing themselves to sorrow the way some women did.

To lead the entire household down that path would be Devil's work.

And that thought reminded him of his purpose now.

"I have come here," he said, "to appeal to you. Father to father, neighbor to neighbor. Puritan to Puritan."

Proctor continued to whittle. Corey hadn't moved. Only Porter seemed interested, his gaze following Putnam as he paced back and forth.

"On a single night our village has lost a barn to fire and a child's life. Forces of darkness are upon our village."

Proctor's hand stilled, and he looked up. Corey's eyes narrowed. Putnam had finally reached them.

"Our differences must be put aside. Now," he said. "Reverend Parris was sent here to protect us from Satan's forces. I am asking for your support of him."

Parris was the one who understood, who knew what they were facing. Certainly these men could see that. They had been recalcitrant in the past, but they could not be now—not when the safety of the entire village was at stake.

"If you give him your support," Putnam said, "the other dissenters will follow. Our minister needs us all behind him now."

"Our minister?" Israel Porter asked. "Half the Village worships in Town, as they always have."

Anger flared in Putnam, and he struggled to suppress it. This was no time for animosity. This was the time to set animosity aside. Surely these men could see that.

"It is time the Village splits from the Town," Putnam said. "They no longer serve the Village's interests. It is why we have our own minister."

41

John Proctor set his whittling on his lap, but he still clutched the blade as if it provided him a defense. "The *Village's* interest? Don't you mean the Putnams' interest, Goodman Putnam?"

They had made this argument a thousand times, and it had done no good. Putnam was worried that the discord in the village was what had attracted Satan in the first place. It was well known that a lack of charity attracted the Devil.

"I am appealing to you Puritan to Puritan," Putnam said. "There is a dark force amongst us. It is time for us to resolve this debate."

"It was the Putnams that brought Reverend Parris to the Village," John Proctor said. "And gave him the land under the meeting house. That was Village land. It was not yours to give away."

"The Village Committee voted it," Putnam said.

"Your Village Committee," Israel Porter said. "Made up of all your brothers."

Putnam shook his head. He had come here to solve a problem, not make it worse. Surely these men could understand that.

"The Village needs its own minister," Putnam said. "The Reverend Parris serves us."

"He has refused to grant church membership to many of us." John Proctor's face was growing red. He was getting angry.

But so was Putnam. "That is only because he requires proof of repentance before—"

"He has refused to baptize our children!" Israel Porter shouted. "You had no right to give away

Village land to a man such as this. You had no right to promise him our taxes. He does not serve our Village. He serves Putnams!"

"Hear me," Putnam said. "We must put this debate behind us at last. Satan's forces have descended upon Salem. What will happen if we are not united to meet them?"

Proctor's knife fell. It landed among the wood chips, point down. Another Devil sign.

All four men stared at it, and Putnam wasn't the only one who shivered.

Betty Parris held a paring knife in her small hand. She was peeling potatoes beside her cousin Abigail Williams. Abigail, at eleven, was two years older and faster at the work, which frustrated Betty.

Abigail was also telling stories, and Betty didn't like it.

They had been whispering so Tituba, stirring dinner in a kettle over the fire, could not hear them. But Betty wanted Tituba to hear now. She was tired of Abigail's stories.

"It isn't true," Betty said loudly.

" 'Tis," Abigail whispered. "While you sleep."

"Tituba, is it true?" Betty asked. "Indians will cut the hair from our head?"

"Not just the hair," Abigail said, "like this."

She held up a potato and peeled its skin back with her knife, slowly, letting the skin curl away from the meat. Betty felt her stomach churn. She could picture the way the scalp would separate from the head.

Tituba wasn't watching. Betty wished she would. She wanted this to stop.

But Abigail wasn't ready to quit.

"Why do you think Mercy Lewis is the Putnams' maid?" Abigail asked. "Her parents were scalped. As she watched."

That wouldn't happen to her parents, would it? Betty shivered. Her Papa was a man of God. Nothing could touch him, could it?

"Tituba?" Betty asked, wanting Tituba to step in.

"Her brothers, too," Abigail said. "That's why Mercy is an orphan."

Tituba shook her head, but there was a fond expression on her face. She wasn't as strict as Mama, and certainly not as strict as Papa.

"Abigail," Tituba said, "you mustn't scare your cousin anymore. Listen to Tituba."

Betty let out a sigh of relief. Finally they were done with this story. But every time she peeled the skin off a potato, she saw hair instead.

Mama came into the keeping room, tucking a strand of hair inside her hood.

Finally, someone who would know the answer if Betty asked a question. Tituba didn't always know how things worked in Salem. Tituba wasn't like the rest of them.

"Mama, what is an orphan?" Betty asked.

Abigail made a "be-quiet" gesture with her potato-fisted hand.

But Betty had to ask. "Am I one? Mama?"

44

"Quiet, children," her mama said. "You must not speak unless you are addressed."

"But, Mama," Betty said, trying to go on. Surely Mama had to know how important this was.

"Enough," Mama said. "We are leaving shortly."

She turned her back on Betty. Betty put her knife down. Maybe Mama hadn't really listened.

But Mama was talking to Tituba. "Will you get them ready, Tituba? There is a distemper in my mouth again. I fear my head will burst."

" 'Tis your teeth, Goody Parris," Tituba said. "After cemetery, I make a poultice for the swelling."

They were all going to the funeral of the Putnam baby. Papa would be speaking at it. Papa said last night when he thought Betty was asleep that he did not like speaking at the graves of stillborns. The Bible was silent on whether or not they went with God. It was a matter of interpretation, one the church fought over. Man was born in sin, after all.

Betty didn't pretend to understand all of Papa's concerns. But Mama seemed upset by the whole thing.

Mama started out of the keeping room, probably to finish getting ready.

"And Goodwife Parris," Tituba said, "we are almost out of wood again."

Mama looked at the fire, clearly worried. Betty knew that there was a fight among the villagers about the family's wood and supplies, but she didn't understand it. There was so much she didn't understand.

45

"I shall mention it to the Reverend," Mama said, and the subject seemed closed.

So Betty could try again. "Mama," she asked. "Am I an orphan?"

But Mama never answered her, and Betty got the sense that Mama never would.

FIVE

Thomas's dog yip-yipped constantly. Ann Putnam sat on the wooden staircase, feeling as if she were wearing someone else's body. If she closed her eyes, she could still feel the babe inside of her womb, moving, kicking, *alive*.

She had no idea how he could have been born still. Perhaps one of the Devil's own had sucked away his breath.

Around her, villagers spoke in soft tones, not wanting to disturb her. Nathaniel sat with the other children on the floor. Her little daughter, Annie, watched her father, sitting at the head of the table, his horrible dog yapping at his feet.

Thomas stroked the dog's head, and the dog's tail wagged. Ann watched her husband's fingers caress the animal and remembered how he had crossed his arms at the funeral when she had reached to him for comfort.

She closed her eyes, letting the voices flow around her like a river. The funeral. She still could not believe it had happened. Somehow she had left the house that morning, her arms clutching the small casket Thomas had made. She didn't want anyone else to touch it, not once her child was placed inside.

This boy had been the most beautiful of all of her children, except that he did not have the breath of life to give his face color. She thought of him in the simple casket, wearing the white linens she had made for his first weeks of life, and shivered. He would be so cold.

The men in the village had dug graves before the earth froze, as they did every year. Big graves and small, and she had not watched, for to do so would have been a bad omen. But she had known of it. Her Thomas had come into the house with dirt on his hands after one digging, and he would not talk of it.

She still did not have the heart to ask him if he had dug a baby's grave.

Her eyes flew open. Goody Nurse was pouring drink as if this were her household. Annie was watching her father still, and that dog hadn't stopped yapping.

Reverend Parris sat at the table too, participating in the conversation. They were probably talking of village politics, which seemed to be all they were concerned with. Even Thomas, when he came home after the baby's death, had spoken not of the tragedy or

48

even the barn fire, but the way the other men could not settle their differences.

If Thomas hadn't built the babe's coffin, she would have thought him unfeeling. She knew he was not.

Still, he had tried to take it from her, to carry it in the processional, and she hadn't let him. She hadn't let anyone take it until Goodman Tarbell forced her to give it away at the grave site. Goodman Tarbell had held the coffin for only a moment, and then he had given it away, too.

It had gone into Samuel Parris's hands and seemed to disappear inside his cloak.

She stared at Reverend Parris's hands now, and as she did, the scent of fresh stew reached her. The men were eating. Everyone was eating, except her.

The dog continued to yip. She wanted to put her hands over her ears to shut out that awful noise, but she lacked the energy. Then, voices rose over the dog's.

"Israel Porter cares less about his faith than about making himself rich from Salem Town," Jonathan Walcott said.

"He and John Proctor both," Thomas Putnam said. "They refuse to support our meeting house. They are even discouraging others from paying their church taxes. We promised the Reverend thirty cords of wood in salary. As it is, he will be out of wood before the Sabbath."

The men were still talking politics. Talking about Thomas's bad morning, the morning after the babe died.

49

As if this compared. It did not.

Ann clenched her hands into fists. Even the Reverend Parris, who was supposed to be tending the needy, seemed fixed on this conversation.

Ann could not shut out her husband's voice.

"Since the Porters and Proctors won't support him," Thomas said, "the Village Committee will force the collection of taxes. Those in arrears shall be arrested."

The dog's barking had grown even louder. Thomas leaned over, picked the dog up, and cradled it against him as he would a babe. Ann watched him, unable to remember the last time he had cradled her—had it been before Annie was born?

She looked at her daughter, who was watching her father with the same envy Ann felt. Annie was too old now to seek affection from her parents. She had to learn the ways of the world, and she was failing. So far as Ann knew, Annie still hadn't asked God for forgiveness for the way she behaved the night the babe died.

Ann had. She asked God a hundred times what sin she had committed, what she had done to suffer so at His hands. And He had not answered her, not that she could hear.

"Dear Ann."

The mention of her name made Ann jump. It took her a moment to focus on Rebecca Nurse. Reverend Parris was beside her, of course. He had left the table, perhaps because the men were discussing him.

Or perhaps Goody Nurse had beseeched him to help the poor, sickly Ann Putnam. Rebecca Nurse was like that: so holy, so kind. God never looked unkindly on her.

Goody Nurse peered at Ann with concern. "Have you taken food?"

Ann's stomach turned at the thought. She had taken little food since that horrible night, and what she had taken had not stayed down.

"The thoughts in my head have crowded out the rest," Ann said. "Hunger, sleep. I have no need for them."

"And for prayer?" Rebecca Nurse said. "Surely the need for that has not left you."

Of course. Goody Nurse wasn't coming to Ann because she needed a kind word. Goody Nurse was coming as the Lord's representative, to remind Ann what an awful sinner she was.

"God is waiting to hear you," Goody Nurse looked over her shoulder at Reverend Parris. "Let us pray for her."

She knelt, wobbling slightly. She was so old, and yet she moved like a younger woman. Ann wasn't sure she had enough strength to kneel like that.

But Goody Nurse took her hand and eased her down. "Show God your faith, Ann Putnam."

The Reverend knelt with them, bowing his head as he spoke. "Grace, mercy, and peace from God, our Father, through our Lord Jesus Christ, hear our prayers."

Ann couldn't concentrate on his words. They mingled with the babble of the guests, and all the sounds became indecipherable.

Then a movement caught her eye. Goody Nurse rose and took a wrapped bundle from Reverend Parris. She lifted it carefully and added it to the two identical shapes already clutched in her arms.

Ann's babies! Her precious, lost babies.

Ann reached for them, but Goody Nurse did not see her—or perhaps did not care. She turned and walked slowly from the room. No one else stood there, either. Everyone had left, and she was alone. Horribly alone.

"Why?" Ann Putnam shouted. "Why are you taking them away? Stop. Please stop."

Suddenly, all the people returned, along with their conversation—or the last of it. Their words faded away as they all looked at her, all of them except Thomas, who closed his eyes as if in pain.

"Why are they being taken away from me?" Ann could not contain the words. They had been trapped inside her since the emptiness came, since the babe left only a few nights ago.

Her son Nathaniel hid his face in his knees. Her daughter Annie had put a hand to her mouth.

But Thomas had opened his eyes again. He was looking at Ann as if he had never seen her before.

"Ann!" he snapped. "Contain yourself."

She blinked, her lower lip trembling. Goody Nurse was not standing near the door as she had thought, and there were no bundles in her hands.

But Ann could not forget the faces, the tiny beautiful faces. Thomas hadn't been there for that hopeful moment—not once—he did not know how it felt to nearly die yourself and have nothing to show for it except a reminder of your own sins.

She turned to Reverend Parris. He would have the answers for her. Perhaps the babe's death had naught to do with her.

"Why?" She clutched at his arm. "This innocent was the third."

"Ann!" Thomas said. "Enough."

The Reverend glanced at Thomas as if he—and not God—would guide them. Ann tugged on the Reverend's sleeve to regain his attention.

"Three of my babies dead at birth," she said, softly, only to him. "You are Christ's ambassador, so tell me, why God is doing this to me?"

He turned to her, and she saw no comfort in his face.

"Why?" she asked, even though she knew now that he had no answer.

Six

Tituba closed the door of the woodshed, shaking her head. There was barely enough wood to last the week. Such things these people did to each other, all in the name of right. She did not understand, nor did she really try. They were not her people. She was just forced to live among them.

The air, colder than it had been in days, seeped into the house. The parsonage was poorly built and not nearly as warm as some of the other homes Tituba had been in. She actually thought herself lucky, though; she had her rolled-up bed near the fire at night—and she was probably the only one in the entire house who stayed warm.

As she came round the side of the house she saw Annie Putnam, Mercy Lewis, and May Walcott standing beside the road. Abigail and Betty ran past, giggling, their faces filled with joy, as children's faces should be.

If Betty's papa saw them, he would chastise them for being wanton.

Tituba could not bring herself to chastise them, but she knew she had to say something.

"Abigail, you watch little Betty now," Tituba said. "Keep her safe."

Abigail waved, indicating that she had heard. Then the girls hurried down the road.

Tituba watched them for a moment. Her childhood—until she had been taken—had been filled with joyous moments like that. These girls had to steal theirs.

They were expected to be little adults, but they were not. Sometimes Tituba thought they might break under the strain. And then she saw them laughing, just as they were now, and she was glad for the strength of the human heart.

Behind her, she heard footsteps. She clutched the precious wood closer and turned.

Sarah Good made her way up the road, clutching the hand of her four-year-old daughter, Dorcas. Their clothes were tattered, and the two looked as if they'd been sleeping in someone's barn again.

"Tituba Indian," Sarah Good said, "have you any scraps for us today? My little girl is famished."

Tituba looked at poor little Dorcas, her pinched face reflecting her lack of a home. If ever a child made Tituba want to take her in, it was young Dorcas. The girl clearly loved her mother, but she needed regular meals and a warm place to sleep.

"Come back later, Goody Good. Tituba give you food then."

"You're a good Puritan, you are," Sarah said. "Taking care of your poor Christian neighbors. Not like the others."

She looked behind her, and Tituba did too. Deliverance Walcott stood near the roadside, watching the interchange. Obviously Sarah Good had spoken to her as well.

And then, as if to confirm Tituba's hunch, Sarah Good blurted, "Like you, Goody Walcott. Casting ye own hungry neighbors out in the cold. Do you answer to Satan?"

"Quiet, you old harridan," Deliverance Walcott shouted back. "You're crazed in your intellectuals."

Tituba backed away. It did not matter if Sarah Good was crazed or not. She had a child who needed care. Sometimes these people, who proclaimed their holiness day in and day out, surprised her more than others.

But then, from what Tituba understood of their God, she shouldn't have been surprised at the people's harshness. The God that the Reverend Parris spoke of sounded harsh, too.

She backed into the door of the lean-to kitchen and set down some of the wood in the hall. Then she went upstairs to the sleeping chamber.

Elizabeth Parris was in bed, the side of her face swollen, her eyes closed in pain. Tituba's poultice hadn't worked well on Elizabeth Parris's tooth. Tituba believed the tooth had to be pulled, but Mistress Parris did not want to lose another tooth.

"I would be old and toothless before my time," she had said. But if she weakened any more, Tituba would speak to the Reverend herself, even though it was not allowed.

She put the wood in its basket beside the hearth and started a fire. The room was as chill as the outdoors, and there were not enough blankets on the bed. Mistress Parris had to be cold.

"You mustn't waste wood on me, Tituba." Mistress Parris did not sound like herself. Her voice was weak, and the swelling in her mouth made the words sound wrong.

" 'Tis not a waste when you are so sick," Tituba said. "A room this cold only makes you worse sick."

"I'll be fine for a while," Mistress Parris said. "The Reverend says that we shall soon have all the wood we need. The Village Committee shall see to it."

Tituba did not believe it. She had heard many things when she was running errands in the village square. People believed she was invisible, that she did not hear their words or understand their talk. They said things in front of her that they would not say near any other member of the Parris household.

She had known that for some time, and she had been keeping it to herself. But she could no longer.

"I hear talk in the Village," Tituba said. "People say Salem Town does not want a minister in Salem Village. That is why no wood for us. Two times before us, preacher here then gone away. Bad anger in this place. Bad omens, more and more."

Mistress Parris seemed small in her blankets. She did not say so, but she believed in omens too. She had been raised on Barbados, like the Reverend. She knew about these things.

"Bread not rise twice this week," Tituba said. "Just like before the hurricane."

"That was Barbados, Tituba," Mistress Parris said. "You can't be superstitious here. That won't happen to us again."

But she did not sound so certain.

"Bad omens," Tituba said, and Mistress Parris closed her eyes.

Israel Porter stood in the center of a group of men, staring at the notice posted on the wall of Ingersoll's Tavern. Giles Corey had pointed the notice out to him when Porter had arrived. The Putnams' man had put it up just moments before.

Every man in the tavern—and there were quite a few—had gathered around the notice. Most were reading it to themselves, but all repeated the important phrases for the men who had never learned their letters.

"Those in arrears will be arrested?" Samuel Nurse read. He was standing beside Israel Porter. They had become allies of sorts. Porter liked Nurse and thought him sensible.

"Arrested for keeping my own wood to myself?" Giles Corey glanced at Israel. "Can the Putnams do that?"

Israel nodded. "They are the Village Committee. They can do it."

A hand reached around Porter and snatched the notice from the wall. Porter turned in time to see John Proctor tear the notice up. Samuel Nurse watched in shock, and the others moved away.

Porter did not feel like having a drink after all. For all his talk of reconciliation, Thomas Putnam had once again shown that he did not know how to work with others.

John Proctor walked beside him, still clutching the notice. Giles Corey kept pace, but Samuel Nurse kept his distance, unnerved by their defiance.

"Goodman Porter!"

Porter looked up to see young Joseph Putnam running toward them. Joseph was Thomas Putnam's half brother and was sixteen years younger. He, along with their father's second wife, Mary Veren, had inherited the bulk of the Putnam estate.

When he reached them, John Proctor held up the crumpled notice.

"Has your brother instructed you to protect his notice?" Proctor's voice was mocking. "Are you going to arrest me, Goodman Putnam?"

Joseph frowned at the crumpled paper as if he did not know what it was. "No, I am only half a Putnam, Goodman Proctor. 'Tis something I am reminded of almost daily."

Joseph turned to Porter. Porter felt his stomach clench. He did not know what this young man had to do with him.

"It is not Village business I wish to discuss with you, but this. . . ." Joseph pulled a small wrapped object from his pocket. He handed it to Porter.

Porter took it, felt the slight weight of it, and frowned in confusion.

" 'Tis an Indian carving," Joseph said. "The finest I have yet found. Might you give it to Lizzy?"

Porter unwrapped the carving and looked at it. It was fine. Young Putnam was watching him, eagerness on his face. And then the light dawned.

"After all these months of admiring her," Porter asked, "you could not find a way to give it to her yourself?"

Joseph looked at the other men, then shifted. "I could have, yes, but . . ."

His voice trailed off. He was nervous. Porter felt a slight rush of power.

"But you wanted me to know your interest in my daughter is official?" Porter asked.

Joseph took a deep breath, glanced at the other men, and blushed. "Yes, sir, I did. It is."

Porter was touched by the young man's nervousness. He remembered doing this same thing many years ago with his wife's father. The old man had tortured him then, making him wait days for an answer.

Porter could not do that to this young man or to his own daughter, who admired Joseph so much that it was painful.

"I shall give it to her," Porter said kindly, "with my blessing."

Joseph exhaled loudly. The other men looked

60

down, suppressing smiles. Everyone knew that young Putnam had very nearly asked for Lizzy's hand.

Joseph nodded once. "God be with you, then."

But Porter wasn't done with him. "And Joseph, I expect you to pay me a visit sometime soon. An official one."

Joseph smiled. "Yes. I shall, sir. Thank you."

He ran off, all grace and energy, a young man in love. Porter watched him go, and clutched the carving.

"Did you feel the air shift just now?" Porter asked his friends. They nodded. They might have a Putnam on their side now.

"Everything," Porter said quietly, "has just changed."

SEVEN

It was cold, but the sun was out. Annie Putnam hadn't felt such a glorious day in a long time. She liked the way the wind bit her cheeks and moved her hair beneath her hood. She had a small basket over her arm, and even though she was working, she felt free.

Mercy Lewis, Abigail Williams, Betty Parris, and May Walcott were near her, gathering roots and nuts in the woods. The woods felt safe with her friends nearby.

Annie felt better as well. Her house had been an awful place recently. Her mama had been crying herself to sleep at night, and once she had complained to Papa that her breasts ached with milk for the dead babe. Papa had turned away, as if he did not want to hear it.

At that moment, Annie had touched her own flat

chest, wondering at all the things that awaited her. Once she had thought them pleasant. Now she doubted that they would be.

She raised her head and let the wind brush over her. If only she were a man, she could have power and control and freedom to walk through the Village the way her papa did. People would listen to her and do as she asked.

But she was not a man. Already there was a division between her and Nathaniel. Nathaniel would never be asked to gather nuts. 'Twas woman's work, like helping with childbirth.

Annie shuddered, feeling the sadness and fear inside her rise again. She didn't want to think about that. Not now.

Instead, she moved closer to the other girls and let their conversation flow over her.

". . . a butcher," Mercy Lewis said. "And we'll live in town and every night go to bed with a full belly."

"I should like to marry a tailor like Goodman Cummings," Abigail Williams said. "A husband whose hands are fine and always clean."

"Cleaner than your own?" May Walcott asked. "How shall that look?"

May pointed to Abigail's hands as she dug in the dirt for roots. Abigail looked and frowned, realizing that May was right.

The girls laughed, Annie too. The laugh felt good. It was a relief after the terrible days. But it also felt wrong. She wasn't sure what her mama would think of her joy.

After a moment, Abigail laughed with them. Then she threw a clod of dirt playfully at May, who ducked.

"I want to marry a preacher like my father," little Betty Parris said. She sounded so sincere. She was such a gentle thing. Annie liked her but thought she was almost too young to be with them.

"You shall marry no one because you cry too much," Abigail Williams said. "Only sinners cry."

" 'Tisn't true." Betty teared up. Annie wanted to put a hand on her arm to comfort her, but knew better. Once Abigail started in on Betty, there was no stopping her.

"There are the tears now," Abigail said. " 'Tis proof you are a sinner. See?"

Abigail laughed, and the laugh was mean. The other girls joined in. After a moment, Annie did too.

"Sinner's tears!" the girls chanted. "Sinner's tears."

Annie mouthed the words because she didn't like the look of pain on Betty's face. It seemed that Betty wanted to cry, but she was afraid to now—afraid it would mean she was a sinner.

Annie remembered how hard she had cried the night the baby died. Had it been her sin, her fear, that had killed him?

Then a bird shrieked in the distance. The laughter stopped, and everyone looked around. May Walcott looked scared, as if the bird reminded her of something frightening.

"Did you hear that?" Mercy Lewis asked.

Annie clutched her basket closer and listened. So

did the others. From somewhere in the woods came the bird call again. It was unnaturally lovely. Annie wasn't sure she had ever heard anything like it before.

May Walcott's face had gone white.

" 'Tis a woodpecker," Abigail said.

"It can't be," May Walcott said. "It is nearly November."

The girls pocketed their roots and moved toward the sound. Annie was the only one with a basket, and she wished she weren't carrying it. It felt clumsy; it got in the way.

She wasn't sure what May Walcott was afraid of, but she had an idea. May claimed she'd seen Indians in the woods the night of the fire, and they had made sounds like an owl's hoot.

Annie felt caught between fear and excitement. Indians? Or a beautiful bird no one had seen before? She wanted it to be the bird, because the thought of Indians was too awful.

Then Mercy stopped, rolled her eyes, and shook her head. " 'Tis William Proctor."

Annie felt her breath catch. William Proctor was such a handsome boy. "Let me see."

She pushed forward, and there he was in all his glory. He was four years older than she was—a majestic sixteen—and he seemed perfect. He was standing beside the Proctors'maid, Mary Warren, and he was making the bird calls for her amusement.

Annie felt a stab of jealousy and then wished it away. Mary Warren was no one important, after all.

Annie came out of the woods and put her hands on

her hips, smiling at William. "You had us fooled, William Proctor."

She almost told him that he had frightened May, but she didn't think that would be right. May would deny it anyway. No one else seemed to have noticed.

"He can mimic any bird you could name," Mary Warren said. "Ask him."

William blushed as he looked at Mary. Annie didn't like that either.

"Not any," William said.

"Do a wood owl," May Walcott asked. Her color was good again. She was no longer scared.

William shifted his feet, looking uncomfortable. His blush deepened, but he prepared anyway. He licked his lips, listened for a moment as if he could hear the bird in his head, and then he called an owl's hoot.

The girls laughed, and Annie thought she had never heard anything so wonderful.

"A barn sparrow," Abigail asked.

"A whippoorwill," Mercy said. "Oh please, William."

"Can you do a love bird?" Annie asked, astonished at her own forwardness.

William glanced at Mary Warren, who smiled shyly at him. Annie willed him to look her way, and he did then, nodding, and starting the love bird's song.

It was perfect. He was performing for her. She clasped her hands together, wondering if he knew how talented he was.

The other girls tried to mimic him. They couldn't make the sounds, and they laughed at their own ineptitude. Annie didn't like the way they were interrupting him or the way he was looking at Mary out of the corner of his eye.

William continued to call, and the laughter grew. It sounded wild, out of control, and she remembered how the Reverend said joyful noises should only be made unto the Lord. They were not worshiping here. They were mocking—and it was wrong.

William smiled at Mary, and Annie could take no more.

"Stop it!" she said. " 'Tis sinful!"

Everyone did stop. She saw hesitation on May's face, and Abigail frowned. William was watching Annie as if he hadn't seen her before.

"But it is fun," Betty Parris whined.

"Slothful merriment is the Devil's pastime." Annie had no idea why she had felt sorry for Betty. Betty was tearful, just as Abigail said. She had no idea how anyone could put up with her. "It is sinning."

"But—" Betty said.

Annie grabbed Betty's thin shoulders and shook her. " 'Tis against God's will."

Betty's eyes filled with tears, but she held them back somehow, her face turning red. Her shoulders felt small in Annie's fingers, and Annie let go.

She hadn't expected her emotions to get away from her so quickly. She scarcely felt like herself lately, and this made it seem even more so.

The others were staring at her, even William. He

seemed almost angry that she had spoiled his fun. Well, someone had to. He was flirting with a maid in the woods, and that would lead to sin. Just like all this wild laughter.

Even though she had participated in it. Encouraged it even.

She felt heat rise in her own cheeks. She hated this, hated the way they all made her feel. She was right, and they didn't even seem to know it.

But no one spoke to her, and after a moment she turned and ran away from them.

The woods did not seem like a refuge. Annie could hear the voices behind her, talking about her and about how strange she was. They did not understand what sin could do, the way it could affect everything.

Mama had been talking of sin a lot these last few days. Mama believed that sin had caused the baby's death, caused all the deaths, that God was frowning on them. Annie's family wasn't particularly merry, but they sinned in other ways.

And she didn't want anything to happen to her friends. Although she was no longer sure of William Proctor. Flirting with Mary—and she nothing more than a maid. How could he do such a thing? And the way he had looked at Annie. Surely he would never smile on her again.

Without realizing it, she had reached the road. As she climbed the embankment she heard a horse's hooves clomping and the rattle of a cart. The Reverend Parris's booming voice reached her as if he were speaking to her alone.

". . . Puritans, we are a people chosen specially by God!"

Sometimes Annie hated that. It meant that God gave them special attention, special notice. She didn't want the special notice.

She knew such thoughts were blasphemous, but she couldn't help them. She couldn't stop them.

She reached the edge of the road and realized she had run to the Village square. People were gathered all around it, but they were eerily silent. They were watching the cart approach.

"But that it is meant we are held to a higher standard by Him."

The Reverend was standing beside some people she could not see clearly. But she saw her mama on the fringes of the crowd. Mama did not look herself—so wan and tired. She had her cloak pulled close.

Then Annie looked at the cart. In it were men and women oddly dressed, with strange hats on their heads. Two women followed the cart, and for a moment, Annie thought they wore the same odd clothes.

But they wore no clothes at all.

Her cheeks heated.

She stepped even closer so that she could see better. The scene fascinated her and made her ill at the same time.

The cart had stopped in front of the Reverend. He was speaking to a group of people who were being loaded onto the cart to join the others.

"When you fail Him," he said, "with your unseemly speeches, you are a sinner. With your theft, you are a sinner."

Annie now saw the hats, and she could read the words on them. One read *Unseemly Speeches against the Church*, and another, *Stealing Food*.

She crept closer. There was writing on the backs of the naked women. It said *Unholy Fornication*.

Annie did not know exactly what fornication was, but she knew it was a horrible sin. The women looked humiliated and cold; their skin was bluish and covered with goosebumps. Annie looked at her mama, still on the fringes of the crowd. She looked saddened but not appalled.

"With your unholy fornication," the Reverend was saying, "you are a sinner. With your doubts about God's presence, you are a sinner."

Mama's mouth dropped open, as if she thought the Reverend were speaking to her.

"But not only a sinner. You are a sinner worse than others because you have been chosen by God, and yet you failed him."

This time, Annie felt as if the Reverend had heard her thoughts in the woods. The heat in her cheeks deepened. Mama shook her head and slipped through the crowd, disappearing. Annie did not want to go after her, did not want her mama to know she was here.

"And you have failed me," the Reverend said, as if all of the sinners had hurt him personally.

Annie stood on her tiptoes. She recognized the last

70

sinner being forced to enter the cart. It was Mary Godfrey. Someone had hit her. Her lip was split, and her face was badly bruised. On her forehead, someone had written: *Railing and Scolding Husband*.

The Reverend did not look at Mary. He was speaking to all the sinners. "You shall be taken from village to village so all can see your sins. As you are exposed to your more righteous neighbors, ask thyself this: God has chosen me to purify you and lead you to Him. But with your sins you chose to follow Satan and not me? Why?"

Mary Godfrey kept her head high. Her eyes were moving as she walked among her neighbors, but mostly out of nervousness. Then Annie realized that someone was walking beside the cart, talking to everyone within.

Bridget Bishop. Papa had once said she was pretty, but she was no longer. She had a strange face, and even stranger eyes. Her lips moved as if she were uttering something—an incantation, perhaps. Mary looked at her quickly, hesitated, then glanced at the Reverend. He hadn't seen Bridget Bishop yet, but Mary seemed to be taking solace in Bridget's words.

Annie wondered what the Reverend would say when he saw Bridget Bishop, but before he did, a man's voice rose above the murmuring of the crowd:

"Keep away, you filthy hex!"

Annie looked in the direction of the voice and saw Ezekiel Godfrey, Mary's husband. He shouted, "Avert your eyes, Mary."

Annie looked at Mary to see if she had heard. She

didn't move, but Bridget did. She slipped an amulet around Mary's neck. Annie recognized its design. The Parris's maid, Tituba, said such amulets provided protection.

Mary passed into the crowd, near her husband. He raised a hand to her, and she ducked immediately, clearly afraid of him. Annie's stomach clenched.

"You listen to me, you insolent wife!" Godfrey shouted. "Not to that witch woman."

The Reverend seemed oblivious to everything going on around him. He was still speaking to the crowd. Many of them had rotted vegetables in their hands, and while Godfrey shouted at his wife, they started throwing them at the sinners.

Annie's stomach clenched tighter.

"What causes you to turn away from the path of righteousness I am leading you toward—the path that leads to God?" the Reverend asked. "And become sinners?

The sinners didn't flinch as bits of tomato and rotted potato hit them in the face. The naked women seemed oblivious to it, as if the cold and humiliation were already too much for them.

"Why?" the Reverend continued, and he sounded duly perplexed.

Annie shivered. These people were worse than she could ever be. They had done terrible things. Maybe they were why such shame had come to her family. Maybe it had nothing at all to do with her or Mama. After all, Bridget Bishop sinned right in front of the Reverend, and he didn't see it.

Annie would make him see it.

She took one of the roots she had gathered and threw it at the cart with all of her strength.

"Shameful sinners!" she shouted.

The root hit Mary in the face, right on one of the bruises, making her wince. So much for the Devil's protection. Annie felt herself grow taller. She was doing what adults did.

She was using her own power to save her people.

EIGHT

Lizzy Porter's hands were buried in dough. Mama insisted on kneading each loaf of bread until all the flour lumps were gone—no one wanted to eat bread and get a mouthful of flour, she would say—and so the task usually fell to Lizzy. She had the strongest hands of any of her siblings.

They were crowded around her in the keeping room, helping prepare dinner. The cooking fireplace was stoked and burning hot. Lizzy's back was warm, but her face was cool.

The family's maid, Lita, also kneaded bread. She had a good technique, rolling and slapping the dough on the wooden surface. But Lizzy's was more delicate.

Outside, the clomping of horse's hooves caught

her sister Enid's attention. Enid dropped the bowl she was holding and headed for the window.

She let out a giggle.

Lizzy's sister Jane hurried to the window then, and giggled also. She elbowed Enid, and they both looked back at Lizzy.

Lizzy couldn't stand it anymore. She left the dough, wiped her hands with a towel, and walked to the window. As she reached the window, Enid said breathlessly, " 'Tis Joseph Putnam come to ask for Lizzy's hand."

Lizzy felt her heart flutter, but she made sure not to change her expression. "Stop it. There could be a hundred reasons why he would call on Father."

She leaned closer to the window to see Joseph tie his horse to a post. What a fine figure of a man. She particularly liked his eyes. They were very warm, and he was kind. So many men, even young men, were not kind.

"But only one reason that matters," Jane said. "I believe Enid is right. You shall marry a Putnam."

"He is the richest of all of them," Enid said.

Lizzy blushed. She couldn't help it. She knew he was rich, but she didn't care. She liked his kindness better.

"Both of you must stop," she said. " 'Tis obscene to talk this way. Lita, tell them to stop."

Lita continued slapping the bread dough on the table, but she smiled. "Everyone knows young Joseph has been courting you. And the blush in your face is confirmation enough."

Jane and Enid started jumping up and down. "Goodwife Putnam," they both said. "You shall be Goody Putnam."

Lizzy's blush grew deeper. She'd dreamed of that name in the dark, when her sisters slept beside her.

"Aye, but 'tis part a curse." Lita hadn't broken the rhythm of kneading the dough as she spoke. Lizzy's dough lay in a neglected lump beside hers. "A wife of his must cope with Thomas and Edward. Brothers-in-law such as these shall be a constant chafe for a poor wife."

Lizzy hadn't expected such words. She frowned. "But why, Lita? Why are they so hateful to Joseph? 'Tis heard everywhere."

The girls left the window and crowded around Lita. She finally stopped kneading, seeming to enjoy the attention.

"Because," Lita said, "when their father died, he left Thomas and Edward out of his will. Instead he left most of his estate to his second wife and their only son, Joseph. They will never forgive him. And he has no other family."

She smiled again and stroked Lizzy's cheek. Lizzy leaned into her hand.

"You will be all of it for him," Lita said, and Lizzy closed her eyes. It was her dream—and now, it seemed it would come true.

A family of her own, and one that would be mostly hers. With Joseph, a kind man. And enough money to keep her comfortable for the rest of her life.

What more could a woman ask for?

*   *   *

Joseph Putnam had always thought that Israel Porter's home was one of the most beautiful in the area. It was large enough to have not only a magnificent hall, but a parlor as well. The parlor clearly wasn't used as much as the hall, judging by the chill, but it seemed pleasant enough.

When Joseph had come into the house, Porter had brought him here instead of staying in the hall. Now he knew why.

Porter had led him to a large window with a view of the town. Beyond lay the harbor, a bit of gray with masts on the horizon.

"Over that rise is the port of Salem Town," Porter said. "You are aware of that, yes?"

Joseph smiled. "Have you asked me here to give me a lesson in geography?"

"Of course not," Porter said. "The future."

The future? Joseph looked at the other man expectantly. Porter was much older, and he had a confidence many in Salem did not possess. Perhaps it came from his wealth, or perhaps it came from his knowledge. Joseph wasn't sure which.

"Your grandfather and mine were the richest men in Salem," Porter said. "I believe yours once owned over seven hundred acres of land."

"Yes, it was that much," Joseph said.

"And today," Porter said, "except for you, not one of the Putnams has enough land to support another generation. The Putnams believe they have been wronged by their neighbors, and they bring lawsuit after lawsuit. They believe God has turned his back on them, so they hire their own minister. Anything but the truth."

Joseph did not move. He wanted to nod. He had always privately thought these things about his half-brothers. They were bitter men who took no responsibility for their own lives.

His father had known that. Before his father died, he had pulled Joseph aside. *Joseph*, he had said. *You are the only one worthy of the Putnam name. You will put it to good use, and be the best Christian you can be.*

"New England's wealth is not going to come from the land," Porter was saying. He extended his hand toward the harbor. "That is the future. Trade. Shipping. And commerce. Not farming. If the Putnams weren't so stubborn they would have seen this when my father did. I mean no offense."

"None taken," Joseph said. "I am more outcast than Putnam."

"I know that," Porter said. "It is why I shall accept your request for my daughter in marriage."

Joseph felt as if his heart had stopped. He suddenly could not take a breath. This was the second time Porter had mentioned an offer. Joseph had meant to do it someday, but he had been working up his nerve.

Porter smiled at Joseph's discomfort. "As soon as you get around to making it, that is. I would like to offer you the future."

Joseph couldn't put it off any longer. The old man was giving him a chance, right now. It didn't matter that he hadn't rehearsed the words.

"Lizzy? Marriage?" Joseph said, trying to gather himself. "May I? Rather . . ."

His discomfort seemed to amuse Porter. Joseph cleared his throat and tried again.

"Goodman Porter, I would like to offer my marriage for your daughter's hand. Or rather . . ."

Porter grinned. Even though Joseph had not finished, Porter shook his hand.

"It is all right," Porter said. "Your words are nonsense, but your meaning is quite clear enough. I accept your request."

Joseph let out a small sigh. He had not expected this to be so easy. He'd heard tales from other men of their future fathers-in-law denying their pledge or making them wait for a long time before getting an answer.

But Porter did not seem to be that sort of man. His expression softened at Joseph's confusion.

"A father is blessed when he can make a marriage that is rich in love," Porter said. "And in this case, with a marriage of Porter and Putnam assets, we will bring the future to us. Let me not pretend that does not please me as well."

He extended his hand again. Joseph took it, and they shook. The agreement was made. Joseph was going to wed Lizzy Porter, the prettiest girl in all of Massachusetts.

He was a very lucky man.

Ann Putnam had never been so tired in her life. Her entire body ached, as it had since the failed birth. She was still embarrassed by the scene she had caused at the funeral, and Thomas had not let her forget it. He reminded her that women should reflect well on their families, implying that she did not.

She had left the house earlier that day and stumbled onto the unfortunate scene in the Village square. Reverend Parris had seemed genuinely confused by all the sinners. Thomas had hoped that Parris would be the answer to all their ills, but Parris seemed to have no answers—at least none that Ann had heard yet.

Then she had met Rebecca Nurse. The elderly woman had seen Ann's confusion and had taken it upon herself to help her. Ann did not like Goody Nurse, although she was hard put to say why. The woman stank of sanctimony, and it seemed genuine.

It would have made Ann feel better to see a bit of human frailty in Rebecca Nurse.

Still, Ann leaned on the old woman as they walked back toward the house. A horse was tied to the rail outside. Joseph's horse. Ann flinched. Whenever her brother-in-law visited, there was trouble.

Goody Nurse didn't seem to notice Ann's new distress. She was talking, as she had been since they'd met in the Village square.

"The Lord has given us the gift of much work to do, and yet we must also take time for ourselves," Rebecca Nurse was saying. "To do nothing but walk. Like this. It will ease your heart and make you forget."

Nothing would make her forget. Apparently, Goody Nurse did not know these things.

"And what will make my body forget?" Ann

snapped. "My breasts are still full with milk for the child. My arms ache to hold him. How much walking until my body forgets this?"

Goody Nurse did not rise to the bait. Instead, she patted Ann's arm. "The good Lord does not let us suffer forever. Have faith in that."

"Faith," Ann said to herself.

A loud crash came from the house, followed by her husband's voice. "No! I forbid it. Do you hear?"

Ann recoiled in shame. She knew that scenes like this never played in Goody Nurse's house.

She slipped her arm from Goody Nurse's and said, "I must take leave. Forgive me."

And Ann ran toward the house. She did not want Goody Nurse to follow her or to hear any more. Her family was the subject of enough gossip. The last thing they needed was even more.

She pulled open the door to find her husband leaning over his brother Joseph. Joseph's face was white, as it always was when he was frightened—and Thomas often frightened him.

"A Putnam shall never marry a Porter," Thomas shouted. "Never."

Joseph's mouth worked before the words emerged. " 'Tis my right to do—"

"I am the eldest," Thomas said. "I shall say what is right and what is not."

Annie and Nathaniel ran to Ann and grabbed her skirts, hiding in them for protection. Thomas had been getting angry like this a lot lately. It was bad for her, bad for the family.

"Thomas," Ann said. "Whatever—"

"Leave us!" Her husband said, waving his arm to keep her back.

She wasn't going to leave. To leave, she would have to cross the room and mount the stairs, somehow taking the children with her.

"Joseph wishes to marry Lizzy Porter," Annie whispered to her mother.

The whisper carried across the room. Joseph looked at them, his eyes—so like Thomas's—defiant. "And I shall."

Then he stood up straighter, as if his own words had given him courage. He faced Thomas. "I do not need your permission for this or any other decision I make. Shout, strike me—it makes no difference."

Joseph tried to push past Thomas, but Thomas wouldn't have it. He grabbed Joseph and flung him at the wall.

"No!" Thomas shouted.

Joseph hit the wall with a thud. Thomas strode forward, his right hand already making a fist.

This had gone too far.

"Thomas!" Ann said as she hurried toward her husband. She used the last of her strength to pull him away from his half brother. Annie and Nathaniel scurried for cover.

It was wrong, wrong, to have the family so fearful and divided.

"Have you lost your senses?" she said.

Thomas turned on her. "He and his whore of a mother have already taken the property that was

82

rightfully mine by God's law and order of birth. He shan't also marry the daughter of the sinner who designed it to be thus stolen."

"Joseph is in love with her," Ann said. She had been jealous of that from the start. Thomas had wooed her, and maybe he had even liked her once, but he had never loved her. "Everyone knows it."

"Love!" Thomas shouted. "Are you blind? This is Israel Porter's design to steal more of my land. He will trade his own daughter for it."

"Liar!" Joseph pushed closer, obviously spoiling for a fight as much as his brother was. "Don't speak thus of her."

Thomas whirled on him. "Israel Porter was the executor of your mother's estate. Do you believe he has not been planning this for the eighteen years of your life?"

"Hold your tongue!" Joseph said. "You shame yourself with such slander. It is you who has wished me ill for all my years."

And to Ann's shock, Joseph—the gentle and kind Putnam brother—shoved Thomas with all of his strength. Thomas raised his fist to strike Joseph, but Joseph caught it in mid-air.

He held it tight. "If you raise your hand to me again, I swear to God you shall lose it."

Ann believed him. And secretly, she cheered on her brother-in-law.

Nine

Thomas Putnam whipped his horse again. The animal was foaming at the mouth, its barrel chest heavy, the breath coming out of its nostrils in steamy vapor, but he didn't care.

He had to get to Israel Porter's house now.

Despite the snow that was falling thickly on Salem Village, there were too many people in the street. He wanted to whip them out of his way, although he did not.

Instead, he shouted at them and ordered them to move. They did, scurrying toward the buildings like rats.

Who did Porter think he was, forcing the marriage in such haste? Had his daughter fornicated with someone else and gotten with child? Did they seek to blame it on Joseph?

Or had Joseph sinned with the Porter girl himself?

Putnam hadn't thought to ask that when Joseph had come to his home nearly a week earlier to announce his engagement. A week was not enough time to plan for a life together. But Putnam doubted that Porter wanted these children to have a life together. All he saw was the merger of the households and the power it accorded him in the village.

Putnam whipped his horse harder, speeding down the road to Porter's house. It seemed to take him forever to reach that huge building—ostentation that a true Puritan would have been ashamed of.

Of course, Joseph's mount was already tied to a post. Putnam rode past it, right to the front door. He kicked the door with his boot, scuffing the wood.

The door opened wide.

Putnam said, "Let me—"

"You are too late," Israel Porter announced flatly. "They are married."

Putnam's hands tightened on the reins. Porter had planned this. He had made certain Putnam would not know until it was too late.

"You shall pay for this, Israel," Putnam said, each word a curse.

"I have done nothing to bring shame onto this house," Porter said.

So innocent, as if he did not know what Putnam was speaking of. Putnam leaned closer, using the height he gained from sitting atop his mount. "You and that thief brother of yours will pay."

"There is naught you can do," Porter said. "Not

your anger, not another legal suit. You can not harm them now."

Them? Porter included Joseph in this, as if Putnam would want to harm his own brother? His own foolish, very foolish brother, who did not know when he was being used.

Putnam held up his whip. He was tempted to use it, but he did not. "You shall pay for conniving against me, Israel Porter. Let God hear me now. You shall pay for this."

He backed the horse away from the door, then yanked on the bridle and rode off. He had never been so angry in his life. Things were not supposed to go like this. He had ordered Joseph to break off the engagement. And he had all but threatened Porter.

Yet they had gone ahead anyway.

Ann had tried to argue with him, to claim that the boy loved Porter's daughter. As if such soft emotions meant anything. The boy was ruining the village, not even realizing he was doing it.

The snow was falling so heavily now that Putnam could barely see. His horse was wheezing, and he knew he might pay a price for treating it so badly.

Still he pushed it forward. He had one more home to visit.

Thomas Putnam paced back and forth in Samuel Parris's hall. The hearth had a tiny fire, one so small that it was a waste of wood. Putnam could see his own breath as he spoke.

Parris sat while Putnam paced—something

Putnam did not want but did not know how to stop. Parris should show Putnam, the man responsible for his hire, more respect.

"It is no less than a rot in this village," Putnam said. "Has God determined that the Putnams shall inherit nothing but an aggregate of loss? A Putnam child dies, a Putnam barn burned to the ground—and now this."

Parris kept his hands clasped in his lap. His face was an impassive mask. Putnam wanted to see outrage on it, outrage like his own.

"Israel Porter now controls land that was rightfully mine. Were we not to rise as one? Is that not the Puritanism my grandfather came to Salem for? You said it yourself, Satan's hand is upon us. We brought you here to strengthen us. But you have not."

"Do not cast the glare of blame on me," Parris said. "My sermons are leading this congregation to—"

"Then no one is listening," Putnam snapped. Was this minister so feeble that he did not understand his role as community leader? He was supposed to calm these crises, not sit idly by while they went on and on. "You were to restore the godliness and order here. It is why I met each of your demands. I gave you land upon which you sleep each night. Agreed to your salary."

"Agreed to it, but have not yet delivered it. 'Tis winter now. How can I be the minister you want when half of Salem Village does not give the respect I warrant?" He gestured toward the hearth. "Where is my wood?"

The man had the life he deserved. He was a failure, and he was failing at Putnam's expense.

"Where is my order?" Putnam snarled.

Parris glared at him defiantly. Then someone knocked on the door. It was a tentative knock, so faint that Putnam knew it had been made by a woman.

"Samuel," the man's wife said through the door. "People will hear you."

Putnam made himself take a deep breath. This minister couldn't even control his own family. Scripture said that the wife should be subject to her husband, not the other way around.

At least Parris had the good sense to look ashamed of his wife's actions. He did not speak to Putnam, and Putnam felt the immense anger that had brought him here subside.

But he was not going to forget the purpose of his visit here, no matter what happened in Parris's household.

"You shall have your wood," Putnam said. "And I shall expect the return of Puritanism that you were brought to Salem for."

He opened the door, passed Parris's wife—a weak-willed wisp of a woman—and paid her the courtesy that he was bound to, under his religion.

"Good evening, Goody Parris."

She bowed her head, and before she could answer, he let himself out into the frosty night.

Betty Parris was cold beneath the blankets. She hadn't been able to sleep because it was so cold, even with Abigail beside her. And then the raised voices, coming through the floorboards. The way Goodman Putnam had yelled at her father—she had never heard such a thing.

And she knew she wasn't supposed to hear. As the front door slammed, she turned and huddled next to Abigail as much for comfort as for warmth.

"Are we going to hell?" Betty whispered.

"Shh," Abigail responded. " 'Tis a sin to listen to them like this."

That was why Betty had asked. If only Abigail understood. Could a person sin without intending it?

"But I did not mean to listen," Betty said.

"Quiet!" Abigail said. "Do not speak. Do not even think. The Devil will hear and will make you his witch."

Betty rolled away from Abigail and huddled on the edge of the bed. She closed her eyes and willed sleep, but she knew it wouldn't come. Her thoughts wouldn't stop.

She was going to hell. She was tempting the Devil just by breathing. She was sinning all the time.

And she had never been so afraid in her entire life.

Ten

The meeting house was cold, even though it was full. Ann Putnam sat beside her husband in the Putnams' pew, a blanket across her lap. She hadn't been able to get fully warm since the baby's death.

Annie sat beside her, and Nathaniel beside Thomas. Thomas's dog lay across his feet, keeping them warm. At least their pew was close to the front of the meeting house, near a brazier filled with hot coals.

Ann couldn't imagine what it would be like to sit in the back, near the door, with people constantly coming and going, letting the winter in.

The service had been going on for hours now. Normally Ann did not mind this, but it was getting harder and harder for her to sit through. Her body hadn't healed properly, and the middle of her back ached. Her sister-in-law, Edward's wife, had told her it was because of the extra weight in her breasts.

Sometimes Ann thought it was because of the extra pain in her heart.

Behind her, one of the church deacons hit one parishioner who had been snoring softly. Ann knew better than to turn around and see who that had been.

Reverend Parris was in high form this day, working to drive the sin from the congregation. Ann still couldn't get his words from a few days ago out of her mind, and now he was chastising those who had been in the cart, those who had come to his pulpit for forgiveness.

He was standing before Mary Godfrey. Ann had always felt sorry for Mary. She had been so in love with Ezekiel when she married him, and then she had looked so sad shortly thereafter.

All the women in the village knew where Mary's bruises came from, even though she blamed increased clumsiness. Husbands had the right to strike their wives—even the duty, as Samuel Parris would say—but some husbands enjoyed that duty too much.

There was sin in that, Ann believed. There was sin in so many things.

Mary Godfrey's bruises, so vivid that day in the cart, had faded to a pale yellow.

"Please, Reverend," she said, "I have confessed my guilt of unseemly practices. I did covet a bolt of fabric. My husband struck me for it, and I did strike him

91

back. Will you not forgive my sins? I wish to be part of this church."

Ann tucked her hands under the blanket, searching for warmth.

"I have heard enough, Mary Godfrey," Parris said, "By your actions of lustful covetousness you have clearly chosen to align yourself with the Devil rather than with our Lord Jesus Christ. This church does not want sinners."

He waved his hands, and two deacons, who had been standing near him, took Mary Godfrey away. Ann did not turn her head as they pulled her toward the meeting-house door. She had seen this scene enacted too many times in the past.

God did not want sinners, but sometimes He got them long after they had become members of this congregation.

Her eyes teared, and she wished she could lose this feeling of dread, which had accompanied her for so long.

"Who next?" the Reverend asked, and Ann's mouth went dry. She had been meaning to speak to him again, in private, but she had not found the chance. Perhaps here—

Behind her, she heard the sound of a scuffle, and despite herself, Ann turned. Mary Godfrey was fighting the deacons. As Ann watched, Mary broke free and turned to face Reverend Parris.

"No!" she shouted. "I have sinned. Now I have repented. Why won't you hear it?"

The congregation started murmuring. Ann could

hear her own shock mirrored in her neighbors' words. The Reverend Parris was God's representative. His decision was final.

"Mama?" Annie whispered.

But Ann had no answers for her daughter. She did not say anything. Instead, she watched in growing fascination as Ezekiel Godfrey stood.

"Mind your place, wife," he shouted.

But Mary Godfrey ignored him, proving that she had not, after all, repented her sin. A wife should never disobey her husband. Ann had learned that lesson quite painfully.

Mary pointed a finger at the Reverend. "Where is your forgiveness? Can you claim before God that you have never sinned yourself?"

Ann's breath caught. She could not believe that anyone would dare to ask a minister that.

The Reverend Parris seemed shocked as well. He stared at Mary as if she had seen inside his soul.

His reaction disturbed even Thomas, whose fists clenched on his thighs. His disapproval of Parris had grown in recent weeks, and Ann wasn't sure why. Her husband had stopped confiding in her long ago.

Voices rippled through the meeting house—reactions to Mary's accusation, to the Reverend's silence.

From the back, someone shouted, "Speak, Reverend."

The Reverend Parris blinked at that voice as if coming out of a sound sleep. Then his face regained its confidence, and on top of it, anger.

The anger relieved Ann. It gave him the strength a minister should have.

"Sinner!" he said to Mary. "If you are resolved in your way, be assured that you are going to a bottomless pit. You are going to dwell with the devils and the damned and be tormented with the flames from Hell, where you shall be filled brimful in soul and body with the wrath of God."

Mary Godfrey flinched at his words, but they relieved Ann. Mary Godfrey clearly had sinned, and she was continuing to sin through her anger and her challenges to her husband's authority. The Reverend Parris was right to tell her what would become of her.

He whirled on the congregation, facing them as if he were filled with the Holy Spirit. "Who next wishes to be heard?"

Several fearful Christians stood. The deacons carried Mary Godfrey out, and no one looked at her, sinner that she was.

Ann did not stand, but she spoke anyway, almost without volition.

"I do," she said.

The Reverend's gaze met hers, and she thought she saw a sudden fear in his eyes. She felt her husband tense beside her, and Annie gazed up at her as if hating the attention her mother was drawing.

"Speak, Ann Putnam," the Reverend said.

Now that she had the floor, Ann was reluctant to speak her most secret concerns before the congregation. She knew it was the Puritan way, but she had always hated airing private feelings before the others.

Still, she had asked for this, and the Reverend had given her no answers when she sought him alone. So she would try here.

She stood slowly.

"I fear," she said, and the final word caught in her throat, as if it did not want to emerge. She made herself swallow and start again. "I fear that there is some weakness in my conviction. I know not what, for I am diligent in my prayers and righteous in my actions. But something . . ."

Her husband shifted in the pew, his eyes downcast as if he did not want to hear his wife's words. Annie was watching her with horror. Ann resolved not to look at her family. She made herself focus on the Reverend.

"Something has strained my soul," she said, "and this is why they die. They are innocent. Not even a single breath taken. So it must be my guilt that is causing this. Help me. Help me find absolution. I beg this of you, Reverend."

Reverend Parris studied her as if he could see right through her. For the first time in weeks, she felt hope rise in her breast. He was God's representative. He would know how to help her.

He had to. There was no one else.

"Heaven is large, Ann Putnam, if you are virtuous enough," Reverend Parris said, his voice gentle. "But there is just one way into this happiness. It is narrow, with a little gate. And if you miss this gate, you lose all your labor and shall never come to salvation."

He did understand, then.

"That is what I fear, Reverend," she said. "But how—"

"We are born into sin." The Reverend spoke the words that had been haunting her. Her three dead children, born in sin, unable to redeem themselves. Her heart twisted, and she realized he would not offer the comfort she sought.

But she said nothing as he went on. "We must through much tribulation enter into the Kingdom of God. We are not to lie upon a bed of ease, but to engage in a field of war. And endure to the end. Do not lose your faith, Ann Putnam."

She was trying not to. That was why she was speaking to him. Couldn't he understand that? "But Reverend . . ."

He turned away from her. She let her voice trail away, but she had not finished. He had not really answered her, just as before. And she so needed answers.

"Who next wishes to speak?" Reverend Parris asked.

Others stood, but Ann could not bring herself to sit down. Her hands twisted against her apron. Her husband leaned forward, studying his horrible dog, and the Reverend scanned the congregation for some other sinner.

Annie grabbed Ann's sleeve and tugged.

"Sit down, Mama," Annie said. "You have called enough attention to yourself."

She spoke loud enough for the entire congregation

to hear. Admonished by her own daughter. Ann's cheeks flooded with color, and she sat, burying her face in her hands.

The keeping room was cold, as it had been lately. The sermon book lay closed and neglected on a nearby table. Samuel Parris could not bring himself to copy that day's sermon inside.

Instead, he kept hearing Mary Godfrey's voice, echoing over and over inside his head.

Where is your forgiveness?

"Samuel?"

His wife's voice covered the voice in his head. He blinked, and the room came into focus. He was sitting at the head of the table, Elizabeth across from him, looking concerned. Betty sat beside him and Abigail on his other side.

No one had touched the food.

"Have you not heard a word?" Elizabeth asked.

He had not. Mary Godfrey's accusation had possessed his mind.

Betty was watching him with fear. He had never seen actual fear on his daughter's face before—at least not when she looked at him. He stroked her cheek to soothe her.

His actions were so uncharacteristic that his wife seemed even more concerned. He could tell from her tone of voice as she spoke his name again.

Perhaps he had handled things wrong in the meeting house. After all, how did a man know when God worked through him? Did he feel different? Did he speak with his own wisdom or with wisdom granted by God?

Surely a man would feel different with God's hand upon him.

"Do you think," he asked his wife, "I am truly chosen?"

His little family stared at him as if they could not believe his words. His doubt seemed to frighten them more than his certainty did.

Elizabeth watched him with loving concern, but he saw his own fears reflected in her eyes.

She doubted his calling.

They all did.

ELEVEN

Ann's cloak was not warm enough for the chill in the air. She walked in the snowy path left by the other women as they made their way to the village square. The days when merchants' carts arrived were always big events.

Ann used to look forward to them, but this day she could barely convince herself to leave the house.

Every goodwife in the village seemed to be here, picking over merchandise, gabbing with the merchants, bargaining. Ann heard bits of conversation as she approached—requests for a different type of fabric or a particular stitching tool.

A circle of women gathered around the first cart. They were having a conversation, and it didn't seem to be about the goods before them. Ann slipped in among them and started looking at fabric—some good wool that would make nice undergarments for her children.

Her surviving children.

Her hand lingered over some linen, beautiful in its whiteness, and she thought again of her dead son's face. It took her a moment to realize the conversation around her had stopped when she reached the cart.

She raised her head, about to turn and see what was going on, when the conversation started again, this time much louder.

"It is not enough for him to sue me for my land for all these years?" Sarah Osborn spoke. Ann recognized her querulous voice and realized the woman was intentionally speaking loud so that Ann could hear her. "Now Thomas Putnam is ordering my wood to be taken for the minister's salary."

Ann stiffened.

"How much wood are the Putnams themselves tithing? If any," Martha Corey said. " 'Tis all anyone is discussing."

Ann felt tears sting her eyes. She moved away from the cart toward the other one, but she couldn't help a glance over her shoulder. The women who had been standing behind her were trying to hide their smirks but not doing very well.

She hurried away. At the other cart, women were discussing the benefits of echinacea root and the value of the guinea. She stopped and sorted through some cooking tools. Her household didn't need much, but she could always use more knives.

The voices blended, and she did her best to shut them out so that she couldn't hear more innuendo and gossip. But Martha Corey and Sarah Osborn couldn't speak that loudly, and after a few moments, Ann relaxed, searching for a good, solid blade.

Near her, she heard a woman ask, "Have you the root of verbena and oil of flaxseed? It will cure distempers of the womb and solve the mystery of stillbirth."

Ann turned toward the speaker. Bridget Bishop stood in the group of women. The pale light of the sun seemed to shine only on her. She smiled at Ann. The smile had warmth.

"There is no transcendence in suffering," Bridget said.

Ann blinked, feeling unsettled. Were the words spoken for her? Were they spoken at all? She wasn't sure.

She couldn't bear to be at the market any longer. She gathered her cloak around her and fled.

The rest of the day passed as if in a dream. Her mind kept returning to Bridget Bishop's words, to her calm serenity as she had looked at Ann. Ann knew Bridget Bishop's reputation. 'Twas said she was a witch, but Ann's grandmother would have called her a wise woman, a healer who knew arts lost to men.

Such women sinned, so the church said. But the church was providing Ann with no answers. Ann was beginning to suspect that Samuel Parris had none—and he was God's chosen. She was tempted to go to the meeting house in Salem Town, but her husband would not approve.

Thomas had gone to their bedchamber before her. She checked on the children, made sure the hearth fire was banked low, and then went into the bedchamber herself, intent on speaking to her husband.

He had been so angry of late. Joseph's hasty marriage preyed on him. Thomas saw it as a betrayal. He might not have felt the betrayal so strongly if the child had not been lost.

The third child.

She shuddered and pushed open the door to the bedchamber. The room was nearly dark. A single candle illuminated the gloom. Thomas was on his knees beside the bed, his hands clenched in prayer. Something fell from his cheek and landed on his hand, glistening as it ran down.

A tear? Ann had never seen Thomas cry.

She stepped inside, feeling as if she could connect with him for the first time in months.

"And what if God does not listen?" she asked.

Thomas sucked in his breath and whipped around. He had not known she was there after all. She felt doubt grip her. He wiped at his face hastily, furtively, but she saw that she had been correct. It had been a tear that had fallen on his hand.

"Are you bewitched, woman?" he asked. "You entered without a sound."

She closed the door as he stood. He sat on the side of the bed and began to remove his boots as if nothing had gone wrong.

"Did thee hear my question?" she asked quietly.

"If God does not listen," Thomas said, "then we may as well not exist."

She nodded. "It is what I have been fearing these weeks."

He turned toward her, and his face regained its rigid lines. "Do not speak of it again. They are the words of an infidel."

Ann felt his criticism like a slap. She moved away from the door. He finished undressing and slipped into bed, his silly dog already in place at his feet.

Ann was glad this day was over. She undressed as well, leaving the bottom layer of garments on, just as her husband had done. She blew out the candle, crawled in beside him, and nestled her feet against his.

Even the bed was cold.

"It will snow tomorrow," she said. "There is a ring around the moon."

Thomas did not answer, but she knew he was awake.

"There is talk in town," she said, determined to tell him what had happened that day. Maybe she would even mention Bridget Bishop. "Our neighbors are angry about the taxes. They say——"

"You must not listen to what they say," he snapped, his voice louder than it should have been. The children would hear if he was not careful. "There are many who wish to harm this family. They will find fault with every advance a Putnam makes. They always have."

It was such a sore spot with him. She should not have tried that tack.

She wondered just how angry he was with her when he said gently, "Go to sleep, Ann."

He turned away from her, but the gentleness gave her hope.

"Thomas?"

He didn't move, but she could feel him listening.

"Will you touch me, Thomas?" she asked. "Like a husband. You have not since——"

She couldn't speak of the child's death. She wasn't really able to.

She continued in a whisper. "Let me know you do not blame me. To know that would remove the pith of my suffering when these weeks of praying have done naught."

She touched his shoulder, felt him move slightly, as she did.

"Comfort me, husband," she said, "and I shall bring you another child."

He put his hand over hers, but the gesture was not a prelude to something more. It was a caution. "What comfort is it when it brings but stillness and grief to our home?"

She heard her own pain echoed in his voice.

"Go to sleep, Ann."

He kept his hand on hers, but she did not want the touch now. She was embarrassed and saddened by his reaction. She rarely approached him, and now that she had, she learned he did not want to risk more children.

Did not want to risk her giving birth to more dead children.

She pulled her hand from his and closed her eyes, knowing that sleep would not come and this terrible day would never end.

There were dead babies everywhere and midwife Morse was making her hold them. Annie knew she was dreaming, but she could not stop. Then a door slammed, and she fled the room in her dream, sitting up before she was fully awake.

Mercy Lewis slept near her, snoring softly. The house was silent, but Annie knew she had heard a slamming door. She got out of bed, ignoring the cold, and made her way to the window.

Her mama was crossing the yard, her winter cloak wrapped around her. She looked thin and frail against the dirty snow.

Mama never left the house at night. But she had been acting strangely since the funeral.

Papa did not seem to know that. Someone had to make certain Mama did not shame them.

Annie slipped her feet into her shoes, threw her dress over her head, and grabbed her cloak. If she hurried, she would be able to see where Mama was going and perhaps stop her from getting into even more trouble.

Ann felt like a sinner when she contemplated coming to this place. Now that she was here, she felt both free and hopeful—and terrified of being caught.

Bridget Bishop lived at the far edge of the village, in a place so remote that no one came unless they had to. Her home was little more than a pitched roof over a hole dug into the ground.

Still, smoke wisped through the small chimney, showing that someone was awake.

"Bridget Bishop!" Ann called out softly. "Bridget Bishop, will you receive me?"

After a moment, a hatch in the roof pulled in, and Bridget Bishop stepped into the night. She seemed even more powerful than she had that afternoon in the square.

Ann felt small. "I am Ann Put—"

"I know who you are," Bridget said. "What business have you with me?"

She was not welcoming. Ann had thought she would be welcoming. "I do not . . . I am afraid."

"Then turn to your God, church woman," Bridget said. "Pray for your mercy there."

"I have tried," Ann said. "I am a church member, yes. And I have prayed all my life. Harder when the girl child died after but five days of God's grace. And more religiously after the second died in my arms."

Ann took a step closer. Bridget Bishop did not move, but watched her with eerie eyes.

"I feared a breach in my faith was responsible," Ann said, unable to stop what she had started. "So I doubled and trebled my faith and my prayers and my church-going and my righteousness. Every day. And still . . ."

Her voice broke. She wanted to reach to the other

woman, but she did not. She did not want to be rebuked again.

"He has let another innocent die. Why? This is the answer to my prayers? Why?"

Bridget Bishop's face had softened. "Know what people call me?"

Ann nodded.

"You would be excommunicated if you were found here." Bridget Bishop's tone was gentle. "Are you not afraid of hell?"

"I care not that you are called a witch," Ann said. "And I am in hell already. Tell me why they are dying. You know."

Bridget studied Ann for a moment. Tears were streaming down Ann's face, but she did not know when they had started.

Bridget touched Ann's face and wiped a tear away. The simple humanity of the gesture made more tears come.

"I am not a witch," Bridget said, "although 'tis what I am called. But I do know what none else has uttered to you. You are not to blame."

Ann grasped Bridget's hand and held it to her cheek for a moment. *You are not to blame.* How long had she waited to hear that?

She still wasn't sure she believed it.

"Come inside," the witch said to Annie's mama, "and I will tell you all I know, Ann Putnam."

And then, without looking behind her, Mama went inside the witch's hut.

Annie leaned against the base of a nearby tree, shivering in the darkness and the cold. She couldn't go in there after her mama.

There was no saving them—any of them—from this.

Everything was wrong, and Annie did not know how to fix it.

TWELVE

The meal was not as fine as Ann wanted it to be. She had not been supervising her home well enough lately. She had been so distracted, and it showed everywhere—in the food, in the dust along the edges of the floor, in the silence around the dinner table.

Only her husband and son sat at the table. Her daughter and the maid, Mercy Lewis, who seemed to be growing increasingly lax, ate wherever they could find a place. Mercy stood.

But Ann saw Annie huddled by herself, her plate untouched, and an expression of great intensity on her young face. Ann had never seen her daughter look so—well, frightened, perhaps would be the best word. And her daughter's intensity seemed to grow each time she faced Ann, so Ann soon stopped studying her.

Thomas's dog yip-yipped the way it always did at suppertime. For a disciplined man, Thomas suffered a lack of discipline where that mangy animal of his was concerned. The yipping always grated on Ann, but she didn't dare tell the dog to be quiet. Thomas was the only one who gave it orders.

Ann served the platter to Thomas and Nathaniel. No one spoke. The atmosphere was tense. Thomas hadn't spoken to Ann all day.

She felt that he knew about her trip to Bridget Bishop's. But he could not. He had been asleep before she left the house. Asleep and blaming her.

Her heart twisted.

Nathaniel reached for another piece of bread, and she caught his hand. "Wait for your father."

Nathaniel looked at Thomas, but Thomas did not seem to hear the interaction at all. He continued to eat.

The dog yip-yipped again, and the ghost of a smile touched Thomas's mouth. He leaned down, picked up the dog, and placed it in his lap. The dog's tail wagged.

Thomas's great hand stroked the dog's neck, and the dog seemed to lean into the movement. So did Ann, before she caught herself. Imagine being jealous of a dog.

The dog yipped softly, and Thomas fed it some bread. The dog's tail wagged even more, and this time, Thomas did smile fondly at it.

Then the dog whined. Ann frowned. She'd never

heard a dog whine while it wagged its tail. It took a moment for her to realize that the whine came from behind her.

She turned. Annie was staring at her father too, watching his every move, and whining. Then Annie started yipping, sounding for all the world like Thomas's dog.

Everyone turned and looked at her, but Annie didn't seem to notice. She kept on yipping.

Ann couldn't tell whether her daughter was making that sound to mock the dog, or for attention. Either way, it was a horrible thing to do.

"Annie! Stop!" Ann snapped.

Annie yipped even louder, as if her mother's words made her crazed. Her eyes were round and wide and fixed as she continued to stare at the dog.

Ann's throat went dry. What was wrong with her child?

"Enough!" Thomas commanded. "Are you possessed, child?"

At that, Annie stood and shouted, "Bridget Bishop is a witch!"

Ann's mouth dropped open. She felt as if her soul had been bared for all to see.

"What?" Thomas asked, confused now.

Annie started chanting: "Satan's witch. Satan's witch. Satan's witch."

Thomas spoke over her. "What is this of the witch woman?"

Ann clenched her hands tightly. The world was spinning.

"And all know of her evil," Annie said, but she wasn't speaking directly to her father. She was still staring fixedly, speaking as if she were in a trance. "Bridget Bishop is a witch."

Ann had had enough. In two steps, she had reached her daughter, and shook her hard. "Annie! Hold your tongue or you shall be—"

Then her daughter slumped in her arms. Ann still held her shoulders, uncertain what to do next. Annie looked up at her pitifully. Ann had the sense of a lonely child trapped inside Annie's eyes.

Annie opened her mouth and whimpered—small yips like the dog's when it wanted to be held.

Ann was breathing shallowly. She had no idea what to do. So Ann did nothing, holding Annie by the shoulders while she bayed like a small dog.

Samuel Parris crouched before the fire. He placed more split wood on it, glad he could afford the firewood. The fire roared. A hard-earned fire, much needed in the depth of winter. At least his home wasn't as cold as it had been only a week ago.

He turned to his wife, who lay in their bed, ill as she had been off and on these past months.

"You shall feel better with the warmth now," he said.

Elizabeth smiled at him. "Yes. I am stronger already. Thank you."

A mere thank you? Did she not know how hard he fought for this wood? How diplomatic he had had to be? He had not known before he took the ministerial position here in Salem Village how much politics were involved in the Lord's work.

He felt that every movement of his was judged. One mistake and his family would freeze.

"There is plenty of wood in the shed," he said. "Have you seen? The congregation is gathering around me now. In time, this place will seem like our home."

Elizabeth closed her eyes. It was clear she did not want to hear of this.

"I am tired, Samuel," she said. "I must rest."

He studied her for a moment. He knew she was ill, but he needed the support of his family. He couldn't do this alone.

"You have no faith in me, do you, Elizabeth?"

Her eyes fluttered open, and at first he thought he saw annoyance in them. She licked her lips, as she often did when considering her words.

"Salem shall be our home when our congregation supports us of their own will. If it is not divine inspiration but threat of harm that moves them . . . Samuel, how does this bode for us?"

He shook his head. He had been right. She did not have faith in him. He shoved more wood into the fire before controlling his temper enough to speak.

"I will not fail," he said finally. "I will lead them to divinity. If you do not believe this out of faith in me, then I shall have to prove it to you."

"You do not need to prove—"

"God has brought me here, Elizabeth," Parris said. "He took away our farm in Barbados to give me this.

Yes, my brother has my family's estate, but I have this. God's role for me is to come to Salem to save His chosen people. If I fail, Puritanism fails forever."

She seemed to sink into the bed with each word. He didn't want her to cringe from him. He wanted her to agree.

He stood. "That is my task. No less. Do you understand?"

She didn't answer. After a moment of silence, he headed for the door. But he could not resist a parting remark.

"You may lack faith in me," he said, "but God does not."

Thirteen

The great room of Ingersoll's Tavern was hot. Almost every man in Salem Village packed the place. The roaring fire in the great hearth, combined with the heat of all those bodies, made the tavern the only comfortable place for miles.

Israel Porter sat near the fire, Giles Corey and John Proctor beside him. Porter's new son-in-law, Joseph Putnam, stood near the back along with Samuel Nurse and Goodman Tarbell. Thomas Putnam stood in the center of the room, yelling at the men as if they were his congregation, but no one was fawning on him now.

Porter watched the scene with a faint smile. Things were finally going his way.

"You have dared vote me off the Committee?" Thomas Putnam asked.

"And your brothers and cousins," John Proctor answered with a grin.

A cheer rose up from the men around. Putnam looked shocked, as if he couldn't believe how many people hated him.

A man should look at what he did before he judged himself holy. That's what Porter thought. Joseph Putnam was watching his half brother, anger glinting in his eyes.

There was no love lost between those two, for which Porter felt a great relief.

"You cannot steal our property, Thomas Putnam," Giles Corey said.

"It is time for new leadership, Thomas," Israel Porter spoke in an even tone and the men quieted to listen to him. Who was in charge now—Thomas Putnam? Porter had to struggle to keep his smile from showing.

Putnam saw it anyway and glared as all the men shouted their agreement with Porter.

Thomas Putnam held up a hand for silence, and when he did not get it, he shouted, "Our village must have its own minister. Do you not see the erosion of our standings while Salem Town grows fatter? 'Tis against the will of our Puritan God—"

"Thomas Putnam!" John Proctor shouted, breaking his speech. "You mistake your own self-interest for God's will. This hypocrisy must stop!"

Putnam did not spare him a look but continued as if Proctor hadn't spoken. "Are you not righteous Puritan men?"

116

"Give Parris your own wood, Thomas Putnam," someone shouted from the back. "We already have a meeting house—in Salem Town."

Beside Porter, Giles Corey shook his fist. "You have gone too far, Thomas Putnam."

Men yelled their agreement, and several slapped the tables, adding to the din. Porter let that go on for a moment, then he used his tin mug to call the meeting to some kind of order. He banged the mug on the table until the men quieted.

"From this day forward, the Salem Village Committee shall now consist of my brother, Joseph Porter. . . ."

Cheers greeted his words, all except for Thomas Putnam, whose face turned red.

"No, you cannot!" he shouted.

Porter continued as if Putnam had not spoken. Porter had to yell even louder to be heard over the cries and cheers.

"My brother-in-law, Daniel Andrew . . ."

"I am a Putnam!" Thomas shouted, trying to drown out Porter. "I will bring back the Puritanism of my grandfather. We will stand as one against the profiteers."

But Porter would not be cowed by any man. He made sure to say the name that stung the most next. "My son-in-law, Joseph Putnam . . ."

The cheers increased and became "Ayes." More than one man waved a fist in triumph.

Putnam watched it all, his eyes glittering with an anger so vast that it made Porter worry for his sanity.

"You will not neuter me with your votes," Thomas Putnam yelled above the din. "I. Am. A. Putnam."

Yes, he was. But Porter's gaze met his son-in-law's. The problem was, Thomas was no longer the important Putnam.

Joseph was.

The sleeping chamber seemed like an oasis of calm after the scene in the tavern. Joseph Putnam had never in his life been in such chaos. It was exhilarating and frightening at the same time.

Even though he had always been his father's favorite, he had never been in a situation where Thomas had been so badly put in his place. Thomas had seemed all-powerful to Joseph until the last few months, when Joseph took control of his own life.

He smiled at that life now. The hearth fire was large and warm, illuminating the room Lizzy had made so comfortable. The bed on which they'd consummated their vows was lovely, well apportioned, and high.

Lizzy lay in it now, pillows against her back, her face radiant in the candlelight.

As he came in he followed their ritual, snuffing the candles she had lit one by one. He had done that on their wedding night, and she had proclaimed the action a courtship all by itself. So he continued, believing that courting his wife was the only way to ensure contentment in their life together.

She smiled as he made his way closer to the bed. But as he was about to snuff the last candle, he saw that her eyes were worried.

"What is this?" he asked. "Are you not well again?"

His mother had never gotten this sick during her early days.

" 'Tis my head that is uneasy," Lizzy said. "I have heard that your brother's fury has not abated and that the Village is split, like a ripe melon."

Joseph kissed her forehead tenderly, then stroked her belly.

"Shhh, wife," Joseph said. "Our baby will not want to be born into such a place as you make Salem sound."

He lay beside her and gave her his best smile. "Do you fear I shall be as poor a Committee leader as I am with your spinning wheel?"

She grinned. "Then the Village shall be as knotted as our flax. If only our village were no more than the four corners of this room."

"Then imagine it is," Joseph said. "And I shall never let harm enter."

She leaned her head against his shoulder for a moment, then stirred with concern. She was not going to let this topic rest. "I am afraid, Joseph. It is not just Thomas's black air. Something is happening in the Village, and all are aware of it. The Tarbells' corn rotted overnight in its crib. And Abigail Williams saw a small bird that she swears was a witch's familiar. People are saying that Satan has come to the Village because it is impure."

His brother had started that talk. Another sin to lay at Thomas's door. Joseph stroked Lizzy's hair.

"Shhh," he said. "Do not listen to people talking."

"The fear is everywhere," Lizzy said. "I can feel it myself. And with our child coming—"

"You are safe, Lizzy. And I would lay down my life to keep you that way." He had to make her understand that. He knew that the best way to have a healthy baby was to keep his wife calm. That way they could both make it through the travail—if not with ease, then at least alive.

"And what of your brother's anger?" Lizzy asked. "Do you not fear that?"

"I fear only the thought that someday you will stop loving me," Joseph said.

She studied him for a moment. Her gaze was sincere, and he could see the moment when she realized that he meant his words.

"Then you have nothing to fear in this world," she said.

Samuel Parris sat at his desk, the parchment document clutched between his fingers. Beside him a candle guttered, but he did not have the strength to pour out some wax.

He was staring at the signatures, all of them from men he knew, all of them people he had thought would acknowledge him and his leadership.

Thomas Putnam stood behind him, reading over his shoulder, telling him the bad news as if he couldn't parse it for himself.

"With this petition, they have taken a new Committee leader," Putnam said. "Their first act will be to void the tax that pays your salary. And they intend to reclaim the land under the meeting house. They believe it was unrightfully given to you."

Parris sat taller in his chair. These men did not understand his life and his requirements. He was not a farmer as they were, nor was he a merchant. The living he made, he made with his mind, with his soul.

He was God's representative in Salem Village, and it was God's rule, not his, that required them to provide for his family. He could cite scripture passage after passage proving that claim, but he felt he should not have to do so.

They should have known better.

"These are the men who would wage war on a Puritan minister?" he asked.

Putnam nodded. "And this is far from over. We shall form another petition."

"Obviously they are in need of our prayers." Parris did not want to discuss this any longer. He had been fighting this battle since negotiating his contract with Salem Village when he first arrived.

That the battle had gotten worse was not his fault. It was the fault of the man standing behind him, the man to whom he owed so much, the man he dared not contradict.

Parris folded the petition and placed it between the pages of his Bible. Then he rested his hands upon it.

Putnam looked as if he wanted to continue the conversation, but after a moment, he nodded. He seemed to understand that Parris was not going to indulge him further.

"Yes," Putnam said, heading for the door. "Well, good night."

When the door closed behind him, the room was still. But only for a moment. Parris's children giggled in the keeping room. And then he heard splashing water.

He closed his eyes, willing the noise to stop. It did.

Then, as if it moved of its own volition, his hand removed the document from his Bible. Parris stared at the signatures again, going down the list.

> Israel Porter
> John Proctor
> Joseph Putnam
> Samuel Nurse
> Giles Corey

He forced himself to stop. To continue would be to invite hatred, which would only increase the Devil's invitation to this hateful place.

He wished that he and Elizabeth had never come here. Sometimes, Lord help him, he longed for Barbados and the life that had been promised him. The warmth, the luxury. Elizabeth hadn't been sick there, and their marriage had been good. . . .

The children giggled again—raucous out-of-control laughter, the kind that implied an unfettered merriment. They were not doing God's work, either. Such laughter had dangers to it.

He slipped the document back into his Bible, set the Bible aside, and pinched out the guttering candle. The giggling continued.

He could take it no longer. He stormed to the keeping room, yanked the door open, and froze.

A large tub filled with steaming water stood in the center of the small room. To his surprise, Betty and Abigail were outside the tub, fully dressed. They had not seen him yet. They were flicking water and laughing, their giggles high-pitched and wrong.

But he was not watching them. He was staring at the woman in the tub. She was beautiful. Her breasts were high and full, her shoulders arched just so.

He couldn't remember the last time he'd seen a naked woman, one who did not have words of her crime written across her back. Just a naked woman enjoying a hot bath on a cold winter evening.

But this woman was not his wife. It was Tituba.

He should have closed the door and left immediately, but he could not bring himself to move. He had not realized how lovely she was.

After a moment, Tituba looked up and saw him there. Her smile faltered, and he could tell from the expression on her face that she recognized the lust in his eyes.

Then the children realized she was no longer playing. They turned toward him. Betty looked upon him as if he were someone she didn't know.

"Papa?" she asked.

But he could not speak to her. Nor could he remove his gaze from Tituba's naked breasts.

FOURTEEN

Tituba sat in the back of the meeting house, as she had been forced to do each Sabbath of her servitude. She wrapped her arms around her legs. It felt good to sit. She stood too much. But it was cold here, very cold in back, where the warmth from the braziers did not reach. She had no blanket to bring with her, and her winter cloak—Goody Parris's cast-off—was so thin as to be useless.

Usually, Tituba used the hours of the service to think her own private thoughts. She kept her mask on, of course—the one she wore for these people so that they would not know who she really was. No one knew. No one could.

She was little more than a convenience to all of them. Except Betty, of course. In many ways, Tituba had had to act as Betty's mother. Goody Parris had been too sick to mother her since their arrival in Salem.

Tituba studied the girls now. They were all squirming in their pews, and more than one looked surreptitiously toward the door as if thinking of escape.

This was not Tituba's religion, although she never spoke of her beliefs to anyone. She parodied and mimicked the speeches of the Christian folk around her as best she could, and did not let them know she thought their religion harsh and unforgiving.

But she understood it well enough. After all these years, she had to. She knew all of its boundaries. And she knew, on this day, that the good Reverend Samuel Parris was treading on the edges of them.

He was in a fine frenzy, leaning forward on the pulpit, spitting hellfire. His shiny gaze had found Betty at least once, and Abigail too, and all their friends. She had never heard such vehemence in his voice before.

"Children lie!"

The words reverberated in the meeting house. Even though it was packed, the entire congregation was quiet.

"Children covet. They are not too young to know evil. And the souls of evil children are not of value."

Tituba had to struggle to keep from shaking her head. Children were innocents. They did not deserve such a sermon, particularly when they were not the ones who sinned.

"They are not too little to die," Parris went on. "They are not too little to go to hell."

More squirming. Tituba watched as the children in the congregation felt the weight of Parris's judgment.

"Do you have sin in your hearts?"

He did. She had seen it in his eyes when he walked in on her bath. And she had known what he wanted.

"Children." Parris pounded on the pulpit. "Do not lie to me. God will put out His wrath upon those who lie. Glance at your neighbor, right and left. Are they pure?"

The congregation looked, just as he said. But Tituba did not. She knew they were not pure, not in the way this religion meant. Like other human beings, they wanted to enjoy their lives, and this religion denied that enjoyment.

Oh, they were not pure, and she did not want to be. So she did not look at anyone except the grand sinner himself.

"Are you pure?" he boomed. "Oh, sinners. Hell is a terrible place. And it waits for you."

His words echoed. Ann Putnam and her little daughter, Annie, looked down simultaneously, but that bear of a man who ran their household, Thomas Putnam, sat even straighter. What was it about these people that made them refuse to take responsibility for what they were, even though their religion required it of them?

Did the righteous Reverend Parris know he was talking to himself and not to his children?

He turned the pages of his text, paused, and studied it for a moment. Tituba held her breath.

Then he looked up, the maliciousness in his gaze shining even worse.

"Know ye this," he said, "I am to make the difference between the clean and the unclean so as to purge the one and confirm the other. I shall be your guide on Earth. I shall lead you to the narrow gate of Heaven and into the grace of God for eternity. I know sinners. And I know the righteous."

He scanned the congregation as he spoke, as if he were imparting a personal message to each one there. Then his gaze met Tituba's.

Unlike the others, she did not look away. She did the same as she had in her bath. She met him as an equal. She let him see past her mask to her contempt and her dislike of him.

With her eyes, she told him that she knew the darkness hidden inside his heart.

Lizzy Putnam had never been to the empty meeting house. Before going inside, she looked over her shoulder, hoping that no one saw her. Neither her father nor her husband would like that she had come here.

But she could not get to the meeting house in Salem Town. And she needed to speak to a man of God.

She pulled open the heavy door and stepped inside. It was dark, and seemed just as cold inside as it was outside. For a moment she thought she was alone, and then she saw movement near the communion table.

"Who approaches?" The voice belonged to the Reverend Parris. He sounded startled.

The door closed behind her. " 'Tis I, Reverend Parris. Lizzy Putnam."

Her eyes adjusted to the darkened interior. The meeting house looked bigger than she had expected. When it was full, it always felt crowded and small to her.

The Reverend Parris was standing near the front, and he looked less official than usual. Almost approachable.

"I was hoping," she said, "you would allow a moment to speak in private."

"About?"

He sounded guarded. She finally stopped in front of him. He seemed to relax when she reached the thin light of the candle he'd been using.

"Pray do not think me crazed, Reverend," she said.

He folded his hands over his coat. "Speak, child. I can think nothing until you confess."

"I . . ." Her mouth was dry. Maybe she should have told Joseph of this. But their marriage was still so new, and she didn't want him to think ill of her. " 'Twas a dream I had. It woke me in a terrible fear, without breath. Without my wits perhaps, as well."

The Reverend Parris didn't move. His expression remained the same, as if he were listening and withholding judgement until she was finished.

"I have told no one," she said, "and shall not if you advise. I am afraid, Reverend."

"Of your dream?"

"If it was a dream." She broke into a sweat just remembering. "Someone was there. In my room. I was sure of it, but could see nothing. And yet I knew with as much surety as I know you are standing flesh and blood here in front of me now."

She touched his arm in demonstration. He looked down at her hand, and his face was in shadow.

"I knew someone was there," she said. "What is happening, Reverend? Was it a witch? Or a familiar? I have heard of these but dare not speak of it. To naught but you."

He took her hand in his cold one, surprising her. Then he looked into her face the way no one but Joseph ever had, as if he were trying to memorize her.

The thought made her uncomfortable.

"We shall keep your secret between us," the Reverend said, sounding like himself, and convincing her she was wrong. She was imagining a variety of things that were not there.

"But it was a dream?" she asked. "Am I bewitched? I shall wish never to sleep again until I am certain."

The Reverend Parris leaned toward her. His grip on her hand tightened. She resisted the urge to back away.

"I have studied you often on Sabbath," he whispered, and the hair rose on the back of her neck.

If he had been any other man, she would have slipped her hand out of his, but he was the minister.

He was thinking of her soul, not of anything else.

"I have watched the devotion of your prayers," he was saying. "You are lovely of spirit and complexion, and it is likely that Satan would covet one as pure as you."

His words did not comfort her any more than his actions had. He had never made her feel like this before, almost as if what they were doing was unclean.

"Pray with me now, and I shall keep thee pure." He took her other hand and pulled her closer. Every muscle in her body tightened, and it took all her strength not to run away. "Know that the godly bask in the fellowship of other pious people as well in the light of God. Give me your faith."

Then he bowed his head toward hers, his forehead brushing hers. His posture seemed reverential. The problem was hers, not his. She had to remember that.

Slowly, she bowed her head, and joined him in prayer.

Ann Putnam stood in the chicken coop. When she had first come in to gather eggs, the familiar stench had nearly made her gag. She wasn't certain she would be able to finish her chores.

Then she heard something, turned, and saw a small egg rocking back and forth. She'd watched chickens hatch before, but never had one so fascinated her.

She stepped toward it and saw the beak quiver as it pecked its way out, the downy gray crown, and then the full chick as it wobbled out of the remains of its prison. Alive. Healthy.

Breathing.

Carefully, she reached toward the newborn, wanting to touch it, to feel its tiny heartbeat.

Then a hen cackled and threw itself at her, flapping its wings protectively. Ann took three frightened steps backward, hitting the other edge of the chicken coop. She put a hand to her throat, her breath coming hard.

She'd nearly had her face scratched. She'd seen what happened to people who had gotten too close to angry hens. One of her third cousins actually lost an eye.

Ann had been cautious of hens since then. It was amazing she'd forgotten all her training.

She had been so focused on the miracle of birth.

The hen still watched her, hovering near the chick. Ann gathered herself, holding her emotions in check. She couldn't lose her concentration that way again.

Then she nodded to herself and went about the mindless day-to-day tasks that were her life, gathering more eggs and placing them in her basket.

Annie Putnam moved closer to the table so that she could see the water glass. Abigail Williams had blocked her view. But, then again, it was Abigail's house; she had the right to stand wherever she wanted.

Betty Parris stood near the door, keeping watch. The whole idea of doing this made her nervous.

But then, everything made her nervous.

Mercy Lewis and May Walcott were on the other side of the table and could see even better. This time, May took an egg, broke it open with one hand, and dropped it into the water.

They all bent over the glass as the egg coagulated.

"It looks like an apron," May said. "A cobbler's apron."

"No, 'tis a scythe," Abigail said. "Look at it here."

She pointed at the sharp edge, and Annie leaned in even closer. It did look like a scythe.

"You shall marry a farmer," Abigail said.

May made a face, as if she did not like that news.

"Wait," she said. "it is not finished turning yet."

Abigail leaned back, so sure of herself as always. "'Tis a scythe."

It looked like a scythe to Annie. This was taking too long. If they argued over the glass, the way they had with Mercy's, then they'd never get to her. They'd be discovered first.

" 'Tis my turn now," Annie said.

Betty Parris turned toward her, eyes wide. "Shhh," she said, putting a finger to her lips.

"Quiet, Annie," Abigail whispered at the same time.

"We shall be discovered," May whispered.

They were taking a risk, doing this in the Reverend Parris's house. But it was the best place to do anything unusual. Tituba never said much, and Goody Parris was always in her room. The Reverend Parris was at the meeting house. So unlike Annie's house, where someone was always home.

She didn't know why everyone was getting so upset at her. Then she heard a faint, quavering voice call, "Tituba?"

It was Goody Parris. They had moved her to the keeping room for the day so that she would be near the cooking fire.

"Tituba!" she called again.

"We should stop before we are found," Betty whispered.

As if Tituba would do anything. Annie glared at her. "Quiet. 'Tis my turn next."

" 'Tis the Devil's game we play," Betty whispered at her. "Our souls will be blackened, and we shall go to Hell. Tell her, Abigail. God hears us."

"God hears nothing," Annie said. Her mama was proving that. She should have been stricken down when she walked to Bridget Bishop's, but she wasn't. If God heard everyone, then no one would sin. "No one hears us. No one."

Betty started whimpering, as if the very idea frightened her.

"Quiet, Betty!" Abigail said. "I told you it is your crying that shall send you to hell."

May Walcott looked from one girl to another. "Maybe Betty is right," she said.

Annie had had enough of this. She knew this was what would happen. It would become her turn, and she wouldn't get a chance to play. Her whole life had been that way lately. Everything was going wrong. Even the little things.

She grabbed another egg.

"I want to see who I will marry," she said stubbornly, making sure her voice was louder than it had been when everyone shushed her.

The girls all stared at her, horrified, but she didn't care. She broke the egg into a glass, and in spite of themselves, the other girls leaned in to look, just as she knew they would.

Slowly the egg fell into the water, coagulating, finding the form of the man Annie would love.

Betty glanced nervously at the door, then back at the table. Abigail crossed her arms—

And suddenly, Mercy gasped.

" 'Tis a dead man's coffin," Mercy whispered.

It was. It was square and boxy and horrible. Annie's stomach turned. The other girls gasped as well. They had seen it too.

They had seen everything.

Annie felt tears prick behind her eyes. It was a bad omen. Everyone knew it.

She felt as fragile as the eggs they'd been breaking.

"It hasn't finished turning," Annie said, even though she knew it wasn't true. She sounded just as May had when she saw the scythe.

"It has too," Mercy said.

"Mercy is right," May said.

"Liar!" Annie shouted.

Betty made a shushing gesture with her hands, but Annie ignored her.

" 'Tis a coffin," Abigail said.

Betty burst into tears. "I told you."

Annie stepped toward her, feeling like slapping

her. Didn't Betty know she was making things worse?

Betty was crying wildly now, making huge gasping noises. Abigail's face had turned red. Mercy was running toward the door, and May was wringing her hands together. Only Annie stayed by the table.

"Betty!" Goody Parris called from the other room. "Abigail!"

Betty made a terrible choking sound. "She is coming."

If the adults found this, everyone would be in trouble. They were playing with black magic. What would Annie's father think?

"Throw it out!" Annie whispered.

" 'Tis too late," Mercy said.

"No one will know," Annie said.

"She is coming!" Betty cried. "She will find out."

May turned on Annie. "God knows. 'Tis a coffin because you have sinned."

How did she know? How did she know what Annie had done?

"Throw it out!" Annie shouted.

She slapped at the glass, and it flew through the air, moving so slowly that Annie thought she could catch it. She wasn't able to.

The glass hit Abigail and drenched her, covering her in the sin. Abigail looked both furious and panicky. Frantically, she tried to wipe the egg off her.

"Witch!" Abigail screamed. "Look what you have done!"

But May wasn't watching Abigail. She was watching Annie. May had an intense look on her face. "You have sinned," she said to Annie. "We shall go to Hell because of you."

" 'Twas not my game," Annie cried. " 'Twas Abigail's."

Abigail backed away, shaking her hands and trying to get the watery substance off them. She tried to speak, but only an odd panting noise came out of her mouth.

Mercy was running around, trying to clean up the broken eggshells and water. Then there was a crack.

She had broken another.

Annie looked at her in horror.

"Betty!" Goody Parris called.

She could hear them. Goody Parris could hear them, and she might discover them. How awful would that be? Annie felt her stomach churn, churn, churn, and her head ached terribly. She felt tingly and strange, as if the sin in the room were taking her too.

Betty's cries became more hysterical, getting louder and louder as she lost control of herself.

May shook her violently. "Quiet!"

But Betty couldn't seem to make herself quiet. She started whimpering, sounding like an animal.

There were footsteps outside the door. Goody Parris. Goody Parris was going to catch them, and tell her mama. Tell her papa. Annie whimpered too, remembering Papa's anger at her, the way he'd looked when she'd cried out about Bridget Bishop.

The tingly feeling was getting stronger, as if the top of her head were going to come off. She was going to be sick or something. She wasn't sure.

The other girls looked as scared as she did.

Then the door latch was pulled from the outside, and all the girls froze, staring at the door.

Betty let out a loud whimper, and that started everyone else. Annie's head ached so badly that she clutched it. Someone was crying. It might have been her.

The door opened—and the girls gasped.

It wasn't Goody Parris. It wasn't even Tituba, who might understand.

It was the Reverend Parris. The Reverend Parris had caught them sinning. Annie screamed, and the other girls cried as well.

But Betty, Betty fell to the floor in a fit, her body pounding the wood as if she could break through it.

The Reverend Parris looked at Annie. Right at Annie as if no one else were there.

"What has happened here?" the Reverend Parris demanded. "What have you done?"

She opened her mouth to answer him, but she didn't know what to say. Something held her throat closed, and she made a terrible choking sound.

The Reverend Parris's face turned red. "Can you not speak?"

He was so angry. He was angry, and he was God's representative, which meant God was angry.

Annie continued choking. She couldn't stop. She put her hands around her head and bent down. The other girls cried around her, and Betty's eyes rolled into the back of her head.

FIFTEEN

The knock on the door sounded frantic, and the person outside didn't even wait for Ann to answer. Instead, the door burst open as she crossed the center hall, and the Reverend Parris hurried in, followed by Doctor Griggs. They were carrying Annie and Mercy. Another girl followed, looking terrified. She was Doctor Grigg's niece, Beth Hubbard.

Ann registered all of this peripherally as she reached for her nearly unconscious daughter.

"What?" Ann demanded. "What has happened?"

"Get them to bed," Doctor Griggs said. "Niece, step here to help me."

Beth Hubbard remained near the door. She did not move, the useless baggage.

Ann kept pace with Doctor Griggs and the Reverend Parris.

"Are they ill?" No one would answer her. She twisted her hands together. "What has happened, Reverend?"

Doctor Griggs looked over his shoulder. "Niece," he commanded.

Ann's gaze was still on the Reverend, but she had her hand on Annie. The Reverend shook his head as if he had no words. He looked afraid.

She had never seen the Reverend—any reverend, for that matter—look afraid.

Ann grabbed her daughter and helped carry her, leaving the men to struggle with Mercy.

"Doctor Griggs. Someone tell me what has happened to my child."

They still didn't answer her, struggling to get the girls to a bed. Doctor Griggs looked very serious. Ann had seen him look like this when her father-in-law was dying.

She turned to Mercy, grabbed her, and looked into her eyes. "Mercy, can you speak?"

But Mercy's eyes did not focus on her.

"They are in fits," Doctor Griggs said shortly.

"Annie!" Ann shook her daughter. She couldn't bear to lose another child. When she realized that, when she realized how much Annie meant to her, she stopped shaking her and pulled her close.

Annie responded to the embrace, leaning into Ann's arms. Ann rested her head on her child's and frowned at Reverend Parris. "They were fine when they left here. What harm did they encounter with you?"

He seemed to grow even paler. "Nothing. They were but gathered to—"

" 'Tis biting!" Annie shouted. She jerked in Ann's arms, writhing as if she were in pain. "Biting. Biting. 'Tis biting my hand!"

She was shrieking and slapping at herself. Ann had to back away for fear of being hit. Then Mercy started shrieking too.

Doctor Griggs bent down to help Annie. "Niece," he said, "step here to help me."

He was trying to hold Annie down, to keep her from hurting herself. Ann stepped in to help as well. Mercy was shrieking. The entire room seemed to ring with their cries.

"Niece!" Doctor Griggs shouted, and looked up. He froze for a moment, and Annie nearly hit him.

Ann's gaze followed his.

Beth Hubbard was staring at her own hand as if it too were being affected. She whimpered.

"Oh, Lord Jesus," Reverend Parris said softly.

Beth held out her hand and started panting. " 'Tis biting me now, too. Oh! Oh!"

The Reverend looked from one to another, horrified. Ann's own head hurt, and all she could think as she helped the doctor hold down her daughter was *Not another child. Please, God, don't let me lose another child.*

Lizzy Putnam had been in Ingersoll's Tavern only a few times, mostly to find her father. Such places were forbidden to women, although there were women who came here. They were just not women of Lizzy's ilk.

But today they were. Ingersoll's Tavern seemed to be the spontaneous gathering place. No one was drinking or secretly gaming. (Joseph had told her of that.) Instead, they were talking, most of them all at once.

Many people she recognized had arrived here first. She had come through the door with Rebecca Nurse, and Lizzy figured if the godly Goody Nurse could come inside, so could she.

Martha and Giles Corey sat near the hearth. Goodwife Proctor stood near them, as did Rebecca Nurse's son Samuel, Goody Glover, Goody Hawley, and Goodman Tarbell. There were dozens of others, some whom Lizzy knew only from passing them on the street.

"They are like animals," Goody Hawley said, "barking and whining and foaming from the lips."

"I heard they were unable to breathe," Goodwife Proctor said. "And more fall to the fits every day."

"I have heard five girls so far," Goodman Tarbell said.

"I heard Mercy Lewis attempted to burn herself in the fireplace," Martha Corey said.

"No," Goody Glover said, "the way I heard it, she flew into it, like a bird. She was trying to fly up the fireplace. It took two men to hold her back."

The crowd gasped at this bit of news. Lizzy put her hand over her belly. She had prayed for the babe

141

within from the moment she knew of it. She had been so frightened. Her father had said there were demons about.

Now she was certain of it.

"Oh, God help the child," Rebecca Nurse said. "It is witchcraft."

Lizzy shivered. She had known that. She had felt it in her own room. And she had tried to tell Reverend Parris, but had gotten the sense he hadn't entirely believed her.

"And little Betty Parris has scratched her arm raw," Goodwife Proctor said. "She cries that she is being pricked. The skin is completely gone."

It scared Lizzy even more that the Reverend's daughter was afflicted.

"Perhaps it is the pox," Goody Hawley said. "She needs a poultice of—"

" 'Tis not the pox that ails them," Giles Corey said. "Nor are they poor innocents afflicted by witchcraft."

His cantankerous voice rose above the crowd. Lizzy had never heard him speak with such authority. Apparently, neither had anyone else, for everyone quieted.

"They are *possessed* by the Devil. They are doing His work."

"You think they are witches themselves?" Goody Hawley asked.

"I think it should not be ruled out."

The crowd gasped again. Lizzy's hand tightened over her belly. Had she made a mistake, going to

Reverend Parris? If the contagion had come from his house, had she caught it? Were those possessed girls going to smite her and her unborn babe?

She wished Joseph were here. She wanted his arm around her, and his gentle voice, telling her it was all right.

But it wasn't all right. It might never be all right.

And the entire crowd in Ingersoll's Tavern knew it.

Tituba stroked Betty's head, singing softly. She sat close to Abigail, touching her gently as well. The girls were lying flat on their beds, unmoving. They stared at the ceiling without blinking.

The only way Tituba knew they were alive was the ever-so-subtle breaths they were taking, small and shallow.

The Reverend stood behind her and watched helplessly, as he had been doing since this crisis began. He had said not a word that Tituba had heard, which she thought as unnatural as the girls' affliction.

She stroked Betty's forehead again, wishing the girl would improve. Little Betty, so fearful, so gentle. Tituba loved her best.

This was not natural. They had been bewitched, but Tituba knew not how. And she didn't know how to break the affliction. She wasn't a wise woman, like some she had known in Barbados. She had been a slave too long, among people like these, who denied their connection to the Earth.

She had been singing to the girls for some time now, knowing that sometimes comforting things broke spells. She had saved this song for last. When she came to the end and they still had not moved, her heart twisted.

"This is their favorite one," Tituba said to the Reverend, "but they hear naught. They do not shut their eyes. They neither sleep nor wake. There is talk now that they have been possessed."

That seemed to awaken him. His gaze met hers, filled with fury. "That is untrue! The Devil is not in this home."

He shoved Tituba aside and grabbed Betty. Tituba stepped back, knowing his anger was not what the children needed.

If she had to wager—a word she never used aloud around the Reverend—she would bet that the girls, deep within their fit, feared the Reverend more than anyone.

He pulled Betty toward him. She had always been his favorite. Tituba held her breath, wondering if he was going to hold her. Maybe that would work.

"Speak, child!" The desperation in his voice took away Tituba's hope. This man offered no healing to the children.

Betty did not move. Her gaze continued forward, unseeing. Parris's face grew red, and he shook her as hard as Tituba had ever seen.

"You will answer me," he screamed. "Speak! You shall not bring shame into this home. The Devil is not here. He does not possess you."

Parris continued to shake her, but her head bobbed up and down like a small doll. She did not move.

Tituba wanted to stop him, but knew she did not dare. He might strike her.

Or worse.

"Reverend?"

Tituba started at the voice. She had not heard anyone come in, as worried as she had been about the children. She turned and saw the elderly Rebecca Nurse standing in the doorway, looking as shocked as Tituba felt.

Rebecca Nurse's presence seemed to startle the Reverend Parris as well. A look of shame crossed his face—real shame, not the shame mixed with lust that Tituba had seen when she was bathing.

"Goodwife Nurse," he said.

She came into the room, brushing past Tituba as if Tituba weren't even there.

"I came to pray for the children," Goody Nurse said. "May I?"

Parris eased Betty back onto the bed, then stroked her forehead as if he had been gentle with her all along.

Hypocrite. Tituba clenched her hands into fists.

"Yes," he said to Goody Nurse. "Of course. We shall both pray. God shall hear our hopes, and in tandem they will be even stronger."

He gave Tituba a pointed glance, as if her presence were part of the problem. She raised her chin slightly but would not leave. Goody Nurse seemed oblivious to the interchange—or perhaps she was ignoring all behavior that she did not approve of.

She walked between the beds and knelt. Parris

knelt beside her. After a moment, Tituba joined them. She would not pray to their god but to her own gods—gods who actually had compassion and might help.

But the Reverend would think that she was praying as he was.

She bowed her head as Parris started the prayer.

"Oh, God," he said, and his voice was filled with raw pain. "What have I done to them?"

Tituba looked up. So did Goody Nurse, who looked shocked. Tituba had answers for him—answers he might not like—but Goody Nurse looked on him with compassion.

"Why, Reverend Parris," she said gently, as if she were guiding him. "You are saving them."

Sixteen

The shovel was heavy. Ann's back ached. She shoveled more snow into the cauldron, even though it wasn't close to full. The last time she'd tried to carry it, she had nearly fallen from the weight.

The winter before, she had been stronger. But the winter before, her life had been so much better.

With each shovelful, she thought of Annie, lying on her bed unmoving. Or if she did move, she would scream that she was being tortured.

Why had God brought all this grief upon their family?

With the house behind her, Ann continued to work, not knowing what else to do. Life had to go forward. She still had one child to take care of.

Nathaniel needed her—or at least, he needed Thomas. Lately Nathaniel hadn't even been able to look at her.

As Ann worked she heard footsteps approach. Out of the corner of her eye, she saw Sarah Good and her daughter Dorcas. The woman had wretched timing. Of course, with all the begging she did, she might not have heard of the afflictions that had struck the village.

Ann pretended not to see them. She kept her eyes downcast, focused on the hole she was making in the snow before her. When the cauldron was full, she would have enough water to heat for a bath.

Annie always liked to be warm. A bath might help her.

"Goody Putnam," Sarah Good called out.

Ann sighed and looked up. She couldn't continue to ignore Sarah Good after she'd cried out like that. "I have nothing for you today, Goody Good."

" 'Tis not what I came for," Sarah said. "I wish to pay my Christian respects to the children."

Ann stopped shoveling, feeling as if the world had suddenly become a different place. She couldn't remember a time when Sarah Good had not come with a tale of woe or to beg for scraps.

"Annie is a good girl," Sarah said. "And the maid, too. Both are godly, and the village prays for them. Might you tell them that?"

Ann smiled, although she still felt wary. She had never had a moment like this with Sarah Good. But sometimes compassion came from the strangest places.

"Thank you," Ann said. "I shall tell them that."

She picked up the cauldron with both hands, feeling the pull in her aching back, and started toward the house.

"Might we see them?" Sarah asked.

Ann stopped in surprise. Sarah Good had never asked to come into her home before.

Perhaps seeing her disbelief, Sarah added, "Dorcas made them a toy."

She nudged tiny Dorcas, who held up a straw doll.

" 'Tisn't much," Sarah actually looked ashamed. "We are poor."

Sometimes kindness was repaid in kind. Ann had always given Sarah scraps to avoid her evil eye and her sharp tongue. She hadn't expected Sarah to remember all that Ann had tried to do for her.

Ann hauled the cauldron as she led Sarah and Dorcas into the house. It was so much warmer than outdoors. Sarah helped with the door, and Dorcas hovered, obviously never having been inside a place like this.

The little girl put her finger in her mouth and stared. Ann walked past her into the main room. The girls lay on a bed set up by the fire. Ann hung the cauldron in the hearth to melt the snow, but Sarah and Dorcas stayed back.

As Ann turned, Sarah was discreetly straining to get a good look at the girls. When she saw Ann watching her, she said, "People have said it has been three days without a bite of food. And not even a word."

"Not a word known to humans, anyway," Ann said.

Ann wiped her face and wished there was something she could do for the pain in her back. Then she looked at her daughter, immobile and lost.

"Grunting like animals is what I heard," Sarah said.

Ann looked up, and frowned. She didn't like Sarah's tone.

Little Dorcas seemed oblivious, though. She held out the straw doll and walked toward the bed.

"I made a doll, Annie," Dorcas said.

"Don't get near them," Sarah snapped.

Dorcas stopped in fear, and Ann felt a surge of anger. She finally understood what was going on. Sarah Good hadn't come here to sympathize. She'd come here to see someone else's misfortune.

"You have come to taunt them with your stares," Ann said.

"Haven't either," Sarah said. "But I don't want my girl to be affected."

"How dare you!" Ann said. "They are not witches."

Sarah wrapped her arms protectively around Dorcas, who looked as if she might cry.

" 'Tis not what is being said," Sarah said. "Look at them. 'Tis not human. Satan possesses them."

Lies! Why was everyone lying?

"Get out!" Ann hurried them toward the door. And as they reached it, she couldn't help but add something. "You listen to me, Sarah Good. Ye shall be sorry if harm comes to these children because of the black rumor of your tongue. I promise—ye shall be sorry."

Sarah looked at her in fear and scurried toward the road, half carrying Dorcas, who started crying.

But Ann did not care about the other woman's child. She had her own to worry about. And what she hated most was the way Sarah had spoken to her silent fears.

Jonathan Walcott wished he could feel relief when he saw Doctor Griggs at his door. But Walcott was beginning to believe the horrible things he was hearing in the village.

His household was in chaos. His other children were terrified, and his wife was panicked. They came forward as Doctor Griggs made his way into the house.

From the main room, Jonathan could hear May's screams. He led the doctor to the bed where May was tied. His daughter, tied to a bed like a common animal. But if he hadn't done that, she would have continued to strike herself. Her skin had welts and sores, which came from her own hand.

Her screams faded into a rant. Only she wasn't speaking English. She was reciting some kind of gibberish. His wife, Deliverance, confessed to him late one night that she worried their daughter was speaking a demon tongue.

The doctor stopped just inside the room and sighed. Walcott pushed him forward.

"It has been thus for two days," Walcott said. "With hands and legs flailing until we bound them to save her own bones. And when she stops she is still as death."

" 'Tis like the others," Doctor Griggs said. His voice held no hope.

"You must do something," Deliverance cried.

Doctor Griggs shook his head. "There is naught to do. My own niece is afflicted."

It was just as Walcott feared. "Naught to do but watch this suffering?"

He wasn't sure he could watch much longer.

The doctor looked at him with compassion. "Well," he said, "there is prayer."

The Putnam family pew had been moved aside to make room for the afflicted girls. All the pews had been rearranged so that the girls were in the center of the meeting house, where everyone could stare at them.

Ann hated any change and would have disliked the new arrangement, even if it had not been caused by something as dire as this. She wanted the familiarity and comfort of her place in the meeting house. Instead, all the benches had been full when she arrived with Nathaniel.

Thomas was already here, having brought Annie, and Ann had joined him in his place near the side of the building. She had no idea how long they'd been there with the rest of the village, praying for the afflicted girls, but it seemed to her that it had been most of the day.

Everyone was here, even those who did not believe that Samuel Parris should minister to Salem Village. People who had never set foot in this meeting house, preferring to go to the meeting house in Salem Town, were here, gawking at Ann's daughter.

Ann put a hand over her womb, remembering her own silent prayer when they'd brought Annie to her. Not another child. Please God. She couldn't lose another child.

But she was—and this time, in a manner so hideous she couldn't have imagined it a year before.

Annie lay on the floor, writhing, while Abigail stood beside her, shouting. Betty was sobbing uncontrollably, and Mercy sat, unmoving, on the floor as if she had died sitting up. May and Beth were slapping themselves and screaming gibberish words.

The Reverend Parris seemed even more panicked than he had days before. His voice did not reflect calm. It echoed the terror Ann felt deep inside.

He stood near the afflicted girls and spoke over the murmured prayers of the congregation.

"Hear us, oh Lord," Reverend Parris said, "Accept, in Your divine grace, the tormented prayers of these, Your worshipful servants."

Then he looked at the girls, at Betty in particular, his gaze anguished.

"Can you not feel it, children? God listens for you. Reveal what is afflicting you."

Ann wrung her hands together and watched her

daughter. Annie didn't even seem to know that Reverend Parris was there.

The girls did not change at all, and that seemed to upset him more. He leaned toward them.

"Can you not speak for yourselves?" he asked, his voice filled with urgency.

"Perhaps they are possessed!" Lizzy Putnam shouted.

Ann felt Thomas stiffen beside her. Lizzy Porter Putnam, Israel's daughter. Porter was poisoning the village through his own children. Joseph put his arm around his new wife. Ann put a hand on Thomas, holding him back. The last thing he should do was get angry in this place.

Then she realized that the congregation's murmurs had changed. They no longer sounded like prayers. They sounded like fear.

"Perhaps," Giles Corey shouted, "the Devil orders them not to speak."

Heads throughout the meeting house nodded. Ann felt terror rise within her. The prayers stopped, and she could see opinions change as if she were peering into people's minds.

They believed they were in the room with agents of Satan! They believed that Annie, her precious daughter, was in league with the Devil.

" 'Tis not true," Ann shouted. "They are afflicted."

At the sound of her voice, Annie's head moved, and she started slapping her arms. "It bites! Satan's familiar is upon me! Biting. Biting. Help me! My face! My face! She bites!"

Annie's slaps moved to her face. The slaps echoed in the suddenly silent meeting house. The other girls started to mimic her cries, and their slaps mingled with hers. Their skin was turning red and swelling with the force of the blows.

Reverend Parris stepped even closer to them. "Who afflicts you?"

"Get it away!" Annie screamed. "Get it away. It is bewitching me."

The pain in her voice made Ann step toward her, but Thomas held her back.

"Who?" Reverend Parris demanded. "Speak!"

Annie screamed, a long-drawn-out sound of such terror that Ann wanted to cover her own face. But she could not. She had to keep an eye on her daughter, just in case there was something else she could do.

Thomas's hand tightened on her arm. She glanced at him and realized that he was reacting just as she had. He wasn't so much holding her back as holding them both in place.

"Who is the witch?" Reverend Parris said. "Show us, child."

Annie's scream turned into a high-pitched keening. She writhed and twisted away from hands only she could see. Then her arms stretched out as if they were pulled.

After a moment, Ann realized her daughter was pointing, actually pointing, at someone in the congregation.

"She is the witch," Annie said clearly.

The congregation gasped just as Ann did. She followed her daughter's finger until she saw who was being accused.

And Ann was not surprised when she saw that Annie was pointing at Sarah Good.

SEVENTEEN

Sarah Good realized that Annie was looking at her. Sarah stood and backed away, Dorcas at her side. Sarah knew she was not the most popular woman in Salem Village, and she was often the scapegoat for things.

It only made sense for Annie Putnam to choose her. Her horrible mother had probably put her up to it.

The girls were still screaming and calling out in their made-up voices. Sarah started for the door, but three deacons grabbed her, imprisoning her arms at her side.

Dorcas started grabbing for the men, not understanding what was going on, begging them to protect her mother.

But Sarah knew. She had known this moment was coming from the time this holy congregation had refused to help prevent her slide into poverty and homelessness.

The deacons started dragging her toward the front of the meeting house. She flailed in their grasp.

"Unhand me," she cried. "I am not a witch."

Samuel Parris pointed at the girls as if he were contradicting Sarah. "Look at them. See how they suffer!"

She wouldn't look. Instead, she struggled and begged, even though she knew from experience that begging from this congregation was hopeless.

Annie Putnam felt trapped in her own mind. Everything happening around her felt like a dream. But she knew it wasn't. She hurt, as she had never hurt before.

The meeting house was silent, even though it was full of people. Most of their mouths were moving, but she could not hear the words.

Instead, she saw Reverend Parris's finger pointing at her. His lips opened and closed, but the words seemed to come out slower than any human could speak.

Seeeee haaaaa-oooow thaaaaaaaay suh-fur . . .

Over his words, she could hear her own heart beating and the other girls panting beside her. And the cackling laugh coming from Sarah Good.

The awful woman was standing right beside Annie, pinching her and sticking her with pins. Her long fingernails scratched Annie's face, and warm blood trickled down her cheeks.

Annie fought her off, slapping at her fingers, moving her hands, but Sarah Good seemed to have a dozen of them. Someone had to help her. Someone had to save her from this witch.

Annie turned to the other girls but saw she would get no support there. Betty was floating in the air, being held up by magic. Sarah Good, with evil power, merely pointed her finger at May, and she was thrown backward.

The other girls were fighting as hard as Annie to keep Sarah away. They were twisting and batting and striking. But it was not working.

Annie screamed for help, her own words sounding wrong: *She hurts us! Stop her! Please!*

And her voice mingled with the other girls, who were shouting too: *She is a witch. Look! Look! Help us!*

No one helped. The congregation continued to shout and point, but they were not even looking at Annie. They were looking toward the back, at three deacons who watched as if nothing were happening.

Sarah Good reached for Annie's eyes, her blood-covered fingernails so sharp that they might blind Annie. She screamed and put her hands over her face to protect herself, but she knew it would do no good.

Not even God could help her now.

Annie Putnam's blood-curdling scream seemed to go on forever. Sarah Osborn hugged herself as the girls' fits seemed to grow worse.

Annie Putnam flung her hands over her face and shouted, "She is blinding me!" But there was no one near her.

No one that Sarah Osborn could see.

There was evil in the air. She could feel it. But the evil was not of witchcraft. It was brought on by fear and pride. Sarah Osborn looked at Samuel Parris. His conservative interpretation of Puritan doctrine had taken them all back—back to a time they or their families had repudiated.

This was like England, from which they had fled.

Sarah Good was struggling with the deacons, and her little daughter clutched at anyone she could.

Deliverance Walcott's voice rose above the din. "Get the witch away!"

Sarah Osborn looked at her, afraid for a moment that Deliverance had been afflicted. But she hadn't. She was referring to Sarah Good.

"Are there others?" Reverend Parris was asking the girls. "Children, speak. Who else torments you?"

The deacons dragged Sarah Good toward the door. Her daughter, Dorcas, followed, wailing. Rebecca Nurse reached out to the little girl.

"Come to me, child," she said, and took Dorcas in her arms, turning her away from the unfolding drama. Thank heavens. Sarah Osborn might have done the same if she were close enough.

The children were still screaming up front. The deacons had brought Sarah Good close to Sarah Osborn.

Sarah Good was screaming, too. "Unhand me. I am innocent. I am a beggar woman, that is all."

And it was true. She was just a bitter, sad woman who had little hope. Sarah Osborn had helped her in the past, and she wished others who had more had contributed as well.

At that moment, Sarah Good's gaze met Sarah Osborn's. "You know who I am, Goody Osborn. Say something!"

Sarah Osborn opened her mouth to speak as she reached toward poor Sarah Good. The deacons glared at her and pulled Sarah Good away.

There was nothing Sarah Osborn could do. Who would listen to her? She wasn't one of the most popular people in Salem Village either.

Still, she had to speak.

"Let her go," Sarah Osborn cried. "These girls are deluded. Do not listen to these creatures."

Reverend Parris didn't even acknowledge her words. It was as if she didn't exist. He was still staring at the girls.

"Who else?" he demanded. "Speak before God."

But the girls had heard her. They had turned toward her, and they seemed lucid to her, just for a moment. All but Betty Parris, who was sobbing so hard she could barely breathe.

"Are there others amongst us?" Reverend Parris demanded.

"Goody Osborn," the girls shouted.

The girls were pointing at her. Sarah Osborn felt a shiver run down her back. Those malicious little creatures. They picked at her because she defended Sarah Good when no one else would.

Even the saintly Rebecca Nurse hadn't spoken up. All she had done was cradle Dorcas.

"No!" Sarah Osborn shouted.

"She is a witch, too," Mercy Lewis said.

"Lies!" Sarah Osborn cried.

"She rides with the first," May Walcott said.

The congregation was staring at Sarah Osborn. She recognized the hatred in their eyes.

"Do not look at me," she said, and she did not know whether she was speaking to the girls, to the congregation, or to all of them. Couldn't they see what was happening? Didn't they know that these creatures could just as easily turn on them?

How could these girls claim she was a witch? She had done God's work her whole life.

Surely someone in this congregation would acknowledge that.

But no one was speaking in her defense. Not the way she had spoken in Sarah Good's.

And why would they, when this was what was happening to her?

Time seemed to have stopped. Annie Putnam was beginning to wonder whether she had gone to Hell. Nothing sounded right. When she heard words, they seemed disjointed—part of another conversation spoken elsewhere.

The congregation was as far away as the moon, and she wasn't even sure she could touch them. Not that she wanted to. She wanted them to help her.

Sarah Good had stopped afflicting her. Instead, she had sent her partner, Sarah Osborn, to do the evil work.

Sarah Osborn stood before her, her eyes strange. "Sign the Devil's book. You have no choice."

Then she opened her hands, and dozens of yellow birds flew toward Annie and her friends. The birds' beaks were sharp. Annie screamed. Betty screamed beside her, and so did the others.

Sarah Good reappeared, attacking everyone, and Sarah Osborn started to help her. Annie fought hard to keep them away, but she wasn't succeeding.

May Walcott fell to the ground, ignoring the blows that landed on her, and crawled forward. She reached Reverend Parris, pleading for his help, and knelt in front of him as if in prayer.

Annie wasn't sure prayer would help any longer. Her entire life felt like one unheard prayer.

Surely, if God loved her, He would have stopped this pain a long, long time ago.

Eighteen

Tituba huddled in her place in the back of the meeting house, watching the chaos before her. She remained quiet, even though she did not think Goody Good was a witch. She was glad that Rebecca Nurse had taken poor Dorcas aside. The child had no one.

Tituba felt as if she had no one either. There was no one she could talk with, no one she could confide in. She stared at Betty and Abigail, knowing the girls were in distress, and knowing that this show was only making it worse.

All she wanted to do was take them home, calm them, and ease the pain they had slipped into.

She still wasn't sure what had happened. She knew something had taken place in the Parris home, but she couldn't tell exactly what it was. She did know that it was the final event in a series—that things had been building badly for some time.

Her ears ached from the girls' cries. Poor May Walcott had climbed across the floor to Samuel Parris, seeking redemption from a man who could not even give it to himself.

Tituba had never liked him, and she was beginning to hate him for what he was doing to these children. The man had no compassion in him at all.

"Save us, Reverend," Deliverance Walcott cried out, her words mimicking her daughter's actions.

"Keep Christ with us," Goody Glover said.

"Reverend Parris, protect us," Goody Hawley said.

And the rest of the congregation joined in—all but Tituba, who knew that he could not bring anyone salvation. Still, she mouthed the words. This was not a time or place to behave differently from the others.

As the congregation cried his name, Samuel Parris turned toward them. Tituba could see the change in his face.

He was enjoying this. He thought it was all about him. She had known he was vain, but she hadn't realized he'd sacrifice his own daughter, whom Tituba thought he loved, for his pride.

He seemed taller than he had a moment ago. He pointed a finger at Sarah Osborn and narrowed his gaze theatrically.

"Sarah Osborn," Reverend Parris said, "the Devil is your master. You obey His commands and are deaf to the utterances of Jesus Christ our Lord. And oh . . ."

The "oh" quivered in a mighty way, and Tituba knew he had planned that break. She had to struggle to keep the mask on her face so that no one in the congregation could see her revulsion. She wanted to get up and scream at the man, to blame him for all that was happening here, but she knew better.

Parris was still yelling at Goody Osborn. "He is driving you to the chambers of death, and hurrying you down the steep precipice of everlasting destruction."

And Goody Osborn looked terrified. The deacons were coming for her now, and she cringed.

Parris was done with her. He wanted more victims. He turned to the ill girls, the deluded girls, and asked, "Who else, children? Who else is amongst us?"

And in the middle of it, Betty, who was crying uncontrollably and had cried off and on for days, looked up. Her gaze met Tituba's, and Tituba knew that she was begging for help.

But Tituba didn't dare go to the front of the meeting house. Right now, she had to protect herself, huddle back here, so that when this hysteria calmed down, she could tend her girls again.

"Name the one!" Parris was shouting. He turned as he did so, and he, too, looked at Tituba. She saw him remember his lust, and then she saw the idea cross his face. "Name the *dark slaves* of the Devil."

He emphasized "dark" and "slaves." Tituba shuddered, but she knew her girls wouldn't betray her.

"Who, children?" he shouted.

Betty's hand fluttered outward. "Tituba?"

It was more a cry for help than an accusation, but of course no one else heard it that way. The entire congregation gasped, and Tituba cringed.

The other girls started screaming her name. "Tituba. 'Tis Tituba!"

And Tituba thought she saw the righteous Reverend Parris suppress a smile of triumph.

Tituba lay on the floor, blood trickling from her nose. She had swallowed even more blood. She covered her head with her arms, but that didn't stop the blows from raining on her.

This time, the Reverend Parris acted like the person possessed. He had dragged her back to the parsonage as the fiasco in the meeting house broke up, and started beating her the moment the door closed.

He took her by surprise, with that first blow to the face, and from there, she hadn't been able to defend herself.

She didn't know how long this had been going on, but she did know that she was getting not only his rage at the events around him but his rage at his own uncontrolled reaction to her nakedness.

She knew that if she didn't stop him, he wouldn't just beat her. He would rip the clothes off her and do much, much worse.

The blows hit her back and her spine. She tried to roll into a protective ball, but he kicked at her.

"Why?" he shouted.

Because you led them to me. You put the idea in their

heads, just the way Goody Osborn put her name in their heads when she spoke up. They aren't girls right now; they are suggestions waiting to be made.

But she said none of this. If any word came out of her, it was "no." She tried to crawl away from him, but he held her as he beat her.

He was stronger than she thought possible.

"Do they lie?" he screamed, his spittle hitting her back. "Confess!"

"No!" she begged. "Please stop."

"Why are you hurting them?"

She could take no more. *He* was the hurtful one. Why couldn't he see that?

Somehow she reared up, out of his grasp, and cried, "Tituba never hurt the children. Loves them like her own."

He slapped her so hard, she fell over backward. She had never seen such crazed fury in his face.

"You have sullied my home," he shouted. "You have brought doubt upon me. You are a force of Satan in my own home."

She tried to get away from him again, but he grabbed her so hard that the skin broke. He shook her and hit her so many times that she couldn't keep track.

Maybe if she started to pray, to act as if she wanted help from his god, he would let her go. He wasn't in his right mind, either. If anything, he was crazier than the children.

It was his insanity that had infected everyone. Only his.

"Witch! Confess and end the terror of this place.

Confess. Or let God strike you dead before you utter another lie for Satan. Are you a witch?"

"I am not . . ."

He slapped her so hard that a tooth lodged in her throat. She coughed, felt it go down, knew that if she didn't do something soon, he would kill her.

"Say it," he screamed, "or know now the wrath of Hell that awaits you for eternity."

She shook her head, but her denials seemed to make him even more frenzied.

"Are you a witch?" He brought up his hand to hit her again.

She ducked, and the word came out of her before she could stop it. "Yes."

He froze. His hand did not come down. He was panting in triumph.

She collapsed on the ground. The only way to stop him was to give him what he wanted. She would deal with the consequences later.

At least she was alive.

And, even though she barely realized it, she hadn't stopped repeating "Yes."

The morning dawned clear and cold. A blanket of pristine snow covered the homes and the tilled, flat farmland. Such beauty, even in the midst of trouble.

Samuel Parris walked beside Thomas Putnam, hands clasped behind his back. The village seemed to be going about its own business. Smoke came from chimneys, men shoveled walks, merchants went about their daily tasks.

Even the usual crowd who frequented Ingersoll's Tavern at this time of day were there, watching him and Putnam through the grimy windows. Parris caught a new respect in their gazes, and he wondered—for the first time since he'd come to Salem Village—if they would listen to him about the sin of too much drink.

"We have filed formal charges of witchcraft against them," Thomas Putnam said. "You shall begin the examinations tomorrow."

"And in earnest," Parris said.

A group of young men passed, doffing their hats as they did so, murmuring words of support to Reverend Parris. Everything had changed in the past few days. Finally the village appreciated him.

He nodded at the men.

"There was a reason I was sent here by the Almighty," he said to Putnam when the men had passed. "Now it is known. After the examinations tomorrow we will be purged of Satan's forces."

Putnam nodded. He did not seem as confident as Parris. But Parris had to convince him. Even if the villagers supported him, Parris knew that support could be fickle.

He still owed his job to Thomas Putnam.

"And," Parris said, careful to keep the sarcasm from his voice, "you shall have your godly order returned to Salem Village."

Two more villagers walked by. They nodded reverently at Parris, as if he were Increase Mather or someone else well known in the colony.

Thomas Putnam noted their reaction and smiled wryly. "And I doubt you will ever again want for firewood."

Parris kept his head down, careful to remain humble. "I am enriched only by God's grace."

Nineteen

A crowd had gathered along the road to the meeting house. Villagers who seemed to have nothing else to do with their time stood and gawked as they waited for the examinations to begin.

Ann Putnam walked with her daughter, Annie. She had her arm around Annie's shoulder, keeping her upright. Annie was very fragile. Her skin had welts on it from the slaps and pinches, and her voice was hoarse.

Ann had made her a soothing tea the night before, and Annie had tossed it across the room, breaking the cup. Mercy had swallowed hers, then let it spew out her lips.

They were not well enough for accusations at the meeting house, but she didn't dare go against Reverend Parris's wishes.

He walked with the girls, half carrying Betty, whose little face was chapped from her tears. He did not support the other child who had been in his care, Abigail Williams, and she seemed as weak as Betty. Beth Hubbard and May Walcott walked together, but none of the girls spoke.

Ann's greatest fear was that they would fall in fits on the snowy road.

"Ann Putnam!"

Ann stopped, keeping her hand on Annie so that Annie stopped too. Ann turned, and saw Goody Hawley hurrying toward them.

Ann had no idea what business Goody Hawley had with her. She frowned, not wanting to stay out here too long.

Goody Hawley reached Ann's side but did not look at her. Instead, she was focused on Annie. It took Ann a moment to realize that Goody Hawley hadn't meant her at all, just her child.

"God keep you, child," Goody Hawley said.

Goody Hawley knelt in front of Annie, then kissed the hem of her dress as if she were a saint. Annie barely noticed, but Ann did.

And found herself almost enjoying her daughter's newfound respect.

Samuel Parris stood in front of his congregation. God had given him much strength that day. His hearing seemed stronger than before, for, despite the girls' cries, he could hear some of the conversations of his parishioners. They talked as if they had been given leave to do so, and he saw no point in silencing them.

The things that were happening in this meeting house were shocking.

Sarah Good stood before the congregation, being examined to see if there was enough evidence to support the charges of witchcraft.

From what Parris had seen the day before, he believed there was enough, but he wanted to be thorough. If there were witches in Salem Village, he wanted to make certain he found all of them and revealed all their malicious acts.

He had been questioning Sarah Good but had opened the floor to the members of his congregation so that they would tell him things he did not know—or could not know. As much power as the Lord gave him, Parris did not have the ability to see everything within his village.

Although he had seen evil in his own household, he had not acted against it quickly enough. That was his sin, and he'd already begged forgiveness for it.

On this day, he would ensure no more evil would happen in his home again.

Deliverance Walcott was standing also, giving testimony against Sarah Good. Parris made himself concentrate on Goody Walcott's words.

"When she passed," Goody Walcott was saying, "she cursed me for not giving her coin. And the next day, another of my hens died. She bewitched them."

"You're a lying gammer," Sarah Good cried. "Your hens are dying of the cold."

Sarah Good had been screaming back at everyone

who accused her, using her evil eye against them. But Parris was proud of his congregation. They would not be silenced.

He scanned the eager faces, knowing that his meeting house had never been this full before. Perhaps he had even gotten parishioners from Salem Town, come to hear the Lord's victory in this place.

Then a small face looked toward his. Dorcas Good, her features too thin for a child of four, cringed in Rebecca Nurse's arms. The child was clearly terrified.

Parris felt a twinge of compassion for her, and then he forced himself to look at Betty. She was drooling and crying, her hair in tangles.

That was what happened to children who saw too much evil.

"Her witch's spell rotted my corn!" Goodman Tarbell shouted. "Overnight!"

"The absurdity," Sarah Good snapped, as if everyone would agree with her.

The congregation became louder as more and more people started shouting testimony against her. Parris could not keep track of all their words.

Besides, he did not need any more evidence.

He slammed his gavel on the table.

"Sarah Good," he shouted, so that he could be heard over the din. "I have found cause enough to have you tried as a witch."

The congregation screamed its support. He continued speaking, although he knew people could not hear him.

But Sarah Good could. That was enough.

"You shall be returned to the prison until that date." He waved a hand at the deacons. "Remove her."

The constables started to take her out of the meeting house, but she shook free of them. They lunged for her, and she clawed at them, drawing blood.

Parris leaned back, staying away from her. The afflicted girls screamed, and the congregation looked terrified.

The constables grabbed her and dragged her through the crowd to the exit. She kicked her feet and shrieked: "Leave me, leave me! Raving idiots. I am no witch. Leave me! You'll all rot in Hell."

Then a movement in the standing congregation caught Parris's eye. People were parting as if they were the Red Sea. Finally, he saw what was dividing them.

Little Dorcas Good pushed through all the people, chasing her mother. The child was hysterical, calling "Mama! Mama!"

Sarah Good looked at her child, her eyes filled with sadness. Parris wanted to turn away but couldn't. She should have thought of the consequences before becoming a witch.

The constables dragged Sarah Good out the door as Dorcas reached it. The door slammed in front of the little girl, and she banged on it with all her might.

No one came to help her.

Parris looked at Rebecca Nurse. She was too far away to reach the little girl, trapped by the crowd.

Dorcas Good slapped her hands against the door, then slid to the ground, weeping.

Sarah Good turned her face away from the meeting house, trying to forget the look in her little girl's eyes. Who would care for Dorcas now? No one would even talk to her so that she could make provision.

The constables dragged her down the steps and into a crowd of shouting people. Finally she got to her feet. As she did, she saw Tituba being led toward the meeting house. Goody Glover walked beside her, saying vituperatively, "Witch! You signed the Devil's book!"

Sarah Good spit into the snow, and people jumped away so that her saliva would not hit them. Goody Glover had never once given her and Dorcas any scraps, but Tituba had always helped them. Tituba was a good woman.

As Tituba drew closer, it became clear that she had been badly beaten.

Sarah Good's eyes narrowed. She had a hunch who had done that.

The constables moved her roughly along and tossed her in the prisoner's cart. Sarah Osborn was already inside, manacled to a cart post. The cold wind had turned her skin raw.

The constables hoisted Sarah Good into the cart. It groaned beneath her weight.

"Do not place that witch so close to me," Sarah Osborn snapped.

Sarah Good looked at her in surprise. They had

been friends of a sort, and she had heard Sarah Osborn defend her. In fact, she knew that was why Sarah Osborn had been accused.

"I am as much witch as you, Sarah Osborn," Sarah Good said as one of the constables shackled her next to Sarah Osborn.

He grinned when he heard her words. "And you'll both be hanging," he said.

Sarah Good looked away from him. She feared he might be right.

Tituba felt dirty, and it was not just because of the dried blood on her hands. She had been standing in front of these people for some time now, and the Reverend Parris had been standing over her, forcing her to tell lies.

Whenever he wanted her to say something, he would hold his arm up, and God forbid, she thought he was going to strike her again. So she would say what he wanted.

But her imagination had just failed her. She admitted that she had hurt the children, just as he wanted her to, and then he asked her why. Why had she hurt the innocent children?

She did not have an answer for that. She wanted, instead, to turn the question on him. Why was he persecuting innocents? But she did not have the courage.

When she did not answer his question, he leaned into her, clearly performing for the crowd.

"And thus you serve the Devil," he said.

She kept her head down so that he couldn't see the anger in her eyes. She was having trouble hiding it, having trouble keeping up her façade. She was afraid of him, and ashamed that she was afraid. She should have had more strength.

He leaned into her. He'd asked her something about serving the Devil. She couldn't remember the rest, so all she did was nod.

"Are there others who do?" Parris asked. "Witches. Are there more amongst us?"

He wanted her to make someone else suffer through this. Wasn't it bad enough that his daughter was senseless, and the other village girls crazed? Wasn't it enough that little Dorcas Good sat by the door, sobbing, with no one to care for her? He was destroying families. Why did he want her help in destroying more?

"Speak, Tituba Indian!" Parris shouted, sending shivers of fear down her body. "Naught will save you now but the truth. You are a confessed witch. Are there other witches among us?"

She could not do it. She could not destroy lives as callously as he had.

She raised her head, blinked, and saw the Puritans of Salem Village. The Christians who claimed to have a compassionate God, yet seemed to know nothing of that compassion.

They watched her with fear and a sort of excitement. She let them see her disgust, but only for a moment. She made her gaze fall on several of them, the ones she knew had no charity in their hearts.

She felt, briefly, the power that she could have if she accused them. The power that Reverend Parris was now abusing.

"Speak!" he shouted.

A few people jumped at the sound of his voice. The tension in the meeting house was high. Several villagers knew that she could accuse them—any of them—and a few were smart enough to be afraid.

"Are there others?" Parris asked.

She looked slowly and meaningfully at Samuel Parris. She let him see the hate in her eyes, and the understanding she had of him. There was evil afoot in Salem. Horrible evil, and it wore God's clothing.

Fear flickered across his face.

"Yes," she said, infusing her voice with meaning. "There are other witches amongst us."

The congregation screamed. The poor afflicted girls shrieked and fell in fits.

Samuel Parris froze in front of Tituba. He knew that she was accusing him.

And for a brief moment, both of them—accuser and sinner—wondered just how far she would go.

TWENTY

Samuel Parris's breath caught. He studied Tituba, the bruises on her face, the dried blood near the corner of her mouth. The marks of his beating covered every visible inch of her body.

It was his right. He could do what he wanted with her. He was her owner.

Her gaze met his, strong and defiant. She was going to name witches.

She was going to name him.

She was going to tell everyone here what he had done.

She knew all his secrets, down to the lust in his heart. She could reveal everything—and destroy him.

Her silence was worse than any accusation could be. Finally, he challenged her.

"For the sake of your salvation," he said softly, "name them!"

The congregation leaned forward. Even the afflicted children were quiet.

Tituba held his stare, but something changed in her eyes. A glance at his fist, a look at him, and then she blinked, looking down.

He had beaten her again. She would not challenge him. She was too afraid of him.

He felt a surge of excitement, followed by real power. Any threat to his leadership was gone now.

"Name them!" he bellowed at her.

She shook her head. He thought of challenging her again, and then decided not to push her. If he pushed her too far, she might actually become defiant again.

He whirled toward his congregation, trying not to seem too victorious. "The Devil orders her not to speak! He still rules her tongue. Take this witch to prison, and let her await her trial."

The congregation screamed its hatred, not holding back at all, as some of them had with the goodwives accused before. The constables approached, and Tituba did not fight as Sarah Good had.

Parris suppressed a smile. He had truly broken her spirit.

"Hang, witch!" Goody Hawley shouted.

"The Devil walks with her," Goodman Tarbell said.

The constables led Tituba through the screaming crowd. She kept her head down. Parris felt an elation that he had never felt before. Perhaps it was the Spirit of the Lord, touching him.

He waved a hand. "Remove these children from the Devil's shadow. Spare them any more suffering."

Ann and Thomas Putnam came forward, along with his own wife and the other parents. Elizabeth shot Parris a look that normally would have deflated him but did not. She resented their presence here. Their house was a mess without Tituba, and Elizabeth was still ill. And she was convinced that too much more of this would cause irreparable damage to Betty.

But Elizabeth was a good wife and did as he told her to. She wrapped her arms around their sobbing, hysterical daughter and led her toward the exit.

"They have served Christ enough for one day," he said, mostly to his wife's back. He emphasized *one day*. He wanted her to know that there would be others.

He was sure of it.

Ann Putnam felt wrung out. The victories that Samuel Parris had achieved that day did not seem like victories to her. She held Annie close and helped her through the gathered congregation. Thomas gave Mercy support. The girls' limbs were twitching, and Annie was too hot.

Ann couldn't tell whether her daughter knew what was going on or not.

People were shouting at them, most of them asking the girls to pray with them. It was as if they saw the girls as something more than afflicted children. As saints, perhaps, touched by God.

"Can you see them, Annie?" Goodman Tarbell asked as they passed. "Can you see their specters?"

If only they could see how touched Annie really was, how ill she'd been, how her skin showed the violence of her affliction. Or the way that Mercy stared at night, as if she saw into the fires of Hell.

"Where are the witches?" Ezekiel Godfrey asked of Annie. "Do you feel them right here?"

Ann moved her daughter forward. Annie didn't react to these cries at all, but Ann did. Each one made her feel odd, in a way she couldn't quite explain, even to herself.

"Save us, Annie!" Goody Hawley shouted.

The crowd pressed against them. Thomas gave her a look that showed his confidence had been shaken. He wanted them out of the meeting house as much as she did.

"I say!" Samuel Parris's voice boomed right behind her. He was walking with them, and Ann hadn't even realized it. "Beware ye now! The Devil has announced His presence in Salem. As of this day, the Devil and His instruments will be warring with double vengeance against our salvation."

He almost sounded as if he enjoyed this. But how could anyone enjoy these horrors?

Ann didn't have time to think about it as the meeting house doors opened, sending in colder air and the roar of an even bigger crowd.

She had never seen so many people in one place. She wanted to stop moving, but the crowd forced her forward, down the steps, her arms around Annie.

"Bah!" A voice rose above the crowd. It was Martha Corey, standing up front. She was looking directly at Ann. "I don't believe it!"

She would believe it if her children were afflicted. But some in the crowd looked at Martha as if they agreed with her. There weren't as many devout people out here as there had been inside.

"How do we know they are not the Devil's witches?"

Ann gasped and moved Annie forward. But she could not suppress a look at the woman. And as she did, she realized Annie was looking too, with that same fixed gaze she had used on Sarah Osborn.

"I shall lead ye from this killing field!" Reverend Parris's voice broke the moment.

Ann shivered herself free of it, wondering what would have happened if he hadn't interrupted, wondering whether someone else, someone like Martha Corey, might have been accused.

The dungeon was filthy and rat infested, and it stank, yet Sarah Osborn was glad she was here and not on the cold cart any longer. At least she wasn't facing her former friends and neighbors, having them stare at her as if she were one of Satan's minions.

Still, she would rather be in her chair in her own home, beside the fire she had built with her own hands. There was no fire here—nothing but wet walls and a chill that never went away.

And to make matters worse, she was forced to share a cell with Sarah Good and the betrayer, the slave Tituba. Tituba cowered in a corner, and Sarah Osborn could take it no more.

She stood over Tituba. "What have you done to us?"

"Had to," Tituba mumbled. She did not look up.

She tried to seem so innocent, and she was not. She was not, and because of her, Sarah Osborn was in this terrible place with the entire village against her.

Sarah Osborn grabbed Tituba and shook her, trying to get her to look up. "We shall hang because of you, witch!"

Tituba finally met Sarah Osborn's gaze. "Tituba no witch!"

"You confessed," Sarah Osborn said.

"He beat me!" Tituba said.

Sarah Osborn froze and saw that she, too, was abusing Tituba because of her own fears. She stared down at the broken woman in front of her. Tituba was sobbing.

"Beat me and beat me," Tituba said. "My own master."

Sarah Osborn let go of Tituba as if the horror the woman had described could flow directly into her. Her master beat her and forced her to confess? Her master? But her master was . . .

Sarah Osborn felt cold as the realization hit her. Samuel Parris was behind this. His evil was infecting the village, not anyone else's. Which meant that the person she normally would have approached for help—the minister—would be no help at all.

Tituba was sobbing so hard that her entire body

convulsed. Sarah Good leaned her head against the dank wall as if she had given up hope long ago.

But hope had been all Sarah Osborn had left. And it, too, was gone.

She sank to her knees. "What is to happen to us?"

She asked the question, but she wasn't sure she wanted to know the answer. Ever.

Thomas Putnam leaned against the wall, his arms crossed. The Parris home was so much more comfortable now that there was enough wood. The fire roared and heated every inch of the best room. Or perhaps the heat came from the argument, which made Putnam very uncomfortable.

Most of Thomas's family members—although not Joseph—as well as Jonathan Walcott and Samuel Parris, were in the room. They had been talking politics for the past half hour now, and it bothered Putnam.

Politics in Massachusetts had become dangerous business. Four years before, when King James II had been driven from the English throne, a group of ministers and merchants had taken the man James had appointed governor of Massachusetts and thrown him in jail.

Theoretically, these men were going to install a government of their own, but they never had. Finally, they appealed to the new English king, William of Orange, for a new charter to govern the colony.

Thomas had watched these events from afar, and they had disturbed him. Massachusetts had been on a knife's edge for years, with the French and the Indians always willing to make war. That the colony no longer had a government meant, in his mind, that it was open for the taking.

He tried not to dwell on that—and usually didn't have to. He could focus on his own small community and make sure everything ran well in Salem Village. But the conflict he had been avoiding had finally come to a head.

Because with no government in the colony, there was no one to enforce the laws. And Salem Village was in desperate need of laws.

Parris didn't seem to understand that. He'd been talking about punishment and sin for the past fifteen minutes. It was as if he had no idea of the political maelstrom around him. He was focused on the accused witches, and the witches only.

"Without their repentance they must be hanged," Parris was saying.

Thomas's brother looked at him with a warning glare. But Thomas had no desire to jump into this discussion, at least not yet.

"There is no law, Reverend," Jonathan Walcott said. "Until the colonies have a charter we cannot even bring them to trial, much less hang them. You know that."

Parris stopped pacing and stared at Walcott. "These are Satan's witches."

"And we are civilized men," Walcott said. "We have no lawful authority."

"We do not have the time to wait on politics,"

Parris said. "We have done without a charter for four years. Today alone, two more girls fell to the fits of affliction."

Someone put a hand on Thomas's arm, but he ignored them. Instead, he cleared his throat and spoke at last. "There is word from Boston that Increase Mather is en route from England as we speak."

"And if the King has not signed the charter?" Parris asked. "We wait for another four years? Without action now, our souls will be consumed."

Thomas studied him for a moment. Parris had a point. And there was another that he wasn't mentioning. So far, they had no idea what sort of government—what sort of charter—the King would force upon the self-governing colony. For all they knew, everything they did before the charter arrived would be for naught.

But Thomas agreed with Walcott. They were lawful men.

"We must wait until Increase Mather returns," he said. "All we can do in the meantime is to continue the examinations."

Parris looked as if he might explode with fury. Every once in a while he got a look in his eye that Thomas did not like. Parris was about to speak, but Thomas did not want to hear any more arguing on this topic.

"Be patient, Reverend," Thomas said, and hoped that admonition would be enough.

TWENTY-ONE

Elizabeth Parris had trouble catching her breath. She put a hand to her back, stopped to rest her basket of wood on the table outside the sleeping chambers, and closed her eyes just for a moment.

She was so exhausted. She should have been lying down, but she hadn't been able to, not since Tituba left. Elizabeth's normally immaculate home was filthy. She simply did not have the energy to attend the examinations, take care of Betty and Abigail, cook and haul and clean.

She hadn't the strength, and they hadn't the money to get a new servant. Samuel didn't even seem to notice. He was so focused on the examinations that sometimes Elizabeth thought he had forgotten that his own daughter was one of the afflicted.

He used to dote on Betty, and now he barely looked at her. Sometimes Elizabeth thought, uncharitably, that the sudden rise in his own status meant more to him than the suffering of his own child.

She took another breath and felt the pain run through her, then opened her eyes. She had to continue. There was no one else.

She picked up the basket of wood and carried it into the sleeping chamber. Betty and Abigail lay on their bed, still as corpses.

Elizabeth stoked the fire, making sure the room was as warm as it could be, then she crossed to her daughter. Betty stared straight at the ceiling, her eyes fixed, her breathing shallow.

Elizabeth sat on the bed and stroked Betty's hair gently. Betty didn't even seem to notice she was there.

"Poor child," Elizabeth whispered. "Can you hear me?"

There was no response at all. Elizabeth leaned closer.

"How can I save you?" she asked.

Again, Betty didn't move. Elizabeth let out a small sigh. It was as if her daughter were gone, leaving her body behind. Elizabeth almost felt as if she were alone in the room.

She brushed her hand over Betty's clammy skin and murmured, "I am afraid."

Betty's eyes moved at that. A small movement, barely discernible, but more than Elizabeth had seen in some time.

"Is that it?" she asked. "You're afraid too? Of what?"

There was no more movement. But Elizabeth went on.

"Of us?"

Betty's lips moved, but Elizabeth couldn't tell whether she said anything. Elizabeth leaned closer, heard the whispered word, and wasn't sure it was correct.

She sat up and studied her daughter, then repeated, "God?"

Betty's eyes focused for the first time in days. In fact, they looked right into Elizabeth's. Elizabeth felt hope mingle with shock.

"You are afraid of God?" Elizabeth asked, just to clarify.

Betty continued to look at her mother. And then, slowly, she nodded. Just enough so that Elizabeth realized her daughter had spoken the truth.

Ann Putnam's hands pressed together, the fingers so cold that her nails had turned blue. Her feet were cold too, but she wasn't going to move. She wasn't done yet.

Fortunately, the meeting house was empty. She wanted to be alone with her God, to get a sense of what He felt about her. But no matter how hard she prayed, she could not feel Him. Was this what God did when He couldn't forgive? He withdrew His presence?

He certainly seemed to have withdrawn it from

their family. Annie was no better, and Thomas could not stay at home. Nathaniel had gone into a world of his own, preferring to spend time in his own sleeping area or outside with a group of boys who almost seemed to run wild.

Ann had lost control of her entire house. Mercy could not get out of her bed either; the girl had disappeared into her affliction as deeply as Annie had.

What would become of them? Was all of this happening because of Ann's sin? She wished she could have a sign of some kind, but God did not give signs to sinners.

A creak made her jump. She spun around, thumping against the family pew.

Rebecca Nurse emerged from the shadows, carrying some rags. She looked like a hag in the thin light. Then she smiled at Ann.

"Goody Putnam," Rebecca Nurse said. "I did not expect . . . 'tis usually empty now."

Ann clasped her cold hands together and nodded. That was why she had come.

Goody Nurse shook the rags, her smile becoming wider. "I have come to pay my respects."

Such an odd way of describing her cleaning tasks. Ann gathered her basket and the edges of her cloak, preparing to leave. "Forgive me," she said.

Goody Nurse put a hand on Ann's arm, stilling her. "Our Lord would surely prefer your prayers to my cleaning for Him. May I?"

Ann slid over so that Goody Nurse could sit beside her on the bench. Ann was just beginning to realize how very cold she had become in this unheated place.

"Are the children improving?" Goody Nurse asked.

Ann shook her head. "I fear not. Some days they give me hope, but then . . ."

"They are in my prayers every day," Rebecca Nurse said.

Ann nodded. Goody Nurse knew how God worked. Ann wondered whether she ever came here and failed to feel God's presence.

"I find much comfort here," Rebecca Nurse said.

Apparently not. Ann fidgeted. Clearly the problem was with her, then.

"I fear I am at fault." Ann was surprised the words had even left her mouth. She would have thought that she hadn't spoken them aloud except for Rebecca Nurse's look of surprise. "I have led Satan to my door. 'Tis why things are happening."

"You have received God's communion in this church," Goody Nurse said, not understanding. "You are one of the chosen—"

"I lost faith," Ann whispered. "My prayers were only words. I turned elsewhere for solace and—"

"Elsewhere?" Rebecca asked.

"I sought the comfort of an infidel," Ann said. " 'Tis why things are happening. I have told no one this, but the rot of it is festering."

Ann touched Goody Nurse's arm. She could feel the tension in it. Goody Nurse looked at her as if she had never known her.

Ann felt her cheeks heat. What had she been

thinking? Goody Nurse was a pious woman. She couldn't possibly understand.

"I pray you tell no one," Ann said. "I should not have spoken, but the ache of my sins . . ."

"Goody Putnam," Goody Nurse said, "God will not forsake you. You have received His communion. Give yourself to God. Reverend Parris will show you the way. Believe in Him, and God will listen."

"But will I be forgiven?" Ann asked.

And, for the first time, Rebecca Nurse couldn't meet her gaze.

"Because hypocrites are the very worst sinners," Parris said, "Christ said to his apostles, 'Have I not chosen you twelve? And one of you is the Devil's disciple.' "

Samuel Parris studied the full meeting house. Thin light came through the windows, and the braziers burned with warmth. For the first winter in his memory, the meeting house was warm during his Sabbath sermons, because people were finally attending in droves. Even people from Salem Town had forsaken their own meeting house and were coming to his.

Some said they wanted to see the afflicted, but he knew it was more than that. He was becoming known as a witch finder. His words, for the first time in his life, had power.

He slammed a hand on his pulpit. "And there are such disciples in this church. Ye who sit right here wearing the mask of piety and yet are not pious. Ye are of your father the Devil. And Christ knows."

Ann Putnam glanced around the room. Parris was getting a sense of discomfort from the woman, but he couldn't tell why. Perhaps the burden of an afflicted daughter was proving too much for her.

"Oh, heretics, time enough, time enough," he intoned. "Have but a little patience, and you shall see Hell in time enough."

Suddenly he heard a thud, and a series of cries rose from the right side of the meeting house. Parris looked over and saw women gathered around the floor. The thudding continued, and he realized that someone had fallen into convulsions.

" 'Tis the Proctors' maid!" someone shouted.

And at that moment, the group parted enough for him to see. Sure enough, Mary Warren was pounding her hands and feet on the floor, just as the other afflicted girls had done.

Parris felt fear and elation mixed. This crisis continued. There was no end in sight.

John Proctor and his eldest son, William, carried Mary Warren into the house. The trip home had been horrible. Mary continued to convulse the entire way. John's wife, Elizabeth, herded the rest of their large brood of children toward their rooms. She did not want them to see what was going on.

John didn't like it either. He'd known Mary Warren a good long time, and he did not believe she was having a witch-induced fit. The fact that he had had to carry his maid into his own house was making him angry. If she had truly been ill, he wouldn't have been as upset. But he had a hunch she was performing for someone, that this was some kind of trickery, and he wanted no part of it.

Her limbs were still flailing as he got her to a bench. Her right hand nearly hit him, and he grabbed it hard.

"Be careful with her," William said.

John had no intention of care. Not at this time. The girl had relied on his charity too long for this nonsense to continue. "Mary!" he said. "Stop this! I'll not have it in this house!"

"They are sticking me," Mary moaned. "Sticking. Sticking!"

"Good Jesus," his wife said as she came up behind them. "She is afflicted."

"She is not!" John snapped. It was precisely that kind of attention he wanted to avoid, and his kindhearted wife was providing it. Well, he made the rules in this house, and everyone had to abide by them.

Even Mary Warren.

He grabbed her flailing arms, shaking her wildly. "Stop it, Mary. You will not be thus in my house. Listen to me, there will be no fakery."

"Father!" William tried to get between him and the maid, but John shook him off. He was still stronger than his stripling son.

John pulled Mary closer. She had to see reason. Now, before this mood of hers infected the rest of his children.

"I shall throw you out of here," he said. "You shall be as homeless as the day I found you."

She didn't stop convulsing. It was as if she hadn't even heard him. He picked her up by her arms and dragged her toward the door.

"Don't!" William shouted.

John's actions seemed to get Mary's attention. She started sobbing, but she wasn't struggling anymore.

Then William grabbed John, pushing him aside. What was wrong with the boy?

John glared at him. "She is not afflicted!"

"I know," William said. "She is with child."

John felt his breath catch. What had Parris been saying when Mary Warren fell into her fit? That heretics sat among them? Of course. In Parris's view, all sinners were going to Hell and could not get redemption.

Mary Warren had shown fear, the fear of her own actions.

She wasn't moving. Not now. Her convulsions had stopped. William bent over her.

" 'Tis mine," William said.

John looked to Mary for confirmation. She was weeping normally now, and she nodded as William spoke.

Her "affliction" was gone.

TWENTY-TWO

Ezekiel Godfrey woke once in the middle of the night. The fire had already burned low. He was huddled on his straw bed near his wife, Mary.

The night was dark. There wasn't even moonlight to see by. He got up, stoked the fire, and shivered once in the cold. Then he returned to bed, wrapped his arms around his wife, and closed his eyes.

Then the moon rose, quickly, as if it had forgotten it was supposed to come up. The white light illuminated the entire room. He saw its meagerness with a clarity he'd never had before.

The room was silent. He couldn't hear the crackle of the fire or Mary's breathing. He couldn't even hear his own breathing. He was about to move when a woman emerged from the shadows.

She wore a red corset and nothing more. He saw all of her as she climbed on top of him. He reached for Mary, but she was far away. He had wrapped his arms around her, and he didn't remember letting go.

The woman on top of him, the woman in the red corset, put one long finger against his lips to keep him from crying out. It was Bridget Bishop. And with the thought of her name, he felt the first stirrings of arousal. He had always found her beautiful.

She smiled at him, then traced her finger lightly over his face. Her hair fell around her bare shoulders, and her cleavage was lovely in her corset.

She drew her finger over his lips again, then parted his lips and played with the inside of his mouth. Her gentle touch became more powerful, and her entire finger went into his mouth. She pushed hard, and he tried to get away, but he could not.

He was choking. He tried to free himself, but he couldn't. He was trapped beneath the woman, and he was going to die.

Then, as quickly as she appeared, she vanished, and with her the moonlight.

Ezekiel Godfrey lay on his back beside his sleeping wife, his breath coming rapidly, and his mouth aching from the force of Bridget Bishop's hand.

Despite the day's chill, Jonathan Walcott was bathed in sweat. He had been working hard all morning, building a new barn. Thomas Putnam, Giles Corey, and Ezekiel Godfrey were helping him. They had finally come to the moment when they could put the new frame on the foundation.

They stood around it, bracing the wooden beams. The beams were heavy.

"Up," Walcott said, as they lifted. "Up!"

Behind him, he heard screams. The men got the last of the frame up before they could look toward the house. May was running across the snow, yelling, "I am on fire! She is burning me! Get her away. Stop, get her away! She burns."

For one odd moment, Walcott thought his own wife was burning his daughter to stop her fit. But Deliverance looked as if she were about to cry. She was chasing her daughter, clearly at her wit's end.

"Stop it, May," Deliverance Walcott shouted. "Come back inside where it is safe for you."

Walcott headed across the snow to catch his daughter. Thomas Putnam was beside him, and the other two men were behind him.

"I don't believe them," Giles Corey said in a voice low enough that he clearly didn't think Walcott could hear him. "I say it is evil mischief."

Walcott felt his jaw clench. If Corey had to live day to day with the fits, his opinion might change.

"It is not mischief," Ezekiel Godfrey said. "Nothing human can make that noise. 'Tis enough to make a sane man lose his intellectuals."

At that moment, Walcott caught his daughter in his arms. May continued to struggle. Deliverance's gaze met his in a look of relief. Apparently she had been afraid she could not catch her daughter.

But May was still in her fit, struggling so hard against her father that he could barely hold her. Deliverance put her hands out to help, and this time, so did May's uncle Thomas, who gripped her shoulders.

"Who afflicts you?" Thomas Putnam asked May.

"Burns and burns," May said almost as if she were having a conversation. "Do you not smell my flesh afire? Stop her!"

"Speak, May!" Thomas said. "Who?"

"Can't see!" May said. "Can't see. The witch. She burns me. The witch, the witch."

May twisted so hard she could barely breathe. She slapped at her father, and he turned his head away, only to see Ezekiel Godfrey's face.

He looked like a man waking from a horrible dream. He touched his mouth, as if it hurt him, and then he frowned.

"I know," he said in a low voice.

Only Walcott heard him. The others were still focused on May.

"Who afflicts you?" Thomas Putnam asked May. "Speak her name!"

"I know who it is," Godfrey said.

And Jonathan Walcott held his breath as Ezekiel Godfrey told them what he knew.

He did not want to help the other men. They did not know her power. But Ezekiel Godfrey knew better than to stay behind. These were difficult times, and his actions might be mistaken.

So he carried a torch, sparks dripping onto his

hand. The night was cold, and the snow was deep out near Bridget Bishop's ramshackle hut.

Smoke drifted out of its chimney, but that did not make it look like a place of comfort. Godfrey touched his mouth again. It ached each time he thought of the way Bridget Bishop had tried to kill him.

Thomas Putnam walked beside him, also holding a torch, and Jonathan Walcott brought up the rear. He had believed Godfrey before Putnam had. But then, Walcott was living with an afflicted girl. He knew how terrible such attacks could be.

The men stopped in front of the hut.

"Bridget Bishop!" Thomas Putnam yelled. "Come out!"

They stood, motionless, waiting for a response. The woods were eerily silent, just as Godfrey's home had been the night of Bishop's attack. How did she make all sound go away? And why?

Godfrey held his torch tightly. The silence was the precursor to an attack.

Then, behind them, an owl screeched. Only there was something odd about the noise, something not quite owl-like.

And Godfrey knew what it was. "She has turned herself into a bird."

Putnam gave him a measuring look, but Godfrey did not back down. Putnam had not felt her awful power. Not yet.

Walcott took a deep breath, as if screwing up his courage. Then he nodded at the others. They walked down the path in the snow to the hut's front door.

Godfrey's heart was pounding. His breath was coming in small gasps. He wanted to run, but he couldn't. He was between the two men on the path.

Putnam pushed the door open and entered. Godfrey couldn't bring himself to go inside. He hovered just inside the jamb, watching Putnam search the small dwelling.

Then he stepped out again. "She is gone," Putnam said. "She heard us coming."

Of course. Godfrey should have expected that, with her great control of noise. She could make sound stronger in the same way she made it weaker.

"She is a witch," he said to the others. "She can hear us breathing from a mile away."

Walcott nodded, looking disgusted. Putnam scanned the woods as if he could see her. But Godfrey looked over his shoulder into the hut. Something had caught his eye.

Then he saw it. The red corset, hanging on a drying rack with some other clothes. He stared at it for a moment, remembering how she had looked in it.

His body responded as it had that first night. In horror at his own reaction, he tossed the torch at it. The torch landed on the corset, setting it on fire, red against red, burning the sin away.

The fire spread quickly to the rest of the drying rack and then to the hut's walls.

Ezekiel Godfrey ran after the other men, his heart pounding so loudly he thought even they might be able to hear it.

TWENTY-THREE

Ann Putnam was preparing the evening meal. The day had been uneventful in the house for the first time since she could remember. No fits, no struggles. In fact, Annie sat near the fireplace, playing with Thomas's dog. Nathaniel, happy that his sister seemed normal, painted her face with charcoal— an old game of theirs.

Thomas was in the next room, doing some work. He had been in a foul temper for the past day, ever since he'd helped his brother-in-law with his new barn. He wouldn't tell Ann much, except to say that May's fits seemed to have grown worse.

Ann wiped the sweat off her brow with the back of her hand. She stirred one of the pots hanging on the hook inside the stone fireplace. Another pot needed stirring, and the joint of meat, on its twine in front of the fire, needed tending.

Without a maid, even making dinner was difficult.

Perhaps she could get some help, after all. If Annie were recovering, it might be worth a try.

Ann turned toward her daughter. "Will you spin the meat, Annie?"

Annie tilted her face so that Nathaniel could reach her other cheek. It seemed that she heard her mother but was ignoring her.

That vexed Ann. "Annie!"

Annie leaned toward her brother and tapped her forehead. "Draw more."

Nathaniel froze. He looked at his mother out of the corner of his eye, and she knew what bothered him. He wondered if she sensed Annie's small rebellion, just as he did.

Ann had had enough. She put both hands on her hips. "Child, will you defy your—"

A knock on the door interrupted her. She bit back the rest of the words—no sense in letting the villagers hear her being a fishwife—and crossed to the front door, pulling it open.

Bridget Bishop stood before her, looking ghastly. Her hair fell about her face in wet strings, and her clothing was soaked through. She shivered, blue in the lips.

Ann couldn't take a breath. She wasn't sure whether this was an apparition or a real woman.

Then Bridget said, "Help me, Goody Putnam."

And Ann felt her horror deepen. Part of her

wanted this vision to be an apparition. Then she wouldn't have to speak, wouldn't have to acknowledge that she knew this infidel.

"They have come to arrest me," Bridget Bishop said. "They have burned my home. I have been all night in the forest. Another night and I shall die of cold. You can stop them."

Ann shook her head. She couldn't stop anyone. Besides, the entire village knew that Bridget was a witch. Ann didn't need anyone to know they had a connection, or she'd be accused.

She glanced over her shoulder, hoping Thomas hadn't heard. Instead of seeing her husband, though, she saw her daughter, looking terrified.

All illusion of normality was gone. Annie's eyes had glazed, and she was mumbling. Ann knew what that meant by now.

A fit was coming on.

Ann turned back toward the door, caught between the woman who had helped her and her daughter, whom she couldn't help at all.

"Please, Ann Putnam," Bridget said. "You know I am not a witch. You can stop them."

Annie's body hit the floor, and Ann could almost count the rhythm of the convulsive pounding. Nathaniel screamed for their father, and Ann reached for the door to close it.

Thomas couldn't see Bridget Bishop. He couldn't.

"Why has she come to you?" her husband asked from behind her.

Ann hadn't even heard him approach. She blinked as

207

Bridget Bishop looked up at him. Bridget's next words were for him, even though she addressed them to Ann.

"I helped you, Goody Putnam," she said. "You had nowhere else to turn, not even your God. I saved you."

But Thomas didn't seem to notice what Bridget was saying. He was leaning against Ann.

"Why here?" Thomas repeated.

Annie's fit continued behind them, but Nathaniel had stopped yelling for help. Ann felt guilty that her ten-year-old son was alone to deal with his sister's affliction.

"Ann Putnam," Bridget whispered, "where is your conscience?"

Annie was hissing and babbling. Ann backed up, bumped into Thomas, and pushed past him.

He caught her arm. "Why here?"

Ann looked up at Thomas and saw something in his face that she had never seen before. As if he were waiting for her answer to judge her.

"I don't know," Ann said.

Bridget Bishop's face fell, and she turned, running into the night. Ann let out a secret sigh, thinking that perhaps all of this was at an end now.

But her husband wasn't going to let it go. He ran after Bridget Bishop. And if he caught her, he would learn what Ann had done.

Ann walked back toward the hearth fire. Annie was deep in her fit, screaming and hyperventilating, her back pushed against the wall as though pinned there by a supernatural force.

As she got closer, Ann felt the warmth of the fire. She had just doomed a woman to death.

A woman who had helped her.

William Stoughton sat at his desk in the Boston Office of Magistrates. Behind him, he could see the harbor where the frigate had anchored. He'd heard already that the Reverend Increase Mather had returned with the charter.

Now Stoughton could continue with the duties the colony had assigned him as deputy governor—except that he would be the colony's official governor now.

He stood up, impatient for the meeting to begin. The changes ahead excited him. Although he had been trained as a minister and had worked most of his seventy years within the Puritan structure, he loved politics more, and he knew it well enough to survive the overthrow of the governor and all that had come since.

The door finally opened, and Increase Mather entered. Mather was a distinguished man, who looked a bit weathered after his long journey. In his right hand he carried a leather document case.

Stoughton tried hard not to look at it.

Instead, he crossed the room, hand extended. "Increase Mather, four years have changed you little. Welcome home. I trust the crossing was bearable."

"Only just," Mather said. "My advancing years become all too known to me on the sea."

Stoughton raised his eyebrows in amusement. He had twenty years or more on Mather. "The only thing that makes me feel old is when younger men complain of their advancing years. Please, sit."

Mather looked over his shoulder as he took the nearest chair. "There are matters we must discuss before—"

"Of course," Stoughton said, wishing he could just take the case and look inside. "I trust you have brought good news with—"

"Actually," Mather said, "even before we can—"

"Were you not successful?" Stoughton asked. He couldn't take this blather. Mather was usually a much more direct man. "The charter was signed, yes? We have—"

"Yes, of course," Mather said. "The colonies have their charter. King William agreed to many of our needs, but—"

"Excellent," Stoughton said, reaching for the case. "Then what could possibly be of greater importance than the charter? We have had no formal government for four years. Have you any idea what—?"

Then the door banged open. A man wearing the dandified clothing of a non-believer, and a woman dressed as no godly woman ever would, entered, with Stoughton's assistant at their heels.

Stoughton frowned. He thought he had given clear orders about how his day would be conducted.

"Not now," he snapped at his assistant. "The Reverend and I—"

"I tried, Reverend Stoughton," his assistant said. "But they insisted."

Impatiently, Stoughton turned on the dandified

210

man. To his surprise, he saw the man sizing up his office as if he found it fascinating.

"Who are you?" Stoughton asked.

"This is Lady Phips," the dandy said, deliberately misunderstanding him. "My wife."

"I was not referring to her." Stoughton didn't care how rude he was being.

Mather cleared his throat, looking very uncomfortable. "This is Sir William Phips. He is the new governor of Massachusetts. 'Tis the matter I was hoping to discuss."

Stoughton felt anger surge through him, but he held it back. Mather had been given clear instructions on maintaining the current governmental structure in Massachusetts. On maintaining Stoughton's position.

Then Stoughton realized that the name Mather had given was familiar.

"William Phips, the adventurer, is going to govern Massachusetts?" Stoughton asked in disbelief.

"By orders of the King." Mather did not sound pleased. Stoughton sensed there had been much discussion of this very point in England.

"I assure you," Phips said, "we will find a role for you. There is no reason the work you have done for the Colonies should have to stop."

Stoughton, so good at politics, heard what was being implied. Phips meant to shuttle him out of the political arena—and to do so in a way that would reflect poorly on Stoughton.

Well, Stoughton had been at this longer than

either man. He'd show this Phips how Massachusetts really worked.

"I work for God, Mr. Phips," Stoughton said.

To his surprise, Phips smiled at his rudeness. " 'Sir,' Reverend. Sir William Phips."

Outranked in man's world, but not in God's. Of course, King William would honor this man. But men like this didn't survive in Massachusetts, especially dandified men with ungodly wives.

At that moment, Lady Phips turned toward Stoughton's assistant.

"May we have more wood on the fire?" she asked in a tone that brooked no disagreement. "My husband prefers a warmer room."

Preferred to waste God's resources on comforts of the flesh. Yes, Sir William Phips would not survive long in this colony, where God's people ruled.

Phips was looking at his wife fondly, the expression unseemly in public. Stoughton's jaw set.

"Before we get to matters of housekeeping," Stoughton said, "which is of course no less pressing than the new charter that sits just there on my desk, pray tell what role you envision for me in your new administration. I should like to prepare myself."

Phips turned toward him, his expression placid. The man did know how to play this game, at least a little.

"Witchcraft, Reverend," Phips said. "The news of its invasion into the colonies very much concerns England."

He wandered toward the desk and ran his finger across it as if searching for dust.

Stoughton wanted to tell him to back away, but did not dare. For the moment, Phips was in charge.

"The King," Phips said, "shall be watching us carefully to see that it is handled and without undue disruption."

Stoughton caught the coded warning. He was not to do anything that would interfere with Phips's authority in the transition of power.

Stoughton would not, at least in the transition. But who was he to say what would happen once Phips became governor. Massachusetts had already deposed one governor. The colony could do so again.

"The latest news," Phips was saying, "is that the Devil is not satisfied with just beggars and slaves. He has begun to possess respectable souls. Obviously, His evil hand reaches deeper than we first imagined."

Stoughton froze. He caught the implied threat. Should things not go the way the King desired, the Devil could be found anywhere.

Even in the deputy governor's office.

TWENTY-FOUR

Martha Corey could not believe the crowd that had gathered on her farm. She had never seen so many people standing in front of the door, their feet buried in the early spring mud.

Rain was falling hard, and she was not dressed for it. The constables who had pounded on her door just a few moments ago would not let her grab her cloak.

The men held her arms and dragged her outside as if she were a common criminal. One of the constables held her husband, Giles, back. He was struggling harder than she was.

"Do not be rough with her," Giles said.

Martha knew that there was no arguing with the constables. But she needed the villagers with her.

She was a godly woman. She'd helped many of them.

She saw the wet faces upturned toward her, and those people had to understand that this could happen to them as well. Once they did, she would go free.

She planted her feet hard so that the constables had no choice but to slow down.

"They dare accuse me!" Martha Corey shouted to the gathered crowd. "I am a member of the church. I have received the Lord's communion. 'Tis the girls who are the Devil's agents. You shall see. Let me be tried, and I will prove who is the witch."

The constables pulled her forward, past her watching neighbors. They murmured as she was dragged by, averting their eyes so that her gaze could not touch theirs.

Never in her life had she been treated this way. Never had she felt so alone. She glanced over her shoulder and saw her husband, watching from the door, the other constable holding him back.

His worry affected her, and as she turned away she wondered at her own bravado.

She certainly hoped she could prove her point. Because if she couldn't, she had a very uncertain fate.

They were starving. Sarah Osborn leaned against the bars and cried out again.

"Guard!" Sarah Osborn shouted, "bring us more soup!"

Not that she would find any compassion here. But she wasn't looking for compassion. She was looking

215

for a way to help the other women, who had become her friends.

In the distance, she heard footsteps and the murmur of male voices. She shouted again. Behind her, Tituba stirred. Sarah Good moaned, and some of the other prisoners took up Sarah Osborn's cries.

"Quiet, witch!" the guard said. "Let Satan serve you."

She couldn't see him. Then people emerged in the darkness: three more women, being prodded by long poles. It took Sarah Osborn a moment to recognize them, and even then she wasn't sure her eyes saw correctly.

Bridget Bishop—yes, it was only a matter of time before she would be accused, with her healing ways—looking as if she had been left outside to die, her hair scraggly about her head. Susannah Martin was a widow from Amesbury, long suspected of witchcraft.

But the person who seemed out of place—who looked out of place, with her head held high, unbroken by the accusations—was Martha Corey.

Sarah Osborn had thought Martha Corey was a good upstanding member of the church. A shiver of fear went through Sarah. If they could accuse Martha Corey, they could accuse anyone. Those demented girls were gaining power.

The guards opened the door and shoved the newly accused inside. Bridget Bishop tripped on the filthy straw and nearly fell. One of the older prisoners caught her and helped her inside.

Sarah Osborn moved closer to the bars as the guards pulled the door closed.

"Wait!" she cried. "Goody Good is sick and with child. Bring us soup."

The guards shook their heads and walked off. Sarah Osborn slumped for a moment against the cold iron. Sarah Good might die of this pregnancy. She had been starving when she conceived, and the babe inside was so small no one had known she carried. Now the stress of imprisonment was making her even sicker.

Sarah Osborn wasn't feeling well herself. She had been sickly before she was accused, and being here, in the constant cold and damp, had given her a hollow cough. Even Tituba, who had been healthy when she arrived, wasn't looking well.

This place would kill all of them if they were left here long enough.

At least Bridget Bishop was here now. She knew the healing arts better than the rest of them. She might be able to help.

The new women found their places inside the cell. Only Martha Corey remained standing, looking like a queen among the filth.

Sarah Osborn turned toward her. "Goody Corey? You have been accused?"

Martha Corey nodded. What Sarah Osborn was taking for pride, she suddenly realized, was more like shock. Goody Corey could not believe she was here.

None of them could.

One of the older prisoners, Rachel Clenton, glared at Bridget Bishop. "It was only a matter of time for this witch."

217

Her words echoed Sarah Osborn's thoughts, only with a lot more maliciousness. Sarah knew that none of them were witches, and she'd gone to Bridget more than once for some herbal remedies. Bridget was a kind woman, who did not believe in the Puritan ways but had her own ways of worship.

"Move, slave," Susannah Martin said to Tituba.

Goody Good was lying in the straw next to Tituba. She put an emaciated hand on Tituba's arm, holding her in place.

"This is her spot," Goody Good said.

Sarah Osborn winced. She knew how much speaking taxed Sarah Good.

"You defend a witch?" Susannah said.

"Are you a witch?" Sarah Good asked.

"Of course not," Susannah said. "The girls are lying."

"Then call her Tituba," Sarah Good said. "She is no different than you. We are all as much witch as each other."

Then she put her head down and closed her eyes. Sarah Osborn let out a small sigh. Martha Corey watched the proceedings with something akin to horror.

She was beginning to realize what sort of place she was in.

Tituba ignored Susannah Martin and looked at Martha Corey. They obviously had an acquaintance. It took a moment for Sarah Osborn to parse it out, and then she realized that Tituba probably knew most members of Samuel Parris's congregation, since she had worked in his household.

218

"Is there word from outside?" Tituba asked Goody Corey.

"There are rumors this will be over soon," Martha Corey said. Then the old fire leaped into her eyes. "The fools. They shall learn who is—"

"Over?" Sarah Good struggled to sit up. "Tell us what you know."

"Please, we beg of you," said Rachel Clenton, her persecution of Bridget Bishop forgotten.

Martha Corey studied all of them for a moment. She seemed to gather strength from their attention.

Sarah Osborn smiled. The community of women in this place gave them all strength. She thought it was what kept poor Sarah Good alive.

"There is a new charter," Martha said. "And a new governor."

Everyone moved closer to Martha.

"And he will favor us?" Sarah Osborn asked.

" 'Tis the rumor," Martha said.

Sarah Osborn felt relief that she knew might be false. Still, any hope was better than none.

Tituba clasped Sarah Good's hand in obvious joy. "Did you hear that?"

"And what news from the village?" asked another woman from the back. Sarah Osborn couldn't see who spoke.

" 'Tis almost spring now," Susannah Martin said. "A week ago, I saw the first shoots of crocus."

"Have you any news from Weham?" another asked. " 'Tis where I am from."

The women gathered round to talk. Much as Sarah

219

Osborn hated to see new arrivals, she welcomed them too, and the news they brought of the outside world—a world she feared she might never see again.

William Phips insisted on using the old governor's carriage for his trip to Salem Village. The carriage William Stoughton had been using was hard and uncomfortable. After a long trip in that contraption, Phips would have been unable to walk. He would have suggested riding their horses, but he knew that Stoughton was too old to handle a trip on horse-back, especially in the uncertain weather of early spring.

Phips was regretting his decision now, though. He hadn't realized that being cooped up with Stoughton this long would be akin to traveling to Hell.

Stoughton sat across from him, back rigid, not touching the carriage's plush interior. Phips lounged, determined to remain comfortable.

Stoughton wouldn't even look at him. Instead, he stared out the window and let Phips know of his displeasure at the King's choices.

Once he had read the charter, Stoughton's displeasure had grown. The charter changed Massachusetts's status from a colony to a province. Gone were many of the privileges the Puritans enjoyed. They could no longer outlaw other religions or force people to join their church.

Stoughton was vehement in his complaints against those provisions, but he failed to notice the one that would have the most impact—the one that Phips insisted upon if he were to govern this colony. Now, all men of property had the right to vote, not just Puritan men. The power in Massachusetts was about to shift away from this hard-headed group of religious extremists to people of good sense—exactly the way things were in England.

"We must be nearing Salem Village," Stoughton said. "There is a blackbird out there."

Phips resisted the urge to roll his eyes. Signs and portents everywhere for these people. If only they had used their minds instead of their superstitions, none of these problems would have arisen.

"That would be expected," Phips said, keeping his tone mild. "It is where birds are most comfortable."

"Do you mock me?"

Well, well. Stoughton was perceptive enough to notice Phips's words instead of his tone. Phips made the smile that came to his lips an innocent one.

"I was merely offering a scientific hypothesis," he said.

Stoughton regarded him for the first time. His expression was full of judgement. "Ah, a man of science are you?"

Phips nodded. "I admit, I do find some comfort in the logic of it."

"And is that, Sir William, how you shall govern Massachusetts? With the logic of 'science' as your guide?" Stoughton clearly did not approve. Apparently he was one of those backward thinkers who believed science and God were incompatible.

"A rather modern concept, isn't it, Reverend?" Phips said, unable to resist the jab.

Stoughton looked out the window for a moment, and Phips hoped this part of the discussion was done. Instead, Stoughton was apparently drawing up his next argument.

He leaned toward Phips, his eyes amazingly alert for a man of his years. "The hell we shall be entering soon is a place, I assure you, where your modern logic will have all the impact of a jet of urine into the ocean."

Phips was taken aback by Stoughton's crudity. He thought Puritans disdained all mention of bodily functions, at least in public.

"By that I mean," Stoughton continued, clearly taking Phips's silence for stupidity instead of shock, "it is tepid and rank in the moment but will quickly be proven inconsequential amid the greater waves of faith and godliness. It has always been thus, and it shall always be."

Phips sighed. He was going to have to get used to these godly arguments. After all, the Puritans had come to the new world so that they could create a religious state. That their state was failing didn't seem to bother them. It seemed to turn them inward, make them even more vested in their personal sanctimony.

Stoughton gestured at the window. "We are entering Salem Village, where the Devil has taken residence. The Devil. Modernism will offer no protection for you. Or for them."

The carriage pulled to a stop in front of a house.

Smoke came from the chimney. Phips hadn't realized they had entered the village; he had been that focused on Stoughton's words.

But he could not let those words stand. Modernism had a place here and provided an explanation for the awful occurrences in this community. Unlike Stoughton, who had turned to his Bible and his twisted interpretation of it, Phips had read the transcripts and had studied some of the recent history of the village before coming here.

Past events shed an interesting light on the accusations.

"We are in Salem to find the truth, Reverend," Phips said. "Can you honestly trust you will be able to see it with so much . . . saltwater . . . in your eyes?"

Stoughton looked appalled at the way Phips had twisted his words. Phips merely smiled and stepped out of the carriage

Reverend Samuel Parris's best room was quite nice for being this far away from Boston. He had a godly house, plain and yet comfortable, with a nice fire in the hearth and good sturdy chairs about.

William Stoughton sat in one of those chairs, watching the men he had just met. Some he had known from other colony business. Parris, however, he had not met. The Reverend was younger than he expected, but his face was strong in character.

Thomas Putnam had done some business in Boston. Stoughton found him to be an opinionated man but one he could trust. Jonathan Walcott seemed tired, almost beaten by the events of the past several months. His eyes had dark shadows to them, which he explained away by talking of the stress in caring for an afflicted girl.

Phips had glanced at Parris when Walcott said that. Parris, like Putnam, was caring for two such girls and seemed no worse for the wear. However, Parris had made apologies for the state of his home. The entry was not as clean as could be. His wife had been ill, and his servant was one of the accused.

The girls were of no use now in helping maintain the family, and so Parris was on his own. He had his congregation to tend. It was not surprising that his home was not quite to Phips's exacting standards.

Phips had been bothering Stoughton all day. Now the man was stirring his tea so loudly that the scraping sound made Stoughton want to grab the spoon out of the man's sun-darkened hand.

"I have reviewed the documents of the accused witches," Phips was saying as he watched himself stir the tea. "I am struck by how many of the complaints were filed by you, Goodman Putnam. Perhaps a third so far."

Stoughton stiffened at the implied accusation. But Putnam did not seem upset.

"I shall not let Satan get a foothold in Salem," Putnam said.

"And two of the accusers live in your home?" Phips's question sounded innocent, but Stoughton knew it was not.

Putnam nodded. "My own daughter is afflicted."

"Ah," Phips paused while he stirred some more. "Then it is understandable why you are so vigilant."

Reverend Parris caught the judgment in Phips's tone as well. He glanced at Stoughton with surprise. "We are all—"

Phips tapped his spoon against the side of the tea cup. Even though he was still looking down and pretending to be polite, it was clear to Stoughton that Phips was making the noise to shut Parris up.

"I was also struck, Goodman Putnam," Phips said before anyone else could speak, "by how many of the accused happen to be of families engaged in prior litigation with your family. Land disputes."

Putnam's face turned red. "I hope you are not insinuating that—"

"Nothing," Phips said. "Life is filled with coincidences. They fascinate me."

Fascinate him indeed. He was playing all of them because he believed he was in charge. He would learn. Stoughton said pointedly, "He is a man of science."

All of the Salem men seemed to have caught the insinuation, though. Parris leaned forward. "An evil hand is upon us, Sir William. There is no doubt."

Phips regarded Parris. Phips's expression remained bland, but Stoughton had a sense that the new governor did not like anyone in the room.

Phips said to Parris, "And you have presided over the examinations of the accused, have you not?"

225

Parris nodded. "It has been—"

"Twenty-six examinations to date?" Sir William asked.

"Twenty-seven," Parris said. "We examined another this morning."

"And how many of those examined do you believe are witches?"

"All."

Phips looked up in real surprise. For the first time he did not try to mask his expression. Somehow Stoughton thought this was worse.

"All of them?" Phips asked. "Have they all confessed?"

"Just one," Jonathan Walcott said. "But there is—"

"Twenty-six have pleaded their innocence, and you have believed not even one of them?"

The Salem men exchanged looks. Even to Stoughton, they seemed almost guilty.

But Stoughton knew the ways of witch trials. This wasn't like property disputes, where boundaries could be proven. Witches were hidden creatures, difficult to catch and even harder to hold.

"The guilt of the accused is beyond doubt," Parris said. "We have examined them carefully."

"Examined for their witchcraft." Phips's tone was flat, like a judge leading on a witness.

"Of course," Parris said, obviously not seeing the trap he was walking into.

"Or for their innocence?"

Color suffused Parris's face. He had heard the

226

accusation in Phips's voice, as they all had. The other two Salem men shifted in their chairs.

It was time for Stoughton to step in with this non-believer.

"Governor," Stoughton said, "these are the wives and servants of Satan. Their specters have afflicted a score of innocent young girls."

"Their specters?" Phips sounded incredulous.

"Have the witches turned themselves into birds?" Stoughton asked the men around him.

"Yes," Parris said. "Yellow ones."

"My daughter saw a black one, biting her," Thomas Putnam said.

Clear proof then, to anyone who knew about these things. That witches existed was not in doubt. Everyone knew that they did. They had appeared in Massachusetts before.

What was hard to prove was who they were and who they touched. Stoughton had assumed that Phips knew that, but now Stoughton was not so certain.

"Yes, they are the witches' familiars," Stoughton said, explaining the obvious carefully. "They are suckling from the girls. And snakes?"

"Yes," Jonathan Walcott said. "And cats as well. The girls have seen them."

Phips watched this as if all the men around him had lost their minds. But none of the Salem men seemed to notice. They seemed relieved that Stoughton understood what they were talking about.

Still, Stoughton led them through the evidence,

so that the non-believer would finally understand.

"And have the witches passed into their rooms at night?" Stoughton asked.

Reverend Parris finally understood what was going on. He nodded eagerly, his gaze darting toward Phips. "Even through closed doors," Parris said. "It is how the witches materialize."

Stoughton leaned back, triumphant. He looked pointedly at Phips.

"Those are specters," Stoughton said as if he were speaking to a child.

Phips merely sipped his tea, but Stoughton still felt his contempt. What would it take to convince the man?

Parris watched him as well. "The poor afflicted girls writhe and bend and suffer in ways that defy the laws of science."

"Yes," Phips said in that bland tone of his. "So I have heard."

"You shall see for yourself at the trials," Thomas Putnam said.

"Regretfully, I shall not." Phips rose.

Stoughton hid his surprise. Was this non-believer going to let witches go free? Was he going to damn Salem and the colony? Let it become a witches' haven?

Phips ignored the consternation around him. He set the tea cup on Parris's table. The spoon clinked once on the saucer and then fell to the tabletop. Phips did not pick it up.

"I am," he said, "en route to the frontier. I must

admit I have more experience fighting Indians than witches. For the time being, I shall place my deputy governor in charge of the trials. I should like to see what he finds."

He nodded toward Stoughton. Stoughton felt fury rise in him again, but he suppressed it. So, Phips wanted this over as quickly as possible, did he? He wanted the accusers to become the accused, the victims to submit to their devilish tormentors.

Phips had no understanding of how things were done in Massachusetts, and clearly no relationship with God. Stoughton couldn't change that, but he could continue to enforce God's law, even if the charter claimed that man was now in charge.

Phips was still staring at him. Stoughton bowed his head slightly.

"And I shall be your humble servant," he said.

But Phips had already turned away from him.

"I wish you luck, Reverend." Phips nodded at Parris and the others. "Gentlemen."

And then he left. Stoughton had known that Phips would leave him here, but he had thought the man would return to Boston first. He had no idea that the new governor was going to fight Indians.

Perhaps the idiot would get himself killed.

Then Stoughton sent a silent prayer, an apology for the wicked thought.

Still, Phips did not realize how much power he had just given Stoughton. Stoughton meant to use it all.

He turned to the three locals before him. "You must immediately shackle the jailed witches. This will help contain their specters. A man of science cannot appreciate how dangerous they are."

For the first time, the other men relaxed. Parris even smiled slightly.

Stoughton stood.

"I wish to see the children now," he said.

TWENTY-FIVE

Parris led William Stoughton into the center hall only to find Elizabeth barring the door to the children's sleeping chamber. Elizabeth looked white-faced and fragile. Her illness clearly weighed upon her.

But fury sparked in her gaze, and Parris was ashamed that his wife showed such contrariness in front of a dignitary.

"The children are resting," Elizabeth said as she crossed her arms. "I'm afraid—"

"Their afflictions have been much discussed in Boston," Reverend Stoughton said, attempting to placate her before Parris could even speak. "I should like to study them for myself."

"They are not to be studied," Elizabeth said. "They are neither curiosities or insects."

Parris felt the first stirrings of fury at this woman who was supposed to be his right hand. She was supposed to obey him in all things. He was a man of God, after all, and this—this thing that they faced—was larger than their family.

When he had gained control of his anger, he turned to the Reverend. "Pardon my wife, Reverend. She has been ill for some time now. The fever makes her lose her senses. Come this way."

He pushed past Elizabeth, and as he did, she whirled on him, her own anger clear. He gave her a cautionary look, then closed the door in her face.

Betty and Abigail sat playing in a corner of the small chamber, piling rocks on top of each other. When they saw the men, they set their hands at their sides and did not move.

"They do not seem afflicted," Reverend Stoughton said. "Not as I have heard."

Parris nodded. The periods of calm seemed to surprise people who had not experienced the full measure of affliction.

"There are times they seem normal," he said. "But you can see they are quite thin, and, except for the darkness under their eyes, their skin has turned disturbingly pale from the ordeal."

Especially Betty's. He longed to hug his daughter but dared not. She wouldn't let him touch her, not since shortly before she had become afflicted. These days, she wouldn't even look him in the face.

She was not the daughter he had loved so. That daughter seemed gone from him forever.

Parris set a candle close to the girls so that the Reverend could study them. As the men knelt, Parris felt the girls grow increasingly tense.

He held his own breath. God forgive him, he wanted the girls to show Reverend Stoughton what was wrong, but he did not want to inflict pain on his daughter anymore.

The Reverend looked at them as if they might attack him at any moment. Then he extended a tentative hand toward Abigail.

She shrieked and fell to the floor in a fit, convulsing and panting.

Betty did not move at all.

Parris felt relief at Abigail's fit. The relief was immediately followed by shame.

"I see," Reverend Stoughton said.

After a moment he rose, and watched from a standing position. Abigail continued to writhe, but Betty sat calmly. Parris knelt beside her, afraid to touch her, knowing that if he did, she might fall into a fit too.

"And the calm one is your daughter?" Reverend Stoughton asked.

Parris nodded. "She is not calm, Reverend."

The Reverend peered at Betty and knelt to look at her more closely. Parris watched the Reverend's face as he realized that Betty was not calm but in a stupor.

Reverend Stoughton seemed fascinated by this. He snapped his finger in front of her face, then waved at her, careful not to touch her.

Betty did nothing. She didn't even move away

from him when it looked as if he might strike her.

"Is this typical?" Reverend Stoughton asked.

Parris longed to run his hand over her tangled hair, to soothe her. Sometimes he wished he did not have to take her to the meeting house, but he knew he had no choice. God needed her to help them catch witches, and sometimes God's requirements were difficult.

"She will remain like this for hours," Parris said.

Reverend Stoughton did look at her as if she were an insect, something to be studied. Parris wanted to complain, but he did not. He needed the support of the colony. He needed this man to prevent more afflictions.

The witches had to be stopped, no matter what the cost.

Reverend Stoughton took Betty's small hand. It looked so fragile in his large, wrinkled one. He pulled her arm out straight, then slid the candle flame beneath it.

Parris knew what he was going to do and almost stopped him. Then he remembered his own admonition. God's work could be difficult, painful even. They were all serving God.

The scent of burning flesh filled the room, but Betty did not move. Her eyes didn't even flicker, nor did she cry out.

Reverend Stoughton removed the flame, and Parris felt his shoulders relax. Stoughton touched Betty's hair gently, as if he were apologizing to her.

Then he turned to Parris. "We shall go to trial."

Parris's relief deepened. A man with as much authority as Reverend Stoughton could see the horrors that had been inflicted on Salem. Parris was no longer alone.

The men stood.

"I shall call the slave first," Parris said, feeling the first stirrings of excitement. "She confessed."

"No," Reverend Stoughton said. "We shall save the confessors for last. First I shall call those who believe they can hide from the truth."

Parris looked at him, pleased at the man's brilliance. Of course. Perhaps they might even get some of these desperate sinners to confess.

What a horrible place to give birth to a child. Bridget Bishop knelt between Sarah Good's legs and wished she had a nice clean feather bed to comfort her in.

Instead, Sarah Good lay in filthy straw that hadn't been changed since Bridget had arrived. Before they were all shackled to the wall, the women had tried to use only one section of the cell as a toilet, but that had been impossible lately. Everyone had one arm chained to the rings mounted high in the dampness. Fortunately, the shackles had some give, so that they could move around somewhat.

Even more fortunately, Bridget had been placed near Sarah, so that she would be able to help when the time came.

And the time had come hours ago.

Bridget wiped a dirty hand against her brow, wishing she had more water than the guards had given her. She had washed before starting to help, but that had been a long time ago. At least one of the guards had been compassionate enough to give them the pot of water, and the rags to help with the birth.

But Bridget had been unable to get more out of him, and he had hit her hard when she had asked for more.

Sarah Good was moaning and panting, as Bridget had taught her. Occasionally, she would let out a screech that sounded inhuman but actually gave force to push the baby outward.

Sarah Osborn crouched beside her, helping as best she could with one arm free. Tituba was the most help. She had done this before, although she would not say where.

Martha Corey held a tool they had made into the shape of a knife over a fire's flame, as Bridget had been taught years ago. A small pot boiled over the fire. Bridget guarded that water carefully. It was all they were going to get, and they would need it toward the end.

Martha started to move away from the flame, but Bridget stopped her. "Hold that over the flame longer."

Sarah Good screamed again, and Bridget leaned inward. The baby was crowning.

"Push now," Bridget said.

The head appeared, covered with fluid and blood, but beautiful.

Excitement built as all the women leaned in to see the miracle.

"Push now," Sarah Osborn said. "Yes, push now."

Sarah Good was pushing. The shoulders had come through, and Bridget placed her hands beneath to catch the babe.

"Here she is," Sarah Osborn said.

"It will be a fat girl, Goody Good," Martha Corey said.

Tituba started chanting a song to celebrate the birth. The women leaned in even closer.

The child landed in Bridget's hands, warm, slimy, and alive. She smiled. "I am holding it. She is beautiful, Goody Good."

The baby burst into tears, lusty healthy cries. A miracle inside this dank place.

The women started cheering and applauding. Bridget felt tears prick her eyes. She wouldn't have imagined such joy here.

Then, above the noise, she heard her name.

"Bridget Bishop," a constable said from outside the bars, "are you prepared to confess for your crime of witchcraft?"

Tituba's chant stopped. The cell, so joyful a moment ago, was silent except for the baby's cries. Bridget froze. She knew what this meant. She had already been examined. They were going to try her now, and no matter what she said, they would find her guilty.

She did not acknowledge the constable. She had to help the other women with the final steps of this childbirth if Sarah Good were to survive. There was so much to explain. At least Tituba had done some of this before.

Bridget Bishop made sure her voice was calm as she gave instructions. "You will cut the cord," she said, "then when the boiled cloth is cool enough, you must stop the bleeding. Give her water and—"

"Bridget Bishop," the constable said, his voice echoing in the cell, "if thou shalt not confess, it is your time."

"I am guilty of nothing," Bridget said, not looking away from the new baby and her mother, trying to memorize them, memorize this moment. This was what life was about. Not the hatred she was going to step into.

She stroked the new baby before relinquishing her to Sarah Good. Then Bridget smiled.

"Let her know she is loved," Bridget said.

She touched the head of the newborn a final time before standing. Martha, Tituba, and Sarah Osborn all embraced her. Then Bridget touched the cheek of each woman she passed, saying goodbye.

There was no need. They all knew she would not be back.

Reverend William Stoughton stood in front of the packed meeting house and wished Sir William Phips could be here. Then he would believe the Devil vexed them all.

The girls had just recovered from one of their fits, and they were clumped in the center of the onlookers. The girls were listening, like everyone else, to the witness, Ezekiel Godfrey. He was twisting his hands together, his face red because of the things he had said.

Reverend Parris sat next to Stoughton. Parris had seemed surprised that he would not be able to continue the examinations. But this was a job for the court now—the court in the person of Reverend Stoughton.

Stoughton leaned toward Godfrey. The man told a strange story.

"And Bridget Bishop came to you?" Stoughton asked.

Bridget Bishop did a credible job of looking shocked. "I know nothing of it," she said. "I do not even know this man."

"Liar! Witch!" Her words seemed to anger Godfrey. He turned toward Stoughton, his eyes pleading. "She has come to me in the night, many times. With naught but a red corset above her waist."

Bridget Bishop shook her head. "I did not!"

"I did not," the girls mimicked.

Bridget Bishop looked at them, shocked. The rest of the congregation watched in silence.

Stoughton folded his hands before him. He had heard such things before in discussions of witches. He, unfortunately, was not shocked at all. "And how did she get in your door?"

"Her specter flew in," Godfrey said. "Without a noise. Not a single sound. Who else but a witch could do this?"

The crowd shouted its agreement. Stoughton did not nod, but he wanted to. These were godly people who understood what they were facing.

Bridget Bishop's face was red, probably with embarrassment at being caught. "It was not me."

"It was not me," the girls mocked.

"Confess, Bridget Bishop," Stoughton said. "There is spectral evidence against you. And we have heard the accusations of the girls. You afflict them."

Bridget Bishop's calm gaze met his. Maybe he had been wrong. Maybe she had not been embarrassed. She was much too calm for a woman who had just been accused of witchcraft.

"They are mistaken," she said.

"They are mistaken." The girls mimicked her position as well, tilting their heads as she did.

She turned toward them. "Must they mock me?"

"Must they mock me?" The girls asked, continuing their behavior.

Bridget Bishop pointed at them, and shouted, "Stop this evil mischief. You must stop it now!"

The girls cringed as she pointed, falling into screams and fits, as if her finger were actually hurting them. Some fell and writhed on the floor, the others cringed and covered themselves.

All but little Betty Parris, who sat motionless.

Stoughton thought little Betty's plight the worst of all.

"Why do you bewitch these children?" he shouted over the noise.

"I do not," Bridget Bishop shouted back.

The congregation quieted, but the girls did not. Their cries were grating. Stoughton wondered how Parris had put up with it all this time.

"Look at them," Stoughton said. "Are they not under your spell right now?"

Bridget Bishop's mouth flattened in disapproval. "They are making mischief."

Ezekiel Godfrey stood. "And you will say I lie as well?"

Bridget Bishop did not respond to that.

Godfrey turned toward the court, clearly upset. "As my wife sleeps beside me, she flies in, putting herself atop me."

The congregation cried out in horror. Bridget Bishop faced them, her expression one of fury.

"Confess, Bridget Bishop," Stoughton said. "Are you a witch?"

"No!" She sounded offended that he even asked.

He raised his eyebrows. "Then why has no one defended you? Not a person."

Bridget Bishop looked into the congregation as if she were looking at a specific person. Thomas Putnam's wife, Ann, mother to one of the afflicted girls, lowered her eyes.

Good woman. She did not want to get cursed by the evil eye.

After a moment, Bridget Bishop sighed. "They are afraid to speak."

"Hang the witch!" someone shouted.

Stoughton nodded. The evidence was clear. He leaned toward her, not afraid of her devilish powers. "Bridget Bishop, the evidence presented here damns you."

She raised her head and stared at him as if she could not believe what he was doing.

He did not let her direct gaze stop him.

"You are hereby convicted of the crime of witch-craft." He paused for emphasis and then added her punishment. "And you shall hang by your neck until you are dead."

The courtroom erupted into shouts over his verdict. The girls continue to writhe in their fits. Apparently, the witch would not loosen them from her grasp even now.

Stoughton looked majestically over them. Let Phips countermand this, the word of God. He could not. Nor could he achieve this kind of popular support.

Only Ann Putnam looked away, or perhaps she had not yet looked up. After all, her daughter had been grievously harmed.

Stoughton wanted to soothe the poor woman and let her know that all would be fine. But he could not. Not yet.

He still had more than two dozen other accused witches to deal with first. And now they would know what they faced in William Stoughton.

TWENTY-SIX

It was spring. The trees were budding, the grass was growing, some flowers pushed their way through the dirt. Normally, Ann Putnam loved the spring.

But she could not enjoy it this year.

She stood next to Thomas on Gallows Hill. Annie was with the other afflicted girls, convulsing and writhing near the hanging tree. Samuel Parris read from his sermon book as if he were inside the meeting house.

Ann could not concentrate on his words. All she could hear was the banging of the carpenter's hammer as he finished the scaffolding near the tree. Above it hung the thickest rope she had ever seen.

She had never witnessed a hanging. She had

heard of them, of course, and knew they were necessary for certain types of crimes, but she had never seen one.

Certainly not one she had had her hand in.

Ann still did not know how to stop this mess. If she stood up for Bridget Bishop, she would be branded a witch, too. But if she did not, she wasn't certain she could live with the guilt.

The cart rumbled up the hill behind her. The other villagers, gathered around the tree, looked down. They wanted to see the condemned on her way to the gallows.

Ann did not look. She wasn't sure she'd ever be able to banish Bridget's face from her mind, so she wasn't even going to try. Not now.

The cart's rumble stopped. The crowd was silent, although they didn't appear to be listening to the Reverend Parris. The only sounds were the ba-bum of the hammer, the drone of the Reverend's voice, and the shrieks of the girls. Ann didn't even look for Annie, even though she wanted to. Instead, she let Thomas look out for their girl.

Ann had to concentrate to remain strong.

The constables led Bridget Bishop toward the hanging tree. She was thinner than Ann had ever seen her, her hair limp and stringy about her face. She was also filthy. Her condition had been hard to see in the dim meeting house, but here, in full daylight, it was obvious.

She didn't look well.

Ann felt the irony of her last thought. As if it mattered that Bridget did not look well. She would not live through the hour.

Bridget Bishop seemed to know where Ann was, because as the constables led her past she looked directly at Ann. Her eyes were still sharp, her face filled with that intelligent compassion Ann had first sought from her—compassion Ann had never been able to return.

Ann looked away.

The constables continued to lead Bridget to the platform. The carpenter finished as Bridget mounted it. He looked at Samuel Parris and nodded.

The constables put a rope around Bridget's neck. Ann was watching again, carefully positioning herself behind Thomas so that Bridget's gaze could not meet her own.

Perhaps it was right that Bridget would be hanged for being a witch. She seemed to have an uncanny ability to seek out Ann and to inflict guilt. She also knew things she oughtn't, and she never tried to join the congregation at the meeting house.

But Ann could not forget the warmth with which Bridget Bishop had greeted her on that awful midwinter night when no one else would talk with her. Surely there had to be good in a woman who would do that.

A breeze blew a strand of Bridget's hair against her face. She stared at the gallows. The hangman stood behind her, getting ready to drop the platform.

Ann closed her eyes, but she could not shut out the sound: the slamming of the platform, the whoosh of air, the creak of the rope, and the startled cry from Bridget Bishop's lips that ended abruptly.

All that remained was the creak of the rope as it swung in the wind, then the gasp of the other villagers and the whispering of leaves.

Not even the girls were crying out.

Only Samuel Parris, speaking as if this were a normal afternoon, seemed unaffected.

"I wish not so much to do as to be," he said. "And I long to be like Jesus. If Thou dost make me right I shall be right. Lord, I belong to Thee, make me worthy of Thyself. Amen."

Ann opened her eyes.

Bridget's body swung in the wind, her face contorted. There was no life left in her.

And Ann could have saved her. She could have done something, reached out to her, helped her escape, done something.

But she did not know what.

A breeze blew a strand of Bridget's hair against her face. She stared at the gallows. The hangman stood behind her, getting ready to drop the platform.

This time, Ann did not close her eyes. She was going to watch, to see her own sin made manifest. But at the last moment, she turned away and heard the slamming of the platform, the whoosh of air, the creak of the rope, and the startled cry from Bridget Bishop's lips that ended abruptly.

The cry echoed in her mind, like the cry of a newborn babe. Then a hand touched her cheek. Lovingly, gently. Ann leaned into the tenderness, and turned.

246

Bridget Bishop smiled at her and stroked her cheek. For the first time in months, Ann felt tranquility, but beneath it, she also felt confusion. She did not remember this. It felt wrong.

The cry still echoed, turning into a baby's giggle.

Maybe this was how everything really happened. Maybe the past few months were simply a nightmare, a bad dream, something she was finally waking from.

She turned toward Bridget. "Is there forgiveness?" Ann asked.

Bridget turned slowly away. Ann reached for her, not wanting to lose her again. But then Ann froze. The back of Bridget's head held another face. It too was Bridget's face.

But this face was pale and still, dead.

Ann gasped and stepped away in horror. Finally she could see all of Bridget. She was dressed in white linen, a horrible parody of swaddling clothes, and in her arms, three bundles, also wrapped in white.

Ann didn't have to see their faces to know that Bridget was holding her babies.

"No," Ann cried. "What have I done?"

An eerie whisper answered her. "I shall pray for you, Ann Putnam."

Ann gasped at the voice—

And sat up in bed, disoriented. She clutched the blankets to her chest. She wasn't sure whether she had had a dream or not because she still heard the voice.

I shall pray for you.

Ann whipped her head around, looking for the

speaker. A white-haired woman sat in the chair in the darkest corner of the room.

Ann clutched the blankets tighter. "Who are you?"

Then a hand touched her shoulder. She jumped and turned.

It was Thomas. "Ann?"

"What is she doing here?"

"Who?" Thomas asked.

Ann nodded toward the corner—and then realized it was empty.

She couldn't believe it. She had heard the voice, seen the woman. She pulled away from Thomas and got out of bed. She hurried toward the corner, but no one was there.

Then she started to pace. What was wrong with her? What was wrong?

Thomas shook his head. "Go back to sleep, Ann."

"I dare not," she whispered. "I am plagued by what I find there."

She stopped near the corner, hating it, hating the chair and the silence.

" 'Tis too dark in here," she said. "Did you not see her?"

"Who?" he asked.

"I do not know." She hadn't gotten a good look at the white-haired woman's face. "Are you sure you did not?"

He stared at her, then shook his head no. She saw fear in his face—fear for her, for her vision. The same look he sometimes gave to Annie when the fits became too much.

Ann understood now what was happening. "Then 'tis a witch's specter. She looks at me, awake or asleep. I fear I cannot escape her. The dread of her is in my thoughts. There is no forgiveness."

"Who means to harm us?" Thomas grabbed her by the arms to still her. But his sudden movement startled her more. She couldn't look at him.

"A specter," she whispered, "means to harm. The one. The white-haired one."

"Who?"

She looked at him, terrified and uncertain. He stared back. She knew he wanted answers, and she had none to give him.

At least none that made sense in the normal world.

Elizabeth Parris poured steaming water into the big tub, her muscles aching from the load. At least the night was relatively warm. She hated bathing the girls when she could see her own breath.

Abigail and Betty were already in the tub. Elizabeth had put them there before she filled it. Neither girl was in fits at the moment, but neither seemed very lucid. Betty was sedate, as she had been lately, as if everything were too much for her.

Elizabeth started with her child. She wiped the girl's skin clean, getting the mucus and the filth off from the meeting house floor. Then she lifted Betty's arm to wash beneath it and found a large scab.

She examined it in the firelight. It was a burn. She'd seen enough of them to recognize the way it purpled the skin. It had to have been painful. No one

249

had tried to treat it at all, not with butter or with cold water.

Even the simple movement Elizabeth had just made had to hurt.

She looked at Betty, and to her surprise, Betty looked back. Her expression was resigned.

"Who did this to you?" Elizabeth asked gently.

Betty's eyes lowered, and Elizabeth knew she was losing her.

She turned instead to Abigail, careful to keep her voice low and warm. "Do you know?"

The two girls exchanged frightened looks, as if they had done something very wrong and were expecting her to discipline them.

"The big man," Abigail whispered.

Elizabeth frowned. Big man? What big man? She thought of all the men who had been to the house recently, and only one could remotely be called big.

"Reverend Stoughton?"

Her words echoed in the small keeping room. For a moment, no one moved.

Then Betty said, "It was God." She looked up at her mother, her expression lost. "We were bad."

Bad? Bad? They were children, not adults who deserved this. Little girls who had lives ahead of them, who should have been learning how to bake and preparing for their futures as wives.

Elizabeth rocked back. She had prepared for her life as a wife, but nothing had prepared her for this—this moment when she realized the situation God had placed her in.

She had to choose her child over her husband. And then she realized she had no choice at all.

Samuel Parris sat in the best room, working on his next sermon. He chose his words even more carefully than usual, knowing William Stoughton would be listening.

Perhaps, when this crisis was over, Stoughton would recommend Parris for a new, larger congregation. Perhaps Parris would move to the ranks of ministers whose words were repeated throughout the colony, not just in his own village.

The door squeaked open, and he turned, feeling his face redden. How many times had he told Elizabeth not to interrupt him? Her movements in and out of the room broke his train of thought. These times were difficult enough without one more distraction.

Then he frowned.

She stood before him wearing her traveling cloak. The girls stood on either side of her, clutching her hands.

His wife, his sickly wife, was looking at him in fury.

What had he done?

"I am leaving," she said.

Whatever he had expected her to say, it was not this. "Leaving? You can't."

They both knew God's dictum as given to them through Paul in Ephesians 5:22–24. Wives must be subject to their husbands.

251

"The children can no longer stay here," she said, ignoring her duty.

He could not believe her actions. What was she thinking? "But they must. They are witnesses."

"No," she snapped. "They are children. Not witnesses. Not spectacles. Not things to be brought out and put on display for your purposes. They are children."

So this was what bothered her. It was insignificant and inappropriate. If she had her health, she would know that. The children had their duties before God, just as he had.

"What is this impudence?" he asked.

Her chin set. " 'Tis enough."

"You cannot leave," he said. "I am the minister. Have I not been pained enough already with a confessed witch under my own roof and two of the afflicted—"

"They are not afflicted." Her voice was low and filled with fury. He had never seen her like this. She was acting as if he were her enemy, not her master as dictated by God. She had said the marriage vows before God, just as he had. She knew God's law and what her duties were.

And yet she still contradicted him.

"They are terrified," she said. "Of you."

He looked at Betty. He loved his daughter. He always had. But Betty's gaze did not meet his. She wouldn't look at him—she hadn't looked at him in months.

Was it just a few weeks ago that he had confessed

in a prayer that he felt as if his child were already gone?

His life would never be the same, especially with his wife teaching his daughter to disobey church doctrine.

And with Reverend William Stoughton in town, it could not come at a worse time.

"How will it look?" he said, and then he understood. "You are ill. And your fever."

"No, the illness is in that meeting house," she said.

That was blasphemy. He was shocked to hear it come from the lips of his own wife.

And she didn't stop there. She continued. "It is carried in upon your own fear. And in turn you have infected this village with it."

She was blaming him for everything. For the afflicted girls. For the witches. Everything.

He shook his head. He could not be responsible. He was the minister. He protected everyone.

Elizabeth softened her tone. "Can you not see what you have done here?"

"I am protecting them from Satan's hand."

She shook her head. She did not believe this. She had never believed this, and he had known it. This was just the first time she had made it clear.

"Samuel," she said, the anger clearly gone from her. "They would not need protection if the God you hear in your head offered compassion. Just that."

She gathered the girls to her and turned to go. He had to stop her. She, of all people, had to understand what was really happening.

"It is God's role for me," he said. "To come to Salem to save His chosen people. If I fail, Puritanism fails, forever. That is my task. No less. Do you understand?"

She lowered her head and sighed. He had not reached her after all.

So he fell back on their relationship. He was in charge of this household.

He said as harshly as he could, "You may not leave."

She stopped and turned, a fire in her eyes. But her voice was soft, filled with quiet threat. "Force me to stay, and I shall speak. From my heart."

Accusing him. Telling everyone he had infected this village. Telling William Stoughton. Telling the afflicted, and the faithful. Telling the witches themselves.

His stomach clenched. The failures that had haunted Parris his whole life faced him now.

Her gaze remained steady on his. She meant it. She meant that she would betray him in front of the whole village and, through Stoughton, the entire colony of Massachusetts.

After a moment, she broke her gaze away from his, put her arms around the girls, and led them from their home.

He did not stop her. He could not, and remain himself.

Samuel Parris walked with William Stoughton on the road past the meeting house. The spring day was lovely: birds sang in the trees, flowers were coming up, and the air had a hint of warmth. For the first time in weeks, Parris did not have to wear a coat.

But he did not appreciate the weather. He kept thinking about Elizabeth's face, about Betty's tears, and wondering if he had truly done something wrong.

And now he had to explain himself to Reverend Stoughton—not an easy matter. A minister was to keep order in his own home, something Parris had clearly failed to do. Parris could see that judgment in Stoughton's eyes as he listened to Parris's explanation, which contained a certain amount of truth.

When Parris finished, Stoughton didn't waste an instant in showing his disbelief.

"They have taken seriously ill?" he asked. "Both of them?"

After all, Stoughton had seen the girls shortly before Parris claimed they had fallen ill. But illness sometimes came on quickly—everyone knew that.

And Parris was counting on that knowledge.

"Yes," he said. "It had become too much for them, these past few months. Taking them away was my wife's idea."

He felt his breath catch. He shouldn't be listening to his wife, not at this point. He should have made the decision himself.

Parris added, "She was of the opinion that in their unhealthy state, the children would unfairly sway the judgment against the accused."

He was explaining too much. He knew it. Liars

always explained too much—that was how he was trained to catch them. And here he was, making the same mistake.

Reverend Stoughton had received the same training as Parris—and Stoughton had years' more experience. He stopped walking and peered at Parris.

"There is order in your home, is there not, Reverend?" Stoughton asked.

"Of course," Parris said. "Why should there not be?"

Stoughton studied him for a moment longer, then nodded, apparently accepting the explanation. Or perhaps he did not want to add one more problem to the group of problems they were already dealing with.

They walked in silence for a moment. Then, Parris heard a voice ahead. He squinted, but saw only the usual contingent of people on the street, going about their business.

It wasn't until he turned the corner near the meeting house that he saw Giles Corey standing on the street, appealing to the villagers who walked by.

". . . pass by and do nothing?" Corey was saying to a man, who averted his face and hurried by. "Won't you stop and hear me? My poor wife is innocent. She is a church woman, the same as you. Her only crime was to doubt. Can you not see this? Neighbors, I implore you to see that there is unholy mischief in this."

As he said that last, he turned and saw Parris and Stoughton. Parris felt his entire body freeze with anger. Unholy mischief? Giles Corey was accusing God's authorities on earth of being unholy? What right did he have?

Unless he was as guilty as his wife.

Stoughton's face held an even firmer line.

And Giles Corey closed his eyes, shaking his head slightly, as if he realized he had been caught.

TWENTY-SEVEN

Giles Corey stood in front of the meeting house, his hands shackled. He had hated the accusations here, in a place where he had gone to worship, a place where he had spent quiet time with his wife. A place where he had tended to matters of the soul.

His soul didn't concern him now, either. He knew what state it was in. He believed in God, believed too in the Bible and in the teachings of his religion.

But he had spoken out against Parris and Stoughton, who now sat in judgment on him, and he had realized, much too late, that what was being punished here was not black magic but dissent.

He should have seen the pattern earlier: the attack on people who had opposed Thomas Putnam at one point or another, or had ridiculed Samuel Parris for not being holy enough to guide them. The Parris-Putnam faction had grown strong in Salem the past few years, and Giles Corey had been naïve enough to think that it was simply a passing trend, that at some point or another someone else would become the village's focus.

He had started questioning that when Martha had been arrested. His problem was that he should have questioned it silently, not in public. He had been continuing Martha's beliefs again—she had thought that if the community understood what had gone wrong, every accused witch would go free.

But that wasn't going to happen. Corey could see that now.

It was evident in the people around him. The congregation, some of whom he had known his entire life, had come to be entertained, like Romans throwing Christians to the lions. The judges were here to confirm their own religiosity, using the threat of witchcraft to puff themselves up in importance.

Corey looked at the girls, noting that Betty Parris and Abigail Williams were missing. He had no idea what motivated the girls. In the beginning, he had thought a few had had fits that were real. But he had never believed some of the others—Mercy Lewis or Annie Putnam, or the ones who came later and joined in as if having fits in God's house were a way of holding a party.

He had spoken out on that, too.

He should have held his tongue.

The girls watched him as he watched them. Some

of them seemed quite lucid. Others were having convulsions, and all of them had mocked him at one point or another.

"Giles Corey." Reverend Stoughton called his name, drawing him out of his momentary reverie. "You are on trial for the crime of witchcraft. What do you plead?"

Corey glared at Stoughton. "I shall not dignify this travesty with a plea."

"Guilty or innocent?" Reverend Stoughton demanded.

Corey did not move. It was time that he remain silent. People knew how he felt. The entire village had heard his opinions on the subject.

If he spoke, he would give credence to the accusations. He was not guilty or innocent. *There had been no witchery in Salem*. Only accusations and blackness in the hearts of so-called godly men.

"Answer!" Stoughton boomed. "The court orders you to submit a plea. Guilty or innocent."

An anxious buzz made its way around the congregation. In spite of himself, Giles Corey was entertaining them. He had not planned on that reaction.

Stoughton had gone red in the face with fury. "Giles Corey, by the law of the land you must submit yourself to trial. Guilty or innocent? Answer!"

Giles Corey did not meet anyone's gaze. He wanted the entire congregation to know that its antics were beneath him. He would not play their game.

See what they could do to him then.

"I order the defendant to suffer *peine forte et dure* until he changes his mind. Remove him."

Peine forte et dure? Corey had never heard of that before, but he didn't like the glint in Stoughton's eye. This had to be something in English law that Corey was not familiar with.

It seemed that no one else in the congregation was familiar with it, either. They all talked, their voices blurring as he was dragged toward the door.

Something was about to happen to him—something he didn't understand. Something that he knew couldn't be good.

The rain was cold and damp, an early spring rain that had the whisper of snow in it. William Stoughton stood in it, wet all the way to his shoes.

He did not like being here, did not like the position this witch had forced him into. But he was not alone. A crowd had gathered to watch.

Normally, he did not like the prurient interest of the idle, but he felt it was important here. They had to learn the price of disobedience in his courtroom.

Two constables stood near a pile of slate. They looked toward the crowd—anything to keep their gazes off the man in front of them.

Giles Corey was suffering his punishment, the full price of the *peine forte et dure*. These villagers had been so ignorant of the law that Stoughton was forced to explain how the procedure was conducted, and they had followed his description exactly.

Corey was on his back, spread-eagled, his limbs

tied to four stakes. On his chest were several slabs of heavy slate. He had seemed defiant when the first slab had been placed on him, but he was suffering now.

Rain beat on his bare head, and he panted shallowly. His face was an abnormal color, caused by the pressure to his body and the chill outdoor air.

"Do you plead guilty or innocent?" Stoughton asked.

If the man would just speak, his suffering would end. Stoughton did not understand Corey's stubbornness. A plea would be easy—after all, a man only had two choices in all of life, guilty or innocent.

And no one was innocent, not without God's intervention.

Corey did not answer. But his bloodshot eyes met Stoughton's, and Stoughton thought he saw hatred there.

"Another stone," Stoughton said calmly.

The constables looked at each other as if they were appalled by what they were doing. He would reprimand them later. Still, they bent over, grabbed another heavy slab, and slid it over the top of the pile on Corey.

Corey's eyes bulged, and he groaned.

"Guilty or innocent?" Stoughton asked again, thinking that perhaps this time the man would speak.

Corey blinked, but his lips did not move. It was clear he would not plead this day.

Stoughton couldn't stand another hour in this

driving rain. He turned to the constables. "Three draughts of water today, three morsels of bread tomorrow. Nothing more."

And then he walked through the crowd. For the first time, no one nodded toward him as if he were the king. Instead, they seemed frightened of him.

Their reaction pleased him. He was not here to be popular. He was here to drive the Devil from their midst.

It had been a long, discouraging day.

Samuel Parris stepped inside his home, shaking the cold rain off his coat and hair. The house had a stale odor, and it was as cold inside as outside. He tracked mud across his once clean floor.

It was not the first time he had done this, but he had no time or energy to clean up after himself. It was all he could do to maintain his clothing and his person so that he was presentable in court.

He had never realized the amount of housekeeping Elizabeth had performed following Tituba's confession. Somehow she had managed to keep the household running and to care for the girls. It hadn't been as efficient as Tituba's management, but she had done all right.

Certainly, better than he was doing. Dirty dishes strewn about, the smell of old food, filth everywhere, even on his writing desk.

Then he heard a noise and turned, feeling hopeful. They had come back. Oh, please God, they had returned.

"Is someone here?"

He stepped toward the sound—

—and a mouse scampered past into the darkness.

Parris slumped into a chair, discouraged and lonely, unsure how he had found himself in this place.

No matter what he did, he failed. When he succeeded in his family life, his professional life suffered. When he had finally achieved professional standing, his family life evaporated.

He missed them all, and he did not know how to bring them back.

The rain splashed Giles Corey in the face. The cold drops were the only thing that kept him conscious.

He wasn't sure why he was trying to stay conscious, alone in the darkness, the weight of more stones than he could count slowly crushing his chest.

Perhaps he was afraid he would slide into false sleep and make an accidental confession. Or perhaps this was the last vestige of his stubbornness, which had led him to this place.

He did not regret his decision, even though he had not expected this result.

Besides, the Lord knew he was innocent. The Lord would care for him.

He continued to recite the Twenty-third Psalm, as he had been doing since night fell, wanting to be in a holy state when death finally came.

The words came out in a whisper: "Yea, though I walk through the valley of the shadow of death, I will fear no evil, for Thou art with me . . ."

*   *   *

Time moved slowly, and then suddenly it changed.

It took Giles Corey a while to realize that when time changed, he suffered from short blackouts. He'd had several already, and the sun hadn't yet reached its zenith.

At least it wasn't raining this day.

Reverend Stoughton had been haranguing him for what seemed like hours. Corey had no way to tell the time, so he did not know. But they had placed more slabs on him.

He could not tell the difference any longer—the pain remained the same—but it felt that his chest now touched his spine. He wasn't breathing, not by any measure he understood, and yet he still lived, so he was taking in some air.

"How do you plead, Giles Corey?" Reverend Stoughton asked for what had to be the thousandth time. "Guilty or innocent?"

Stoughton enjoyed this. He had to, or he wouldn't be here so much. There was a light in his eye that had been there the moment he announced the sentence.

Corey noted that the Reverend Parris hadn't been to any of these sessions. The man's stomach was probably too weak to see a man pressed to death for refusing to answer one simple question.

Then Corey realized that everyone—Stoughton, the constables, the crowd (which was smaller than the day before)—had turned to look at the road.

He squinted, tried to move his head, and couldn't. But he could see the hill beyond, and if he concentrated, he heard the clatter of a cart. The prisoners' cart. People would die today on Gallows Hill.

The cart finally appeared in his line of sight, and he felt a jolt. Martha sat in it. She was staring at the field where he lay, and he thought he heard her cry out in grief.

Martha, he thought, wishing she could hear him. She was going to die. And without her, Lord forgive him, he had no life.

He looked up at Stoughton, but the man did not see him. A constable was watching, though. Corey spoke—or tried to—for the first time since they'd started putting the slabs on him.

He had not enough breath to make words.

Still, his lips had formed around them, and the constable had noticed.

"He spoke," the constable said to Stoughton.

Stoughton's eyes lit up even more. He thought he had won. Corey wished he had enough energy left to smile.

Reverend Stoughton bent over and placed his ear near Corey's mouth. "Guilty or innocent?"

Corey used the last of his strength to push air through his lips.

"More . . . weight. . . ." he said.

Stoughton recoiled in surprise. And with that, Giles Corey died, knowing that he would soon join his wife in a much better place than this one.

TWENTY-EIGHT

"Our Father who art in Heaven . . ." Rebecca Nurse's voice echoed in Ann Putnam's ear. Ann bowed her head farther and tried to concentrate on Reverend Parris's voice, but he was far away from her, near the hanging tree.

Martha Corey, Elizabeth Howe, Ann Pudeator, Martha Carrier, and Mary Lacey stood side by side on the gallows platform.

"Let Thy Kingdom come . . ."

Reverend Stoughton stood across from them, his head bowed as well, his stentorian voice overpowering the others. Ann glanced at him through her eyelashes.

"Thy will be fulfilled . . ."

Ann stumbled over the words. She had been

doing that throughout the Lord's Prayer, and it frightened her. Rebecca Nurse didn't seem to notice.

". . . as well in Earth as it is in Heaven."

A hangman stood back, watching the ropes swing before him. Ann wasn't sure he was praying at all.

Finally the Lord's Prayer was finished. The gathered Puritans were supposed to continue repeating the prayer while the accused were asked one last question.

Ann's head pounded. Being here reminded her of her strange visitation (which Thomas believed was a dream) of her memories of Bridget Bishop. Ann hadn't told him everything—she couldn't—and so she was inclined to disagree with his conviction.

It felt too real to be a dream, and sometimes, in her memory, the day slid from the execution to the night itself. She couldn't remember coming home, serving dinner, or speaking to her family. One moment she had been here, on Gallows Hill. The next she had been in bed, beside Thomas, with the dead Bridget Bishop in the room.

Ann shivered. She wasn't sure what was happening to her, her family, or her town, but she knew that whatever it was, it was awful.

Reverend Stoughton stepped before the accused women. He stopped in front of Ann Pudeator as the hangman put the noose around her neck.

"Ann Pudeator," Reverend Stoughton said, his voice carrying over the crowd, "will you confess to your crimes of witchcraft?"

Ann Putnam watched, her hands threaded together. Rebecca Nurse continued to pray beside her, but Ann was just making noise. Her mouth was dry, and she hoped Rebecca Nurse couldn't hear what she was saying.

Ann Pudeator was shaking so hard Ann Putnam could see her. Ann Pudeator opened her mouth to speak, but no words came out.

Reverend Stoughton nodded to the hangman, and he tightened the noose. Ann Putnam touched her own neck, feeling the brush of hemp as if it were happening to her.

Ann Pudeator was still trying to speak, but Reverend Stoughton moved past her and stopped in front of Martha Corey. She had her head bowed, and she was praying.

"Martha Corey," he said in the same stentorian voice, "will you confess to your crimes of witchcraft?"

Martha's prayer grew louder. Ann Putnam could actually hear her voice—a voice that was familiar to her from the meeting house, from the village, from the sewing circles. The two of them hadn't been friends, but they had associated, because that was what happened in a small village.

"And forgive us our trespasses," Martha was saying, "even as we forgive our trespassers."

Her words, even in prayer, had sting. But Reverend Stoughton didn't seem to notice. He leaned toward her, speaking louder.

"Will you confess, Martha Corey?"

She continued to pray. The hangman tightened the noose, and Martha recoiled, pausing before she finished the last line of her prayer.

Then she looked up at Reverend Stoughton.

"Did you not hear my prayer?" she asked. " 'Twas flawless. 'Tis well known that a witch cannot speak the Lord's Prayer."

Ann Putnam felt her own breath catch. She hadn't been able to say the Lord's Prayer this day. She hoped Rebecca Nurse had not noticed.

"You hesitated," Reverend Stoughton said. "Will you confess?"

Martha Corey lifted her head up. Ann could see the age marks and wrinkles in her neck. "I am a woman of God," Martha Corey said. "I am innocent."

Ann Putnam focused on Rebecca Nurse's voice. She was still reciting the Lord's Prayer with the bulk of the crowd.

Ann took a deep breath and made herself join in. "And lead us not . . . lead us not into temptation, but deliver us from evil."

Rebecca Nurse looked toward her. This time she clearly heard Ann falter—and so soon after Martha Corey had mentioned that witches couldn't recite the Lord's Prayer. Ann looked at Rebecca, frightened. But all Rebecca did was give her a warm smile.

Reverend Stoughton had stopped before two more women while Ann was concentrating on her prayer. She had missed their answers, but judging by the fear on their faces, the hangman had tightened their nooses as well.

Reverend Stoughton finally reached Mary Lacey, the last accused witch. She was trembling.

He stopped in front of her, blocking Ann's view of Mary's face. "Mary Lacey, will you confess to your crimes of witchcraft?"

"No . . ." The first word came out as a whisper, then the others were shouted. "Yes, yes, yes. I'll confess, I am a witch. Pray forgive me. I will lay myself before you and beg for mercy. I confess."

Ann Putnam moved slightly so that she could see Mary Lacey's face. The woman had tears running down her cheeks.

The hangman removed the noose, and he led Mary Lacey a step back, away from the swinging rope.

The rest of the crowd continued to pray, but it was clear they were watching as well. Only Samuel Parris seemed oblivious. He continued with the Lord's Prayer. "For Thine is the kingdom and the power and the glory forever. Amen."

Ann Putnam put a hand to her mouth. She couldn't finish the sentence or the prayer. She was stunned at Mary Lacey, stunned at what was happening before her.

Ann couldn't stay here any longer. She turned away from the hanging, saying to herself, "I cannot."

Rebecca Nurse put her hand on Ann's elbow, stopping her. "Do not lose your faith, Ann Putnam."

"Faith in what?" Ann nodded toward the hanging tree. "Is that God's love?"

She moved away, but Rebecca Nurse caught her, and pulled her into an embrace. She whispered, "It is hard for me as well, Ann, but it is a test for us. The path to our God is not easy. This is how we shall show our Puritanism. Look!"

Ann sneaked a glance at the gallows. The hangman was about to pull the trap. She looked away. "I cannot."

Rebecca Nurse held Ann even more tightly to keep her from leaving. Ann had the odd sense that if she left, Rebecca might find it equally hard to stay.

"Ann, stay strong. You do not want to show that you are weak in your faith. Look at it."

"No."

Rebecca Nurse's whispers were urgent. "They sinned against God, Ann. This is their punishment. It is God's will."

Ann tore herself out of the embrace and whispered, "His will? Where is God's forgiveness?"

Rebecca took a step closer, as if she were going to try to capture Ann again. "They have sinned against us, Ann. We are Puritans, chosen by God."

Ann leaned toward her. "Then where is your forgiveness?"

That stopped Rebecca. She looked as if she had been slapped. Ann used that moment to pull completely away. She had to leave.

Rebecca Nurse blinked, and then the calm that was so much a part of her returned.

"I shall pray for you, Ann Putnam," she said.

Ann felt shivers run down her back. Those were the exact words she had heard in her bedroom the night that Bridget Bishop died. The white-haired woman in the corner of the room had spoken those words.

White-haired, like Rebecca Nurse.

"I shall not let you forget you are one of us," Rebecca said.

Ann knew how the others heard those words; Rebecca would not let Ann forget she was a Puritan. But that was not what Rebecca meant. She was referring to all of this—the witches, the hill, everything.

" 'Tis a curse," Ann mumbled.

Then the trap banged open and four women fell, their voices silenced in mid-scream. Only one scream continued. Ann looked involuntarily at the gallows. Mary Lacey stood on the platform, watching four ropes bob and bounce to the left of her. She was screaming and screaming. The hangman could barely hold her.

Ann couldn't take it. She put her hands to her head so that she could hear no more, and she tried to run. Instead, she stumbled and fell to the ground. Just as Annie had. Just as the others had.

She rolled herself into a ball, and her trembling grew into something more.

A convulsion.

Like one of the afflicted.

Samuel Parris removed his coat as he stepped into the Putnam's house. Thomas Putnam took the coat, not saying a word. The man had aged decades in the past year. He did not look like the person who had brought Parris to Salem.

Parris let Putnam lead him to the best room, noting that the Putnam house looked little better than his. Since the executions, Ann Putnam had been afflicted.

Parris had not been able to believe it. He would have thought that another confession would ease the fears, make the afflictions disappear.

But they were not going away. He tried not to think of Betty, wondering if she was returning to the daughter he had once loved now that she was no longer in Salem.

He had no way of knowing. He had had no word from his wife.

Thomas Putnam opened the best room door. The room smelled of illness. Parris stepped inside and stopped, astonished in the change in Ann Putnam's looks.

Her hair was tangled and matted on her head. Her clothing was in disarray. Even her bedclothes were jumbled.

She moved her head back and forth, as she muttered. Parris had to strain to hear the words.

"You must not, you must not . . . your prayers . . . curse me . . . No, no! I will not sign your book."

Above her, the two afflicted girls huddled together in the loft. Parris could just see their eyes, watching in the darkness.

"Three days like this," Thomas Putnam said.

"Who afflicts her?" Samuel Parris said.

Putnam started to speak, but couldn't bring himself to say the words. Finally, he turned to his wife.

"Ann . . ."

She looked over, still mumbling. At least she had some awareness. Her eyes went wild when she saw Parris, and her mumbling grew louder.

"Go! Go! Leave me. . . . You are with her, do not take me. I do not want your prayers. Curses. Curses. I do not want to go."

He felt odd, as if she were actually talking to him, accusing him of cursing her. But he had said nothing against Ann Putnam. She had had a difficult time caring for two afflicted girls, and as far as he knew, she had been godly throughout.

He reached out to calm her, and she batted his hand away. Her slap stung. Like an animal, she hunched against the bed's headboard, getting as far from him as possible.

"Dare not look at me. Curses. You are with her."

She was speaking to him. Directly to him. He felt himself flush.

"Who, Ann?" he asked. "Who afflicts you? Speak!"

"Goody Nurse," she said. " 'Tis Goody Nurse."

Parris took a step back. That was not possible. Rebecca Nurse was one of his best parishioners, a woman of unblemished character. One of the best people he had ever known.

"Ann," Parris said gently, "do you know what you are saying?"

She mumbled, looking away from him, looking crazed, and for the first time since the executions, Parris was frightened. Very frightened. He didn't want Stoughton to hear of this. He hoped no one would.

Ann knew he was there, knew he was there. Reverend Parris alone, thank God; no Reverend Stoughton with him. Reverend Stoughton was even worse. She held her hair in her hands and pulled on it, wishing she were somewhere else, anywhere else, outside of this bed, this room, this horrible village in the middle of the wilderness.

"Do something," Thomas said.

He was talking to Reverend Parris. Did he want Reverend Parris to take her away? Because that was what would happen. That was what would happen if they found out all the things she had done.

"Mama!"

She thought she heard Annie's voice, but that was not possible. Annie was gone, lost to her affliction. She was ill in the same way that Ann was ill. Ann's sin had infected her children, killing three and maiming Annie. Poor Annie.

"Mama?"

Ann looked toward the sound of the voice, pulling at her hair, her clothes, wishing the men would stop watching her.

Annie's voice continued, the prelude to a fit. Ann recognized the rhythm: "No, no, no, no, no . . ."

And then Mercy shouted, "Goody Nurse. You are a witch!"

That was not what Ann meant. The accusation had traveled, and she hadn't wanted that.

Her eyes cleared for the first time in three days and she saw Annie. Annie, leaning over the edge of the loft, her hands flailing—not flailing actually, but reaching for someone to hold her, the way an infant did before it learned to talk.

Annie, who was suffering too—maybe suffering worse, because her whole life was ahead of her. A life lived in this place, with no hope, no compassion, and no way out.

Suddenly, Annie's gaze met Ann's, and Annie seemed to see that Ann understood. Completely understood her daughter's fear. Of the men, of the religion, of their twisted interpretation of the Bible, changing a loving God into one who accepted only death and hate.

Annie started to cry. Not hysterical tears, but real tears. A child's anguished tears. Her arms reached out again, reached for Ann.

"Mama," she said. "Mama . . ."

And Ann wanted to reach her, but wasn't sure how. Nor was she sure how to quiet Mercy Lewis, who continued to cry out against Rebecca Nurse.

Rebecca Nurse had been dreaming of summer. The warm air, the fragrant flowers, the way the sky was so blue it seemed impossible.

She had been ill for the past few days. A spring cold, perhaps, or something else: an exhaustion she didn't want to admit to. She woke slowly, hearing voices in the outer room.

Then her door opened, and her son, Samuel,

stepped in. Sometimes she had trouble reconciling the large middle-aged man with the babe she had bore so long ago. He had been such a happy child, yet he was such a dour adult.

Here, of course, they were all dour. God, it seemed, did not like mirth.

"You must get dressed, Mother," her son said.

She sat up, realizing that they were not alone. Israel Porter stood behind Samuel, looking very uncomfortable.

She smiled at her guest. "Israel, how good of you to visit. You heard I have been feeling poorly?"

Israel Porter shot a look at Samuel, and Samuel sighed.

"The affected have cried out against another," her son said.

Rebecca shook her head. "Those poor girls. I go to God for them each day, and pity them with all my heart."

Israel Porter's discomfort seemed to increase.

"Mother . . ."

Israel crossed the room and took her hand as he knelt beside the bed.

"Rebecca," Israel said gently, "they have cried out against you."

Rebecca leaned against her pillows, unable to take this in. Why would anyone accuse her? She had done nothing. "But I am innocent as the child unborn."

Israel nodded. "There is not a villager or minister who does not know this."

If that were the case, then why was she accused?

"What sin have I not repented of that God should lay such an affliction upon me in my old age?"

"Harm shall not find you, Rebecca," Israel said. "We will not let it."

But she did not believe him. She had seen what happened to the accused. It was much worse than what happened to those who confessed.

She closed her eyes and knew she had to pray. God had seen fit to test her, as He had tested Job, and she had to be strong enough to meet the challenge.

TWENTY-NINE

Israel Porter's house was filled to overflowing. The entire village seemed to be there, although Porter knew that was not true. Only like-minded souls had enough courage to visit this place, because everyone knew what sort of discussion would be on the table.

All of Salem was shocked at the latest accusation. If Rebecca Nurse, one of the most godly women in the village, could be accused, then no one was safe.

Rebecca Nurse's family had also been involved in a land dispute with Thomas Putnam. There were rumors that this was retaliation for all those years of litigation.

But Porter wasn't sure that was what was going on. He wasn't sure of anything anymore.

He was trying to keep order, but it was difficult.

Everyone was talking at once—and the instigator seemed to be John Proctor, who was sitting to his right.

As Porter noted that, Proctor's voice boomed over the din: "I shall not be intimidated by the slander of girls."

"But the witches must die!" Deliverance Walcott shouted.

Porter winced. This was not the argument he had wanted to have when he asked people here. He thought it obvious with the latest accusation that this travesty had gone too far.

"Rebecca Nurse is not a witch!" he said.

The crowd quieted. This seemed to ring true for most of them.

Porter leaned toward Deliverance Walcott. "You know that, don't you, Goody Walcott? You sit next to her in church. Is she not pious?"

Deliverance Walcott's cheeks flamed. She nodded and looked down.

"And you, Goodman Oliver," Israel Porter said, trying to shut down the dissenters. "Goody Nurse gave aid to your wife throughout her final days. Is she a witch?"

Goodman Oliver shook his head.

Porter pushed forward the petition he had written. A quill pen sat in its holder beside the petition, a full inkwell near by. There was enough for everyone. Those who couldn't write could make their mark.

"Sign this petition," Porter said, finally getting to his real purpose in holding the meeting. If they all banded together, they could save their friends.

They could save Salem.

He offered the petition to Deliverance Walcott. "We must not let innocent women suffer. Goody Walcott?"

She backed away, stricken. " 'Tis too dangerous."

And then she fled the house. Much of the crowd seemed to agree with her. They began to file out.

Porter felt his frustration go. Why would these people be cowed by false religiosity? Couldn't they see what was happening?

"Listen," John Proctor said. " 'Tis too dangerous not to sign. If Rebecca Nurse is cried out against, what is to keep you from being next? Any of you? Who will sign it?"

"I shall!" Joseph Putnam stepped from the exiting crowd. He grabbed the pen and bent over the petition. "My brother's family is too much in the center of this. I do not trust that."

Then he scratched his name across the bottom.

"May I sign it, Father?" William Proctor asked.

John Proctor looked stunned. He glanced at Israel Porter, and Porter could see what was going through the man's mind. It was all right to sign for himself, but to have his son and heir sign—to risk losing his family—might be too much of a gamble.

Porter did not move. He couldn't encourage this, but he wouldn't discourage it either.

After a moment, John Proctor nodded. His son, William, smiled, then leaned forward and placed his name below Joseph Putnam's.

*   *   *

Tituba sat in the filthy straw near the iron bars of the cell. It was crowded with women, many of whom she had never seen before—women from other villages, and women who did not get to Salem often. The cell stank, and whatever hope they had all felt at one point was gone.

She had thought the prison unbearable in the winter, but it was worse now—and they hadn't even reached the heat of the summer. No air made it to this part of the cell. There were no windows, and by mid-day—at least, she guessed it was mid-day—when the sun beat down on the roof, the cell got so hot that Tituba thought she would pass out.

She was used to heat. She had spent most of her life in Barbados. But most of the women had not, and the heat was beginning to take a toll.

A clang echoed at the far end of the room. The constables had finally arrived. Tituba leaned her head against the iron bar, remembering the day Bridget Bishop had been dragged from the cell. Just before that, Tituba had been singing, celebrating a baby's birth. But there was nothing to celebrate any longer.

The constable unlocked the door while the second constable waited behind him, not worried that the women would try to escape. Still, a third constable stood watch just in case.

As if anyone could try anything. They were all shackled to the wall, and most were too weak to run anywhere. He barely looked at them, although he did wrinkle his nose at the smell.

"Where is it?" the constable asked.

One of the women nodded toward the far corner of the cell. The constable walked to Sarah Good. Tituba watched him go, looking so out of place in this cell filled with women.

She could barely see Sarah Good. All the feistiness that had put Sarah here had long since left her. She leaned on the women around her, and they comforted her.

Tituba wished she could give comfort, too, but she was too far away.

The constable extended his hand as if he were waiting for Sarah Good to hand him a plate. Instead, she handed him the wrapped bundle of her lifeless baby girl.

Sarah hadn't even named her. She had said there was no point, and she had been right.

Or perhaps it had been a bad omen. Perhaps if the child had had a name, she would have lived.

The second constable was peering into the cell, looking as if he were trying to see more of the women's bodies than was visible. A few of these men had tried to take advantage, but the women had fought them off.

"We shall all die from the stench in here," Susannah Martin said as the constable walked past with the baby.

The second constable reached Tituba's side and his eyes widened. " 'Tis another dead one here."

Tituba sighed. She reached beside her and touched the cold body of Sarah Osborn. Her death had been easy, relatively speaking. She had gone in her sleep.

But Tituba hadn't wanted her to leave. They, along with Sarah Good, had been here the longest, and she was loath to part with her old friend.

The constable set the baby's body on the floor outside the cell. Then both men came inside. They picked up Sarah's body as if it were a sack of potatoes and carried her out.

"Now there is room for the new ones," the second constable said, and laughed. Tituba closed her eyes. She wondered if Sarah Osborn would have a proper burial.

She doubted it.

At least the women had said a few words over her and the baby. 'Twas all they could do.

The third constable picked up the baby's body, and as they started to leave, he shouted, "Bring them."

"Witches approaching." The words echoed down the dark hallway. It made the hair on the back of Tituba's neck rise.

She hated this moment. The moment when they discovered that the nightmare continued, and that every poor woman, every slave woman in the county was being thrust into this place.

The sound of shuffling feet haunted Tituba's dreams. She heard it even when it wasn't happening.

She saw movement down the hallway before she saw who was coming. But somehow, Sarah Good, in her spot toward the back, knew what was happening. She pushed her way forward, coming as close to the bars as her chain would allow.

"Oh, God!" Her voice rose in anguish. "Dorcas!"

Tituba turned. Sure enough, four-year-old Dorcas Good was being led toward the cell. She looked too thin, as usual, and more frightened than Tituba had ever seen her.

Tituba's heart twisted. Just when she thought the evil couldn't get worse.

The cell door opened, and a constable shoved Dorcas inside. Sarah Good managed to reach her and gather her in her arms.

"What is she doing here?" Sarah shouted.

"Get back, witch," he said. " 'Tis your own fault."

"How?"

"You sent her to afflict the girls," he said. "To avenge yourself. They testified to it."

Tituba's mouth opened. How could this be? How could they go after a tiny child like that?

"They lied!" Sarah Good said.

"She confessed, and she's got Satan's mark!" He nodded toward Dorcas.

Dorcas gave him an uncertain look, then held up her little finger. "Satan sucked from me here."

Sarah grabbed her daughter's hand and peered closely. Then she raised her head, so shocked that Tituba could feel it. " 'Tis a flea bite!"

The constable shoved her back and headed for the door. Sarah's panic filled the cell. She screamed, "The child is four years old!"

He disappeared, as if he did not care. How could someone not care? Tituba leaned her head against the bars.

That was what this Puritan God taught.

Dorcas was crying, and Sarah gathered her up, taking her toward the back of the cell.

Then another guard's voice echoed down the hall: "Witches approaching!"

Again the women looked up. Tituba didn't have the strength to move, but she looked anyway. And at the sight of the woman being forced down the hall, Tituba sat up.

"Good Lord have mercy," Tituba said as the door opened and the constable pushed Rebecca Nurse inside. "We are all doomed."

THIRTY

Sir William Phips stood with his arm around his wife in his office. She leaned her head against his shoulder, and he pulled her closer. She was the center of his life, and they both knew it.

They were looking at the portrait of her that he had commissioned. It was finished now, and it was a good likeness. Somehow the artist had captured the fire in her eyes that made her plain features into beautiful ones.

Phips was very pleased.

"Well," his wife said, "at least I don't resemble a mirthless old matron."

Phips chuckled. "My dear, I would have stoned the poor artist myself if he captured any mirthlessness at all."

Behind them, Phips heard a door click shut. He turned to see his assistant, waiting patiently. Phips knew what the assistant was going to say even before he spoke.

This business in Salem was going to dog Phips as much as he tried to ignore it. He had wanted Stoughton to solve the problem, not make it worse.

That was what Phips got for sending the old fool in his place.

The assistant realized that Phips had seen him. "The others have arrived."

Phips sighed. "Oh, very well."

The assistant bowed slightly and left. His wife, knowing how much he hated this particular job, did not comment on it. Instead, she nodded toward the portrait.

"Actually," she said, "it was the old matron part that most concerned me."

Then she shot him a wry smile and kissed his cheek. Phips grinned at her, wishing she could stay here but knowing she could not. He escorted her to the door, opening it just as the Salem contingent walked in.

They barely acknowledged his wife, which irritated Phips. He kissed her cheek and said good-bye, knowing that even this small display of affection bothered the men who were waiting for him.

Then he closed the door and turned toward his visitors. William Stoughton looked the same, tall and unyielding. His elderly face was set in harsh lines. Samuel Parris looked slightly untidy, but Phips couldn't tell what was different—a frayed edge to his coat, a lack of shine on his shoes. And Thomas Putnam seemed to have aged since the last time Phips had seen him.

The strain of the events in Salem seemed to be taking a toll on everyone—except, of course, Stoughton himself.

"Righteous friends," Phips said in greeting, indicating the chairs he had set aside for them. "Welcome to the city."

Thomas Putnam and Samuel Parris took their chairs, but Stoughton did not move.

Phips noted that and gave the old goat a moment to change his mind.

"I have been made aware—" And now he paused, somewhat theatrically, and smiled at Stoughton. "Do you desire a chair less rigid than this?"

He pointed at Stoughton's empty chair, knowing that the Puritans disdained the idea of creature comforts. Even the question was an insult.

But Stoughton did not rise to the bait. Instead, he sat down while Phips waited. Phips nodded his thanks and started to continue, then seemed to think the better of it—or at least, that was how he hoped his audience would interpret his second pause.

"Or would you prefer to stand?" he asked innocently.

"Please carry on." Stoughton's eyes narrowed. "We have traveled a full day to hear your concerns."

Phips picked up the petition that had reached him days before. It had angered him when it arrived, not because of what it said, but because of what it implied.

It implied that Stoughton was failing in his work for the Crown.

"This concerns me," Phips said with great understatement. "It is a petition signed by, among many others, John Proctor and Israel Porter. Educate me as to this strange ferment of dissatisfaction that is growing in Salem."

"We know of this petition," Thomas Putnam said. "It was—"

"I would like to hear it from Reverend Stoughton." Phips kept his tone polite but firm. "Reverend. How goes it in Salem Village?"

"It goes well," Stoughton said stubbornly.

"Well?" Phips raised an eyebrow. "Yet, some of the more respected men in Salem believe that the afflicted girls are not afflicted but lying, and condemning enemies of yours, Mr. Putnam."

Thomas Putnam started, almost guiltily.

"The girls are afflicted," Stoughton said. "I've seen it myself. If you had stayed, you would have seen how these girls are ensorcelled."

"Yet, they manage to accuse," Phips said.

"They tell us who has afflicted them," Stoughton said.

"Often when the accused is doing something else, their specters appear and torture the girls," Stoughton said.

"Specters?" Phips crossed his arms. "How can these girls know that the specters were sent by the accused, not by, say, the Devil himself posing as the accused?"

Stoughton's face turned red. "Are you saying you doubt spectral evidence?"

"Of course not," Phips lied. All of this sounded like nonsense to him, but he had to be political. He was in charge of these people, but he also knew that they had run out a governor four years before. The longer Phips dealt with the Puritan leadership, the more he wondered whether these people were actually rational.

They certainly didn't believe in the God he had learned about in the Church of England.

"But," Phips said, continuing as calmly as he had a moment before, "I shall forbid the hanging of any more persons unless there is proof that corroborates the spectral evidence. You must get either a confession or physical evidence as well. Understood?"

Stoughton's anger seemed to have receded. His expression was almost regal. "We are just and pious men in this room, Governor. We trust that God will not allow us to harm innocent people. You may raise the bar of proof as high as you like. We shall still find the Devil's disciples. God will not fail us."

Phips did not like Stoughton's response, but he did not know what else to do. He could not order an end to these trials, since so many believed in the existence of witches. It had gone too far. And yet, he could not seem to gain control of these so-called judges.

The thing to do, of course, was to preside over the trials himself, but he had a politician's sense that anyone touched by the events in Salem would be ruined by them. He wanted to stay as far away as possible.

"It's not God's failure I'm worried about," Phips said, and let the meeting come to an end.

Midwife Hanna Morse did not want to be in this room. She stood in the near-empty meeting house, beside a midwife she had never met from Salem Town. Hanna had missed the introduction and did not know the other woman's name.

Not that it mattered. They were being called for their expertise on the oddities of the female body.

Hanna was a Puritan in good standing, but she did not like this meeting house nor the direction her religion had taken. Her belief in God was confirmed every time she held a newborn in her hands. But she was not one to find sin and punishment when one of those newborns died. She had supervised enough births to know that many things factored into the mysteries of life and death, some of which the church did not acknowledge.

Since these accusations had started, she had kept her head down and had not drawn attention to herself. She had also stopped recommending some herbal remedies for fear that she too would be branded a witch. Her patients suffered a bit more, but Hanna had seen what had happened to Bridget Bishop, who was a talented wise woman.

Hanna believed that a bit of suffering was little to ask if she could continue her work and prevent as many deaths of mothers and children in childbirth as she possibly could.

She did not believe she should be here, but she knew better than to say no. Her fate was as fragile as the next woman's.

The midwife beside her was very nervous and kept wringing her hands. Hanna hadn't been able to draw her into conversation. What Hanna feared the most was that she and the other midwife would disagree. She wished they had met before so that they could have consulted in advance, but that was not to be.

Still, Hanna wanted to find out where the other woman stood.

"Are you afraid of touching a witch?" Hanna whispered.

The other midwife nodded, her fear so real that Hanna could feel it. Then a door opened, and Rebecca Nurse entered, led by two constables.

Hanna Morse hadn't seen Goody Nurse since her imprisonment. She looked as confident as ever, despite the shackles which held her. She did not meet either woman's gaze but continued to stare straight ahead. The constables shifted at her side.

After a moment, Samuel Parris, William Stoughton, and the six other magistrates entered. Hanna was shocked. She hadn't expected the men to be here. She had thought that she and the other midwife would report back to the court, not perform before them.

The magistrates did not acknowledge the midwives. Instead, the men sat behind their bench looking official.

"Good morning, Goody Nurse," Reverend Stoughton said.

Rebecca Nurse nodded, and for the first time, Hanna got a sense of her fright.

"I must ask you to disrobe." Reverend Stoughton was calm, as if he asked elderly women to take off their clothes before him every day.

Rebecca Nurse looked at him in shock. "I shall not."

"You are to be examined for witch's teats or Devil's marks," Reverend Stoughton said.

" 'Tis not necessary," Rebecca Nurse said. "I can tell you, on my honor as a Christian, you will find none. Reverend Parris, surely you can stop this humiliation. Tell them the number of years I have been a devoted member of the church."

Reverend Parris studied his hands. "It would be better for your chances, Goodwife Nurse, if you allowed the magistrates to determine the truth for themselves."

Hanna Morse felt her own cheeks flush.

"Pray don't make me disrobe in front of them," Goody Nurse said.

Reverend Stoughton's face turned red. Hanna recognized the expression from the trials. He was losing patience. "Rebecca Nurse, you are on trial for the felony of practicing witchcraft. You shall do as the court requests. Let the midwives begin the examination."

Hanna Morse stepped forward. Her hands were clammy. She had never done anything like this before, and it felt so awkward in front of the men. She wished she weren't here.

The other midwife looked equally uncomfortable and more than a little frightened.

Hanna reached Rebecca Nurse first and said quietly, "Forgive me, Goody Nurse."

Then she reached for the closures of Goody Nurse's garments. The other midwife helped. Together they undressed her. Goody Nurse continued to look straight ahead, as if ignoring what they were doing would maintain her dignity.

Hanna did her best to be gentle. She raised Goody Nurse's arm, examined the flesh around her breast, looked at her stomach and legs. She saw nothing unusual, nothing she hadn't seen before on other elderly women.

"There." The other midwife pointed at a small brown lump on Goody Nurse's ribcage. " 'Tis a teat. The Devil suckles there."

The midwife backed away as if she were afraid to touch it.

Hanna peered at the brown lump. It was a larger version of other marks on Rebecca Nurse's body. Old freckles aging poorly or age spots, or, as was common with older bodies, a mole.

"It is not a witch's mark," Hanna said. "It more resembles a mole."

"No, 'tis a teat." The other midwife sounded positive. Maybe Hanna would have been that positive as well if she hadn't known Goody Nurse. Maybe Hanna would have been looking for witch's marks as zealously as the other midwife, forgetting all that she knew about the female form.

"For the record of this deposition," Stoughton said, "make note of the disputed evidence."

Hanna looked up in surprise. Weren't these men going to examine the mark themselves or at least give the midwives a chance to settle the dispute?

And then she was glad they didn't examine Goody Nurse. The men would probably find more witch's marks as well. Hanna wondered how many such marks she'd find on Reverend Stoughton's elderly body.

She kept her head down, in case someone saw the rebellion in her eyes.

Goody Nurse hadn't moved, remaining stoic, as if she were not naked at all. Poor thing. Hanna wanted to wrap her in a cloak and hurry her out of the room.

"Note also," Reverend Stoughton said, "that the witness does not cry, consistent with a witch's inability to produce tears."

Hanna felt surprise run through her. She stole a glance at the men. Most of the magistrates were looking down.

Reverend Stoughton met Hanna's gaze. "Examine the pudendum," he ordered.

She wished she could say no. Instead she knelt along with the other midwife.

"Spread your legs," Hanna said.

And Rebecca Nurse did, closing her eyes against the humiliation.

* * *

Tituba woke to the sound of a single voice. She was groggy and tired, thinner than she'd ever been, and she'd been sleeping a lot since Sarah Osborn died. Tituba had also heard a lot of prayers down here, but not one spoken with such confidence.

"Show me Tenderness, and I shall find God there." The voice belonged to Rebecca Nurse. Tituba sat up and peered around the woman beside her.

Rebecca Nurse was in the center of the cell, her white hair messed, her clothing slightly askew. "Show me Mercy, and I shall find God there. Show me Reason, and I shall find God there."

The prisoners next to Rebecca exchanged a look. Tituba watched them, then saw the outspoken Susannah Martin frown.

"Goody Nurse," Susannah said, " 'tis not a Puritan's prayer."

Rebecca looked at her with the calm that she had been displaying all along. " 'Tis no one's prayer but my own."

"That is blasphemy." Susannah sounded concerned. "God shall strike you."

"No, child," Rebecca said. " 'Tis people who punish. Not God. God is that which finds forgiveness and understanding when others cannot. I see that now."

Tituba smiled and wished she could go to Rebecca, but her chains did not allow it. That was what Tituba had always believed. Too bad it had taken such an extreme measure to show a good Puritan woman the same thing.

From the darkness in the back of the cell, another woman said, "Show me a bar of good lye soap, and I shall find God there."

The prisoners laughed, Tituba joining them. When was the last time she had laughed? It felt good, even down here.

"Yes," Rebecca said, smiling, "even in that small thing. Soap. That is where God is. He is all around us, and within us."

She stroked Susannah's face tenderly. Susannah leaned into the touch.

"Show me laughter," Rebecca said, "and I shall find God there."

For the first time since she had left Barbados, Tituba felt as if she were in a true church. She sat up and listened.

"Show me my children," another woman said.

"And I shall find God there," Rebecca and the others finished for her.

"Show me hope," Rebecca said.

Tituba added her voice to the chorus: "And I shall find God there."

THIRTY-ONE

She felt unclean, and not just because she hadn't washed in weeks. Mary Lacey allowed herself to be led into the best room of the minister's house. She had forgotten how it felt to be in a civilized place with tea on the table and chairs in a semicircle.

She could see that the house had been hastily cleaned. She certainly never would have let a place have corners that filthy, but that had been in the past, before she had been imprisoned, before they had forced her to live in her own dirt for months.

The afflicted girls sat in a group, and Ann Putnam sat with them. The girls were silent, but Mary Lacey looked on them with fright. They had so much power. Did they know they had that much power?

Thomas Putnam, a man who once wouldn't have even looked at her, helped her to a chair. Reverend Parris sat across from her with Reverend Stoughton beside him.

She still dreamed about Reverend Stoughton's face, his look of triumph on the gallows when she had pled to being a witch. She hadn't intended to—she wasn't one, not really; she'd always been a good, religious woman—but something inside her would not let them tighten that noose around her neck. She had confessed almost involuntarily, and somehow that had saved her life.

"Mary Lacey," Reverend Stoughton said, "we have brought you out of prison for this day to help you save your soul."

She nodded, then looked down. She didn't want to look at his face more than she had to. Part of her suspected him of wanting there to be witches, wanting this awfulness to continue forever.

"Tell us of your work for the Devil," he said.

"Thou hast already asked me." She did not want to repeat the lies she had told him just after the others had hanged. It wasn't that she could barely remember them—although that was true—it was that if she continued to lie, she would be committing a real sin, a sin before God.

And then there was that other factor, the one she had thought of when they brought her back to prison. At some point, he might ask for the names of more witches, and she might have to give them. Would it be murder if she sent other people to

301

their deaths—people she knew had no ties to witchcraft?

"Again." Reverend Stoughton's tone brooked no disagreement.

"He came to me," she said, trying to remember what she had said when she was so distraught, "the Devil, as a black bird."

Reverend Stoughton frowned. "Did you not say it was yellow?"

"Oh, yes, yellow." They would catch her in these lies and take her back to those gallows. And she could not bear that. She repeated, with a bit more strength, "It was yellow."

"And?"

"He said he would tear me to pieces if I did not sign his book and serve him. I had no choice. And afterward, I had the Devil's gift of being able to afflict people."

"And who else, Mary Lacey?" he asked.

Here was the question. She did not know how to answer it. She just stared at him as if she did not understand him.

"Who else rides with you?" he asked.

If only she knew names that had already been called—not just the ones in prison, but other names, things the girls had said recently. Maybe then God would not see what she was doing as a sin. But she had no other names.

She was alone, and everything rested on a single answer.

* * *

"Who else rides with you?" William Stoughton asked.

Thomas Putnam felt a tension throughout his entire body. He knew whom he believed to be evil in Salem Village. He clasped his hands together. His daughter watched him, a forlorn expression on her little face.

"What are the names of the witches and wizards that you know?"

The girl wasn't looking at anyone. Until she had given her first answer, Putnam wondered if she had been in her right mind. She had seemed so frightened when she first entered, and those screams she had emitted on the gallows seemed to have come from a place he could not understand.

"Do not be afraid, Mary." The Reverend Stoughton did not sound comforting. Putnam doubted that the man could sound comforting. But he was trying. "They are our enemies and mean to harm us."

Enemies. Putnam had so many enemies. It seemed the village was filled with them. He shook his head, his lips silently forming the names even though he knew she would not say them.

"Who else?" Reverend Stoughton asked.

"John Proctor."

For a moment, Putnam thought he had spoken aloud. Then he looked at Mary Lacey. She looked just as surprised as he felt. She was looking at the afflicted girls.

"And Israel Porter." His daughter Annie was speaking. She seemed so calm. She never accused when she was calm. "They mean us harm."

And they did mean the family harm. They always had. He gazed at his daughter in stunned amazement, and she returned his look. She had just said the names he had been thinking, only she had made them into witches.

Were the connections in her mind that simplistic, then? Just because someone harmed her family, they were witches? It was a child's solution.

He felt a horror run through him. All those nights he had spoken to Parris in the best room of the farm, his daughter asleep upstairs—or so he thought. Putnam knew how sound carried, and he should have been more cautious.

More than once, he had called those men evil.

"Do these men ride with you?" Reverend Stoughton was still speaking to Mary Lacey. She had yet to respond.

But Annie shot her father a private glance. She was doing him a favor, protecting him in the only way she knew how. And she had no idea how this would protect him. Even if the men survived the accusations, they would have to pay for their jail stays and their sentencing.

Weeks in prison had wiped out rich families before. If Proctor and Porter lost their fortunes, they could no longer oppose Putnam.

He felt a kind of elation, even though he knew this was wrong. But it had gone on for a long time before he knew what was happening. No wonder so many of the accused were his enemies.

It was too late to stop now.

There would be other consequences if he tried to tell the truth—consequences that would destroy his family, which he could not abide.

Subtly, as minutely as possible, he nodded encouragement to his daughter.

She answered for Mary Lacey: "Goodman Proctor would tie us to a whipping post. He is of Satan."

Mary Lacey looked trapped, but Reverend Stoughton was still staring at her. He would not believe Annie if Mary did not back her up.

Mary closed her eyes, for a single moment, as if this proceeding pained her. Then she said, "Maybe."

The word was hesitant. Thomas Putnam found himself holding his breath.

"Maybe I have seen Goodman Proctor."

She did not sound certain.

"And he rides with you?"

"Goodman Proctor," Mary said. "He . . . he . . . yes."

Thomas Putnam let out a small breath, and Annie leaned back in her seat. He tried to suppress the sense of elation he felt, but the best he could do was keep it from showing on his face.

He felt almost as if he had won.

"John and Elizabeth Proctor!" Sheriff Corwin's voice echoed through the door. "I have come to arrest you for the crimes of witchcraft."

John Proctor peered through a window. A large number of constables stood outside his home. Other men were rounding up Proctor's cows and taking his possessions. The prisoner's cart stood nearby.

He felt a sense of quiet horror and inevitability. If only others in Salem Village had signed that petition . . .

The sheriff banged on the door. "You must present yourself."

Proctor pulled the door open and stepped out. This was an outrage, and everyone knew it. The sheriff looked surprised at Proctor's fury.

"You shall not."

"Where is your wife?" Sheriff Corwin asked. "You are both—"

"For the grace of God," Proctor said, his horror deepening. He had suspected that he might be arrested for that petition, but she hadn't signed. "She has done nothing."

He tried to pull the door closed so that they couldn't see his wife, but the constables grabbed him. He struggled.

"They shall not accuse my wife when they mean to harm me," he said, fighting as hard as he could. "No!"

The constables had trouble holding him. He felt one of them strike him, and then he heard something that made his heart sink.

"John?" Elizabeth's voice was clear behind him.

The fighting stopped just for a moment, as he turned. She stood there with several of their children, looking confused.

"Get inside, Elizabeth," he said.

He should have taken the family somewhere. They should have left Salem when things got bad, but he had believed in the power of reason.

What a fool he had been.

"Take me, leave her," he said. " 'Tis I who opposed them."

"You are under arrest, Goody Proctor," the sheriff said.

"Get inside," he shouted to his wife, then to the constables. "Do not touch her."

The constables moved toward Elizabeth. John wrestled with the strength of ten men and finally freed himself, standing in front of her.

"You cannot," he said. "She is pregnant with child."

"Remove their things," he said.

"Father!" William ran out of the house to help, but of course it was too late. The constables grabbed him instead of Elizabeth. Two more pushed at the front door, and Elizabeth shooed the other children inside, to get them out of harm's way.

Even as she did that, the constables grabbed her.

"Do not hurt the children," she said. "John, they are taking everything."

"We are confiscating your belongings to pay for your prison term."

"How dare you!" he said, as the remaining constables overpowered him. He couldn't fight any longer.

They managed to drag him to the prisoner's cart and chain him there, along with his eldest son and his wife.

He no longer tried to beg, even though he didn't know what would become of his children. The youngest was barely toddling, and without William, the oldest wasn't even fifteen.

Maybe someone would take pity on them. But who would have enough courage to help his family now?

THIRTY-TWO ☉

John Proctor stood in the accused's spot. All of his demands had gone unmet. No one had sent for the Governor. No one had listened to his cries of innocence. No one had listened to his pleas to set his wife free.

He had spent too much time in that jail cell already, and he could scarcely believe the turn in his fortunes. Just because he had dissented.

Just because he had pointed out the truth.

From this spot in the meeting house, the travesty seemed even worse. The afflicted girls, falling over each other and screaming, didn't seem so much in fits as putting on performances. And the magistrates seemed to enjoy their power.

Besides, Proctor could have sworn he saw a faint

smile on Thomas Putnam's face when he had glanced in that direction. The man was enjoying this, even though his daughter was one of the afflicted.

As she lay on the floor now, froth around her mouth, she barely looked human.

He could see how the other accused had felt intimidated by this, with all the noise and the screaming and the roar of the crowd. But he was not. He was not intimidated by anything.

He could shout as loud as any of them.

He pointed at the girls and yelled, "Lies! All of it!"

The so-called reverend, William Stoughton, did not seem to appreciate Proctor's opinion. As if that mattered to John Proctor. He wanted out of here, and he would fight until he got his wish.

"Do you not see them suffering?" Stoughton shouted. "Right now! Your specter torments them!"

"I see them lying," Proctor said. "All of them, in concert!"

The girls continued to writhe and shout. When he accused them of lying, their "affliction" got worse. It seemed to him that anyone who was truly afflicted wouldn't be bothered by an accusation.

Proctor was about to say so when Stoughton yelled, "I shall prove they are not! Annie Putnam, rise and approach your tormentor!"

Of course he would pick the Putnam girl. Daughter of his enemy and, from all accounts, the person who had damned him to this place.

Samuel Parris helped the child up so that she could walk toward John Proctor. Even with Parris beside her, she could barely manage to cross the floor.

Her head lolled back, her eyes were spinning, her arms were flailing. John Proctor had seen all of his children do such things—when they were two years old and wanting attention.

"By this test, we shall see," Stoughton was saying, more for the gathered crowd than for John Proctor.

These "tests" were as flawed as the spectral evidence. Anyone with half a brain could see that. But apparently, the congregation of Salem did not have half a brain.

Proctor did not know what he could say about the test, even though he didn't yet know what it was. If he accused them of falsifying evidence before anything happened, they would say he had altered the test. If he asked for another, not the daughter of his enemy, then they would say that he wanted someone under his evil power to test him.

He was in a difficult place no matter what they chose to do.

As Parris brought Annie closer, Stoughton explained his so-called test. "Touch him, Annie!"

"No! No!" Annie shouted. "I cannot! He shall kill me!"

Proctor frowned. He wouldn't kill her. But he'd love to get his hands on her father, for the things Thomas Putnam had done to his family.

"If indeed his specter is tormenting you," Stoughton said, "by your touch, you will be rid of his evil."

"No! Help me!" Annie said, seeming to fight. "He is strangling me! He orders me not to touch. No!"

Parris dragged her closer, holding her hand out. She was putting up quite a fight.

Of course, the test was invalid even before it happened. Stoughton had already told her the result he wanted, and Annie Putnam, faker that she was, would give him what he wanted.

The girls gave people like Stoughton a great deal of power, and none of them wanted to lose it.

"Touch him!" Stoughton shouted.

Writhing and shaking, Annie approached. Parris forced her flailing hand closer, closer. . . .

And finally she reached out for John Proctor. He watched her, knowing what she would do. But the rest of the congregation didn't seem to know. They were holding their collective breath.

And, at the moment of touch, she stilled.

She seemed perfectly normal now.

Just as William Stoughton had told her she should be.

Then Annie's eyes opened and looked right into John Proctor's. Her expression was level and calm, but beneath it, he saw something else. Anger? Fear?

Hatred?

Proctor shook his head. Putnam had taught his child to hate unnecessarily.

All around them, the crowd erupted into shouts and screams. Then a commotion caught Proctor's eye. Israel Porter rushed toward Stoughton.

312

Constables caught him before he reached the bench.

"This is insanity!" Israel Porter shouted.

He was right, but no one else seemed to be paying attention to him. Stoughton was too intent on continuing his little game.

Proctor shook his head slightly. No sense in getting Porter into trouble.

"John Proctor," Stoughton was saying over the shouts of the crowd, "you are guilty of afflicting great hurt and committing sundry acts of witchcraft upon the bodies of Mercy Lewis, Beth Hubbard, May Walcott—"

"I have hurt no one!" John Proctor shouted.

Israel Porter kept struggling with the constables. "He is on trial for being in opposition to that family."

Israel managed to get an arm free, and he pointed. The entire congregation looked in the direction of his finger.

Israel Porter was pointing to Thomas and Ann Putnam, sitting in the Putnam pew along with their brothers (all but Joseph), cousins, and other relatives. Thomas tensed as this accusation was made, but he did not move. Ann nervously looked at her husband as if they'd been caught at something.

Then she looked at John Proctor and shook her head slightly. He didn't know what it meant, except that he was doomed. They weren't going to admit guilt. They were too holy for that.

But the congregation was entertained. They

shouted and talked and speculated, while John Proctor stood before them, trying to fight for his life.

Lizzy Putnam had taken it upon herself to clean Reverend Parris's house. Someone had to; the man had been living in filth since his wife left him. She had to admit that she had an ulterior motive: she wanted to do as many good deeds as she could before the baby was born. She had to protect both their souls.

Lizzy didn't tell Joseph about her cleaning. He wouldn't approve, particularly this late in her pregnancy. He hardly wanted her to move around now that the baby was due at any moment. But Puritan women worked in the home, theirs or someone else's, until travail, and although Lizzy had been feeling poorly of late, that shouldn't stop her from taking care of her duties.

She had a bit of a walk to the Parris house. All morning her back had plagued her. She was aching and tired. She would do what she could and leave early. Reverend Parris was grateful when she just cleaned his desk and made the bed. Perhaps that was all she would do.

Little pains stabbed at her as she walked—false labor, her mother said, when Lizzy had complained of the same thing days before—and she was determined to ignore them.

It was a beautiful day, and she didn't have to be inside the meeting house. The trials had been suspended for a few days after John Proctor had made a spectacle of himself, accusing children of lying before God.

She was nearly to the Putnam farm when a pain ripped through her unlike anything she had ever felt. She nearly collapsed, and she forced herself to breathe as Hanna Morse had taught her.

Then the pain passed, and Lizzy stood. She crossed to the nearest fence, and another pain gripped her, followed by a flood of water between her legs.

She had attended enough births to know what that meant. She was in labor, and she was far from home.

She gripped the fence and cried, "Goodwife Putnam! Help me!"

The door opened, and Ann Putnam stood there, looking frail. Then she saw Lizzy and her mouth opened slightly.

"Oh, child," Goody Putnam said, and hurried across the yard as another pain gripped Lizzy. "We'll get you inside. Now."

Joseph arrived home in the middle of the day to find his wife gone. He had no idea why she would leave the house so close to her lying in, but it worried him.

He took the buggy and headed out, determined to find her.

He'd already been searching the village for some time when he came across a crowd of people gathered near the square. He stopped the buggy and leaned off the buckboard. He couldn't see what the people were looking at, and he didn't care.

"Have you seen my wife?" he asked.

Most people shook their heads except for one man, who said, "This morning. I told her she should not be walking so far from home in her condition."

"Where?" Joseph asked, picking up the reins.

"She was approaching the Reverend Parris's home."

Joseph thanked him, clucked at the horses, and started forward. As he passed the crowd he realized what they were looking at.

William Proctor, John's eldest son, was tied neck to heels. It was a form of torture. Blood gushed from his mouth and nose. The Reverend William Stoughton stood over him, saying, "Confess, William Proctor!"

"I have nothing to confess," William managed.

Joseph shook his head, wishing he could get involved. But he had to find Lizzy. She shouldn't be out in her condition, and he had been a fool to leave her alone.

The newborn's cry made Ann Putnam's heart ache. In her last three travails, she had not heard that beautiful sound.

Lizzy Putnam held her child against her breast, looking down. Lizzy's hair was in tangles and sweat still stained her face, but she looked lovely. She was propped up in Ann's bed, smiling.

"Will she cry like this for a long time?" Lizzy was such a new mother that she hadn't even recognized the beginning of her labor. That was what had brought her to Ann's door.

Ann had assisted with several childbirths, but she had never conducted one on her own. Fortunately, Lizzy's first was not traditional. It hadn't taken the entire day, the way most first babies did. From the moment Ann got Lizzy into the house to the moment the babe emerged couldn't have been more than an hour.

Ann could not answer the question. She didn't want to think about the child more than she had to.

"You must rest," Ann said. "You cannot stay."

She began pulling up the soiled linens and cleaning the room. Even though the birth had been quick, they had made a mess.

The baby finally quieted, and Ann felt her shoulders relax. She enjoyed silence for the first time since Lizzy Putnam had invaded their house.

"I have been mistaken, Goody Putnam," Lizzy said.

Ann glanced over, careful to avoid the baby's face. But Lizzy was looking directly at it, tracing the child's features with her fingers.

"It is not possible that this being is of sin. She is perfect," Lizzy said. "She is naught but innocence embodied. She is radiant with it. I fear Reverend Parris is wrong in what he has told us."

Ann felt her tension grow. "Do not speak such words."

Lizzy raised her head, a slight frown on her forehead. "Do you believe the Reverend, Goody Putnam? That we are born guilty?"

"Do not ask me."

"Do you?"

Ann turned away. "Yes, I believe it."

"Look at her," Lizzy said.

Ann couldn't.

But that didn't seem to stop Lizzy. "How could you believe she is not innocent?"

"Because," Ann said quietly. "They grow into us."

She carried the linens toward the door. Once she had a pile, she would start filling the wash bucket, so that nothing was permanently stained.

"Won't you look at her, Goody Putnam?"

Why wouldn't Lizzy leave her alone?

"Please?"

The simple honesty in Lizzy's voice made Ann still. She turned, and looked at the infant.

A flood of emotions rose to the surface: the first time she'd held her own child—Annie, her little face red and chapped from childbirth, her features squinched as she screamed her displeasure at coming into the world. Nathaniel, placid even then, looking around as if he were in a marvelous new place.

And the other three, the lost three.

Ann walked toward Lizzy almost as if she were in a dream. She had two live babies and three dead ones. Not all babies died. Her niece—Lizzy's child—was alive and healthy.

Lizzy smiled at her, and Ann reached out her finger, carefully stroking the baby's downy cheek.

Lizzy was right. This was a miracle. An innocent miracle.

Reverend Parris had lied to her. Babies were not evil and born of sin. They were precious little miracles, given to make this world bearable.

"Do you see?" Lizzy said. "Whatever we grow into, whatever mistakes we make, we still have this inside of us. Somewhere."

Ann nodded, feeling the baby's cheek, longing for the child in her arms. How wrong she had been about everything. How had she let things get so twisted? She was not certain.

Then a banging on the door startled her. She looked up, realizing that she had tears on her cheeks. Lizzy gave her a cautious smile and then hugged her daughter, who had started whimpering from the strange noise.

The banging happened again, louder, and Ann hurried to the door.

Joseph Putnam rushed in. "I have heard she is here. Is she?"

"Yes," Ann said, "And you have a child."

He rushed past her so fast that she wasn't even sure he had heard her. He hurried into the wrong room, where Annie and Nathaniel played by candlelight. Annie gave her mother a guarded look. Ann should have come to her the moment the baby was born. She had forgotten how frightened Annie had become at the stillbirth last fall.

Joseph stopped, confused, looking for his wife. Before he headed into a different room, Ann caught his jacket.

"You must beware," she said.

He was in a panic. "Why? What happened to her?"

"No," Ann said, touched by his concern for his wife. Thomas hadn't even stayed in the house for the last birth. "Not of Lizzy. For yourself. I fear that you will be cried out against."

He stared at Ann, all emotion gone from his face. "Are you threatening me?"

"No," Ann said, "I am trying to save you." And that child who lay in her mother's arms in Ann's bed. This new family, whatever the problems they had, had to remain together.

Ann let go of his jacket. "You should take her now, before your brother returns home."

She nodded toward the room where Lizzy was, and Joseph rushed in. Then Ann turned and saw the expression on Annie's face.

Annie looked dangerous.

Joseph opened the door to his brother's bedroom. What irony to find his wife here with their child.

Lizzy looked radiant. The baby slept in her arms. She smiled at Joseph, and for the first time in months, she seemed to be free of fear.

He walked to her side and looked at his daughter in silent awe. They were both all right. They had survived.

"You may touch her," Lizzy said. "Both of us."

Joseph took his wife and his daughter in his arms, pulling them close, kissing Lizzy tenderly. No one would take this family from him. If he had to disappear once they cried out against him, he would.

His little family would always be safe.

"I am taking you home now," Joseph said.

"Yes," Lizzy said with a smile. "Home."

And together, they cradled their daughter close.

THIRTY-THREE

Ann Putnam stood on Gallows Hill, watching the local children run alongside the prisoners' cart. They were taunting the people inside: two women she did not recognize, Susannah Martin, Sarah Good, John Proctor, and Rebecca Nurse.

Rebecca Nurse's presence made Ann's heart sink. It was her fault that Rebecca Nurse was there. Twice Ann had repaid kindness with extreme cruelty.

She did not know how to repent of that sin.

The crowd ignored the little children, screaming at the prisoners to roast in hell. Even Thomas seemed oblivious. And the ministers let it continue.

How did children go from being innocent creatures, like the babe Ann had seen in Lizzy Putnam's arms, to this? Screaming with unbridled hatred at people they didn't even know.

"Thou shalt die for Satan!" a little boy yelled, his face twisted with fury.

"Thou shalt die for Satan, witch," cried Ann's daughter, Annie. Ann flinched. She knew how they had come to this place—she had been part of it. Her own self-absorption, her own unwillingness to question the world around her, had led them all here.

The cart stopped beneath the scaffold. Reverends Stoughton and Parris stood on it with the hangman. Thomas watched everything as if it had no effect on him at all.

The unloading of the prisoners, the ceremonial leading of them to the scaffold, the dropping of the rope. He did not seem to feel any of it.

Ann had begged him to let her and the girls stay home, but he had not allowed it. He hadn't even brooked any discussion. They had to be beneath the hanging tree, he had said, because they were Puritans in good standing.

As if that still meant something.

The now-familiar ritual began. William Stoughton started with Sarah Good. She no longer looked like anyone Ann recognized. Her form was emaciated. Ann had heard that a baby of Sarah's had died in prison.

And her little daughter was in prison now. Four-year-old Dorcas, who had tried to comfort Ann's daughter.

Repaying kindness with cruelty.

Ann was so overwhelmed by guilt that she missed Stoughton's question, although she knew what he had asked. Instead, she heard Sarah Good's voice, undiminished by the prison ordeal:

"You are a liar. I am no more a witch than you are a wizard."

"Is that your confession?" Stoughton asked.

"If you take my life away," Sarah Good said, "God will give you blood to drink."

Angrily, Stoughton nodded to the hangman, who placed the noose around Sarah Good's neck. Ann winced. With Sarah gone, who would care for Dorcas?

Stoughton didn't seem to care. He had moved to his next victim.

"John Proctor," Stoughton said, "I shall give you one last opportunity to confess your crime."

Proctor, Ann's husband's enemy, took a step forward and spoke to the gathered crowd, not to Stoughton. "I shall neither confess an act that I have not done, nor proclaim my innocence. There is naught you wish to hear from me beyond the accusations that ring in your own head. I shall admit only that I am not ready to die."

The crowd became quiet at this. Some shifted uneasily. One of the little children started to shout, but a parent pulled the child close.

Mary Warren, Proctor's servant, pregnant and in tears, moved toward the hanging tree. Ann looked at her and realized with a shock that all the Proctor children except William were there.

She wanted to make them go home. No one should see their father die like this, particularly little children like most of the Proctor brood.

"Mary," John Proctor said, "tell Elizabeth this will not take her from me. Tell her to believe that."

"Papa!" one of the little children cried out.

The crowd looked stunned. Ann reached for Thomas's hand but did not find it.

For the first time, Proctor looked sad, as if he wanted to reach out to his children and bring them close.

"We shall pray!" Reverend Parris shouted, as if he were trying to break the mood.

But John Proctor, who seemed to know he had the crowd's attention, turned to Parris.

"Only God can giveth and taketh away, Samuel Parris," Proctor said. "Yet on this hour I shall end my days because you have taken God's role upon yourself. Do not expect my last thoughts to be rancorous against you. They are not. I have already forgiven you, for I know you will have your own God to answer to one day."

Parris looked stunned. Beside Ann, Thomas shifted, as if Proctor had spoken those words to him.

"Instead I shall pray, up to the final moment of my being, that we who stand before you today are the last innocent blood to be spilt upon this hill."

Proctor himself nodded to the hangman, yet the hangman seemed uncertain. He turned to Stoughton, but Stoughton was watching the crowd.

The crowd was murmuring, talking. The sense of

voyeurism that always accompanied these events was gone.

Ann wondered if Proctor's words might come true. Maybe they would be set free. She felt something odd and realized that it was the beginning of hope.

Then Samuel Parris stepped forward.

"He is guilty," Parris shouted, trying to regain control. "Do you not see the Black Man beyond his shoulder? Whispering in his ear?"

Parris turned to the hangman and said, "Do it!"

The command seemed almost obscene. After a moment, the hangman came forward and slipped the noose around John Proctor's neck.

Ann could not look at him any longer. As she started to turn away, her gaze fell on Rebecca Nurse. The older woman, gaunt like Sarah Good, still had her dignity.

And, to Ann's surprise, Rebecca Nurse was reciting the Lord's Prayer.

"Let Thy Kingdom come," she said. "Thy will be fulfilled, as well in Earth, as it is in Heaven."

Her voice carried in the silence. Ann remembered reciting that prayer in this very place with Rebecca Nurse at her side, remembered the strength of the old woman as she had held Ann, trying to prevent her from saying things that would get her accused as a witch.

Repaying kindness with cruelty.

This time, Ann didn't even try to pray.

Rebecca did not look at her. "Give us this day our daily—"

"Rebecca Nurse," Parris snapped, "you have been excommunicated. Thou hast no God to pray to. You are condemned to an eternity in Hell."

"—and forgive us our trespasses, even as we forgive our trespassers—"

"She is innocent!"

The voice that interrupted the prayer was male. Ann looked for it, saw Samuel Nurse, Rebecca's son. He was standing at the base of the tree, looking as powerful as John Proctor had.

Samuel Nurse shouted. "Let it stop! This is wrong!"

And it was wrong. Ann clasped her hands together. Constables grabbed Samuel Nurse, but he kept shouting.

When they finally silenced him, Ann realized someone else had been speaking too. Reverend Parris.

"It cannot be wrong," he said, but he did not sound certain. Ann remembered using that tone when she had realized what she had done. Parris frowned. "We cannot doubt. We will have but the void of Hell if we doubt ourselves now. God is not wrong."

Ann bit her lower lip. She knew what he was doing. He was talking himself back into his resolve. If he didn't—if he believed everything they'd done was wrong—then he was about to murder innocent people.

"Rebecca Nurse," he shouted, "thou shall not pray!"

"Let her finish!" someone yelled.

Stoughton whirled toward Parris as if the unknown heckler had awakened him from a dream. Ann saw the panic on Stoughton's face.

"Hang them now!" Stoughton shouted.

Ann could not contain herself any longer. She stepped forward. It was time to take a stand.

Past time.

"Let her finish!" Ann shouted. "She cannot be a witch. She has made no mistakes!"

Thomas grabbed her shoulders and pulled her back, but Ann shook him off.

" 'Tis I who made the mistake!" she cried.

William Stoughton looked at Ann as if she were the Devil herself. Then he shook a hand at the hangman. "Do it! Finish!"

The hangman hung back. This was clearly against protocol.

Rebecca Nurse had not stopped praying. ". . . And lead us not into temptation, but deliver us from evil . . ."

Annie was watching her mother. The afflicted girls were quiet, and Ann could see how confused her daughter was.

Apparently, so could Parris. He turned toward Rebecca. "You have no God, Rebecca Nurse!"

Of all the things to say to her, this was the worst. Rebecca was a pious woman.

"Stop it!" Ann shouted. "She is innocent!"

". . . for Thine is the Kingdom and the power . . ."

"Finish it!" Stoughton shouted at the hangman. "Now!"

"No!" Ann shouted. "She is innocent."

The hangman put the noose around Rebecca Nurse's neck.

". . . and the glory . . ."

All of the prisoners wore nooses now. They seemed comforted by Rebecca's voice.

". . . forever . . ."

The hangman pulled the lever, and the trap opened.

The prisoners dropped.

Ann screamed. And Thomas grabbed her, pulling her away from the hanging tree, silencing her.

As they went down Gallows Hill, she turned to him. "Oh, Thomas," she said. "Who will forgive us now?"

THIRTY-FOUR

Ann paced in the best room of her house. Thomas had made dinner with the help of Mercy, Annie, and Nathaniel. Ann would not do the work. She had to think.

She had to plan.

She had to bring this all to an end. She just didn't know how.

And she was too late to save Rebecca Nurse or Bridget Bishop. And all the others. Sarah Good. What if they hung little Dorcas? What then?

" 'Tis true, 'tis true," Ann muttered to herself, " 'tis a horrible sin. Hear my remorse, hear it, hear it, please God, 'tis true."

"Enough, Ann," Thomas said.

She turned to him. He wanted her to be quiet, but

she could not. She had to speak. " 'Tis I who should be hanging from that tree."

Nathaniel and Annie looked at her in horror.

"Mama?" Nathaniel asked.

"You are frightening them," Thomas said.

"We should be frightened," she said. "What have we done? An innocent woman died today because of me. And you."

"Ann, stop it!"

"No!" she said. "You stop it. A man died today because he opposed you. That is not a crime before God, opposing you. And the others, as he said, you are the root of it, aren't you?"

In a swift motion, Thomas pulled her away from the listening children. He pushed her toward the wall, holding her arms down in an attempt to calm her. His face was close to hers as he whispered, "Do you know what you are saying?"

She did not whisper in return. "Salem Village is being cleansed of your enemies. Israel Porter was right!"

"Stop it, Ann."

"Do you deny it?"

He shook her to get her to listen, but she wasn't going to agree with him. Not anymore. He could beat her if he wanted to, but she would not participate in this travesty any longer.

"I will stop it," she said. "If it means I hang for it, I shall stop this. I shall speak out."

He leaned in ferociously. "Ann, you are not the only one who will hang if you speak out now!"

She frowned. He stared at her as if he expected her to understand. And then, after a moment, she did.

Her horror increased. "Annie?"

She looked across the room at the children. Annie and Mercy were staring at her, wide-eyed with fear.

Ann couldn't just confess. That would doom all of the afflicted girls.

She had to find another way.

William Stoughton rode alongside the cart filled with the afflicted girls. He couldn't have been more pleased with the way the day had gone.

It had started poorly; Ann Putnam had refused to let her daughter and maid accompany them. It had been her husband who had finally placed them in the cart, but then the trip to Andover had been a success. More than sixty witches identified, and the reverend from Topsfield desired their appearance as soon as they were able.

The girls were becoming strong witch hunters.

And they did not seem to be distracted by the adoration of the crowds, people who now followed the cart as it came back into the village. The girls knew their mission, and Stoughton knew his.

There were witches all over Massachusetts, declaring war against Puritanism, but the Puritans were winning.

Because they had God on their side.

William Stoughton sat in Samuel Parris's best room, Thomas Putnam beside him. Parris wished they would stop meeting in his house. Lizzy Putnam hadn't been here since she had her child. In fact, he hadn't seen Lizzy or Joseph since that day, hearing only of the child through the story of Ann, who had helped with the birth.

Not that it mattered. Parris's entire life was in chaos. He hadn't had word from his wife. He didn't know what was happening with his daughter, and no one in the church listened to him anymore.

He didn't approve of taking the girls to other villages. He had gone with Stoughton under protest. Since Rebecca Nurse had been accused, Parris had been questioning everything.

The fact that she had recited the Lord's Prayer so clearly and so faultlessly terrified him still.

Stoughton could sense his change of heart, even though Parris hadn't spoken of it. Stoughton continually tried to draw Parris back into the fold.

"I believe we owe a debt of gratitude to Reverend Parris as well," Stoughton was saying. "Without his work here in Salem we would not be where we are."

It was a curse, a condemnation, not a compliment. But Parris seemed to be the only person in the room who realized it.

"Samuel," Putnam asked, "are you not well?"

There was no honest way to answer the question, so Parris didn't even try.

Tituba sat near Dorcas Good, trying to feed her. It took most of the day to get the girl to eat anything. She had stopped speaking when her mother left.

333

And now, chained to the wall, her eyes roving in every direction, she had clearly gone insane.

Tituba had no hope for the child any longer. Even death would be kinder than this. The child—a sweet innocent thing a few months ago—was an empty shell now.

She had seen too many awful things, and they had broken her.

And Tituba feared that this—the loss of this child—would break Tituba as well.

The idea had come to Ann on the trip to Andover while her daughter was being put through her paces, declaring people to be witches whenever William Stoughton told her to.

If Ann's confession would condemn her own child, then Ann would not confess. At least not in the way Thomas feared. Ann had finally found a way to stop this madness and to protect her family.

But it would cause her daughter some pain first.

Ann sat down beside Annie's bed. Her daughter slept soundly, Mercy beside her. They looked like little angels, so sweet and innocent.

Ann wanted to touch Annie's face, but she did not. Annie couldn't awaken. Not yet. Not before Ann did some play-acting of her own.

"Forgive me, child," she said softly.

She let her own distress build, remembering how it felt to lose control of herself when she had condemned Rebecca Nurse, letting free all those trapped emotions.

Ann started mumbling, slid into gibberish just as she had seen her daughter do, and then tilted her head back, and screamed as she had never screamed before.

She had to wake the village—or at least try.

The entire Putnam farm was filled with screams and cries and moans. Samuel Parris did not want to enter, so he turned to Thomas Putnam, who had fetched him.

"Is her crisis as it was before?" Parris asked.

"It's worse I fear, Reverend Parris," Thomas Putnam said. "I will not lose her to Satan."

Parris took a deep breath, hoping he had enough strength for this. He let Putnam lead him into the best room.

" 'Tis the way I left them," Putnam said.

Annie and Mercy were writhing on the floor, moaning and crying out.

But Ann was at the center of the room—Ann, who screamed so horribly that Parris wanted to cover his ears.

Ann, who had clearly become one of the afflicted.

THIRTY-FIVE

Sir William Phips heard his assistant enter the room before he saw him. Phips was trying to write a missive to the Crown, letting the King know that everything was fine in Massachusetts, but the lies were not coming easily. There was so much that needed work, but nothing that the Crown could help him with, so he didn't even want to ask.

Phips's assistant was in a state. The man could get riled up about nothing, and Phips had told him he did not want to be disturbed.

So Phips did not look up. Finally his assistant said, "The afflicted girls of Salem Village have cried out again, sir. We received this."

Phips continued writing. "It should be directed to the Reverend Stoughton."

"Sir? You should look at this."

Something in his assistant's tone made him look up. Phips snatched the paper from his assistant's hand.

The list of accused witches was long and included some of the most prominent names in Massachusetts. Phips's stomach turned, and then he saw one name that rose up above all the others.

"Oh, good God!" he said, and stood up.

For the first time in the courtroom, Ann Putnam sat with the afflicted as one of them. Although she was not afflicted, she put on a very good act. After all, she had watched Annie for all these months.

Ann was nervous. The meeting house was quiet except for the mumbled prayers that Reverend Stoughton was trying to lead them in. Ann listened for the sound of carriages outside, knowing that the newly accused would be showing up today.

They had sent word of their arrival.

Her hands were sweating, and her mouth was dry. This was a risk, but it was the only one she could take.

Then she heard them: the carriage wheels, the whinny of the teams as their drivers forced them to stop. There was a moment of silence, and then the meeting house door banged open.

Ann turned. A string of dignitaries entered, including the Governor, Sir William Phips. Beside him walked a lovely well-dressed woman. A murmur ran through the congregation. They had not expected this.

But Ann had hoped for it.

May Walcott attempted to fall into a fit, but no one else did, so she quit. The afflicted girls seemed mesmerized by the famous people in their midst.

Phips stopped at the back of the meeting house, forcing everyone to look at him.

The meeting house grew silent, and the silence lingered for what seemed like an eternity.

Then William Stoughton cleared his throat. "The accused usually stands—"

"I believe your work is finished now, Reverend," Phips snapped.

Stoughton did not answer. That surprised Ann. She had expected him to put up more of a fight.

Phips turned to the afflicted girls. "Know thee this woman beside me?"

No one spoke. Ann hoped no one would have to.

"Anyone?" Phips asked.

Guiltily, the girls looked down. But Annie glanced at her mother. Ann continued to watch the Governor.

"She is my wife," Phips said. "Lady Phips. You have claimed that she is the servant of Satan. Which of you cried out her name first?"

None of the girls answered. They were too afraid. Annie clutched at her dress. Ann longed to take her hand but did not.

"I have heard of your afflictions," Phips said. "That you go mute or sightless at will. But you shall not be silent now!"

He took a step closer. "Who first cried out her name?"

He pointed at Annie. "You!"

In surprised fear, Annie stammered. But Ann put her hand on her daughter's shoulder as she stood, silencing her.

"She is innocent," Ann said, facing Phips. "It was I."

He turned to Ann, so much fury in his gaze that she would normally have cringed.

She did not.

"Have you ever laid eyes on my wife before?" he asked.

"No," Ann said.

"And now that you regard her, does she resemble a witch?"

Ann pretended to consider this for a moment. Her plan had worked. The nightmare was finally coming to an end.

She chose her words carefully.

"She seems to be," Ann said, "as much witch as the others."

The crowd gasped. Phips tilted his head at her, as if he were actually seeing her for the first time. He seemed to understand what she was about.

Then he turned away from her and faced the magistrates. His fury had not abated.

"And you, Reverends," he said, almost spitting out the last word, "Tell me. Does my wife resemble a witch in your eyes?"

Stoughton raised his chin and did not speak. But Parris shook his head slightly.

"Perhaps," Parris said, his voice low, yet clear

enough to be heard by all, "we have been deluded by Satan."

Ann Putnam let out a small sigh. She ran her hand over Annie's hair. Annie leaned into her as if she'd always craved affection. Maybe she had. Ann had, so it only made sense that her daughter did. It was time to change, time to show her children that she loved them.

"Deluded by Satan!" Phips sounded appalled. "Is that how you shall have time to remember this sorry episode?"

Parris and Stoughton looked down, humbled at last.

But Phips was clearly not done. "I would say you were deluded by your own fears and weaknesses. And you had the arrogance to call this feeble human delusion God's will?"

Phips turned slowly, facing the entire congregation, drawing all of them in.

"Where was your heart?" he asked. "In your pursuit of godliness and faith, did you ever once press yourselves to heed, if not logic, then simple humanity?"

The impact of his words was instantly apparent. The self-righteousness left the congregation. They too looked down.

Ann pulled Annie closer.

"What horrible forces of this society have so conspired to allow such a perversion of righteousness to take hold and fester here?" he asked. "How have decent men and women followed the shrill, self-righteous call of the falsely powerful and become deaf to the simple voice of their own heart that speaks of decency and kindness and understanding of others?"

Phips's words echoed in the silent meeting house. Ann had asked the same questions throughout the nightmare, but she was getting the beginning of an answer.

They were all at fault—all of them. And she knew, because she had been to Andover and other places in Massachusetts, that such behavior was not unique to Salem.

It happened everywhere—everywhere people stopped listening to their hearts.

AFTERMATH

In January of 1693, Sir William Phips reprieved the sentences of all the remaining convicted witches awaiting execution.

In May of that year, Phips ordered the release from prison of all the accused witches awaiting trial.

Those who could pay their prison fees were released immediately. Samuel Parris refused to pay for Tituba. She was kept in jail until she was sold into a new home.

Because women in that era had few rights and almost no choices, Elizabeth Parris returned to Samuel after the crisis ended, bringing Betty with her. Betty had recovered quickly after leaving Salem, and there is nothing in the historical record that speaks of a relapse.

The in-fighting continued in Salem Village, most of it focused around Samuel Parris and whether or not he deserved to remain as head of the church. The stress took its toll on Elizabeth; always sickly, she contracted a serious illness in January of 1696, and she never recovered. She died in July of 1697.

The epitaph that Samuel Parris composed for his wife is poignant. It reads "Best wife, choice mother, neighbor, friend." In light of the events of 1692, the words "neighbor" and "friend" are particularly sad.

In 1697, Samuel Parris was ousted from the Salem Village church. He moved away and tried employment as a shopkeeper, a teacher, a farmer, and a property speculator. He remarried and had at least one more child, a son. The boy reached manhood but died insane. Parris's daughter, Betty, married and presumably went on to live a full life.

Samuel Parris died—heavily in debt—in 1720.

In the twelve months of the witch hysteria, 156 people were accused of witchcraft, 30 were convicted, and 20 innocent people were killed.

With the exception of one, the afflicted girls disappeared into history. In 1706, Annie Putnam confessed her sins before God and was accepted back into the church of Salem Village.

What this story does not tell you is the true cost of the witch trials in human life, suffering, and damages. In addition to the loss of life and the destruction of families came a hidden cost: the financial one.

Anyone who was imprisoned had to pay for maintenance, fuel, clothes, transportation to and from jail, special court fees, and each piece of paper used in his or her case. The prisoners also had to pay for their discharges from prison.

If the prisoner was executed, other family members had to pay. In some cases, people from other towns had to pay for a loved one's incarceration in Salem.

For decades after the trials, the families of victims appealed to the province of Massachusetts for reparations, and some got them—as many as twenty years later.

Very few of the powerful people involved in the witch hunts apologized, and none were punished for their actions—at least not directly.

Salem Village attempted to go on as if nothing had happened. Soon after the trials ended, the same old fights started up again—but this time, they didn't result in loss of life.

No one knows why most of the accused were women. Theories abound. Misogyny was common in this period, more common than it is now. Legally, women had no standing. They were property, belonging first to their fathers and then to their husbands. Beautiful, desirable women were seen as the Devil's tools, and post-menopausal women, many of whom were widowed, often stepped into a personal power that threatened the men around them.

While misogyny had something to do with the

witchcraft hysteria, it couldn't have caused all the trouble. Other historians theorize that economics had something to do with the accusations. Many of the accused women were single, in a place where women were supposed to subjugate themselves to men. These women were also economically independent and, as a result, often poor. But they made their own decisions and took care of themselves, even when society taught that they weren't capable of such actions.

Women also tended to take care of one another, and some historians believe that this tendency, this unity of women, made the men around them fear a loss of control. The thinking seemed to be that getting rid of the independent women and punishing those who thought for themselves might discourage such behavior in the future.

Indeed, it seemed to discourage independence in the inflicted girls, many of whom went on to have "normal" lives. Apparently, most of them married and had children. Nothing in the historical record speaks to how these girls dealt with their pasts, but one has to assume that their lives could not have been happy ones.

The Salem witch trials marked a turning point in Colonial American history. In some ways, they showed how Americans would react to future threats. This would not be the last time Americans externalized their fears and accused their neighbors of things that did not exist.

The trials also, oddly enough, had one positive

effect. They marked the beginning of a recognized need for rules of evidence in trials. One of the first written rules is bizarre to us now: no spectral evidence. But after seeing how it was used in the witch trials, we know that it is, in some ways, one of the most important.

THE LIST OF VICTIMS

What follows is a list of the victims in the witch hunt. Note that there were 156 victims—some of them entire families. They came from 24 different communities in Massachusetts.

Many confessed to save their own lives. Others fled when they heard they'd been accused. Even the ones who escaped lost everything they owned.

The accused ranged in age from four (yes, poor little Dorcas Good—who lived for many years after her release, completely out of her mind) to their eighties. The victims, though, included newborn infants (like Sarah Good's daughter) and a whole variety of orphaned children, left to fend for themselves.

The names below are taken from the historical record. Generally speaking, the people with only one name are either slaves or babies who were born in prison and died without being named.

In some ways, the toll from the witch trials cannot be accurately measured. The list that follows is just the beginning of the suffering caused by the reaction of the Salem elders to the fits of a few little girls.

EXECUTED VICTIMS

Bridget Bishop
George Burroughs
Martha Carrier
Giles Corey
Martha Corey
Mary Easty
Sarah Good
Elizabeth Howe
George Jacobs
Susannah Martin
Rebecca Nurse
Alice Parker
Mary Parker
John Proctor
Ann Pudeator
Wilmot Redd
Margaret Scott
Samuel Wardwell
Sarah Wildes

VICTIMS WHO DIED IN JAIL

Lydia Dustin
Ann Foster
Unnamed infant of Sarah Good
Sarah Osborn
Roger Toothaker

Arthur Abbot
Sarah Bassett
Sarah Bibber
Mary Black
Mary Bradbury (escaped from prison)
Hannah Bromage
Sarah Buckley
Hannah Carroll
Bethia Carter, Sr.
Bethia Carter, Jr.
Sarah Churchill
Mary Clarke
Rachel Clenton
Sarah Cloyse
Sarah Cole (Village of Lynn)
Sarah Cole (Salem Town)
Mary Colson
Sarah Davis
Day
Mary DeRich
Elizabeth Dicer
Rebecca Dike
Ann Dolliver
Mehitabel Downing
Sarah Dustin
Esther Elwell
Joseph Emons
Thomas Farrer
Edward Farrington

John Flood
Elizabeth Fosdick
Nicholas Frost
Eunice Frye
Dorcas Good
Mary Green
Thomas Hardy
Elizabeth Hart
Rachel Hatfield
Margaret Hawks
Dorcas Hoar
Abigail Hobbs
William Hobbs
John Howard
Elizabeth Hubbard
Francis Hutchens
Mary Ireson
John Jackson, Sr.
Rebecca Jacobs
Abigail Johnson
Rebecca Johnson
John Lee
Mercy Lewis
Jane Lilly
Sarah Morey
Elizabeth Paine
Sarah Parker
Sarah Pease
Joan Penny
Margaret Prince
Benjamin Proctor

Sarah Proctor
Sarah Rice
Abigail Roc
Susannah Roots
Henry Salter
John Sawdy
Ann Sears
Susannah Sheldon
Abigail Somes
Martha Sparks
Mary Taylor
Job Tookey
Jerson Toothaker
Toothaker (daughter of Mary [listed below])
Vincent
Ruth Wilford
Abigail Williams
Mary Withridge

VICTIMS WHO CONFESSED

Abigail Barker
Mary Barker
William Barker, Sr.
William Barker, Jr.
Mary Bridges, Sr.
Mary Bridges, Jr.
Sarah Bridges
Candy (slave)
Andrew Carrier
Richard Carrier

Sarah Carrier
Thomas Carrier, Jr.
Deliverance Dane
Joseph Draper
Rebecca Eames
Martha Emerson
Abigail Faulkner, Jr.
Dorothy Faulkner
Sarah Hawkes
Deliverance Hobbs
John Jackson, Jr.
Margaret Jacobs
Elizabeth Johnson, Sr.
Elizabeth Johnson, Jr.
Stephen Johnson
Mary Lacey, Sr.
Mary Lacey, Jr.
Mary Marston
Mary Osgood
Hannah Post
Susannah Post
William Proctor
Tituba (slave)
Mary Toothaker
Johanna Tyler
Martha Tyler
Mercy Wardwell
Mary Warren
Sarah Wilson, Sr.
Sarah Wilson, Jr.

VICTIMS WHO MANAGED TO ESCAPE

John Alden
Daniel Andrew
Edward Bishop, Jr.
Sarah Bishop
Elizabeth Cary
Elizabeth Colson
Mary English
Philip English
George Jacobs, Jr.

VICTIMS WHO WERE RELEASED OR REPRIEVED

Nehemial Abbot, Jr.
Abigail Faulkner, Sr.
Mary Post
Elizabeth Proctor
Sarah Wardwell

FURTHER READING

Salem Witch Trials is an extremely accurate miniseries that manages to cover, in four hours, one of the darkest periods of American history.

The Salem witch trials were among the most bloody miscarriages of justice that ever happened on this continent. And they created a phrase that we still use today—witch hunt—when we're talking about someone who searches for crimes where there are none.

If you would like to read the history of the witch trials, here are a few books that would be a good start. Most of them read like novels, although a few of the others do show their academic roots.

Also included are some fictional versions of the witch trials and Puritanism. All are classics.

Nathaniel Hawthorne was a direct descendent of one of the judges, so an ancestral guilt floats through his pages. Arthur Miller's *The Crucible* was written during another period of American witch trials: the Army–McCarthy hearings of the 1950s. The only difference: instead of finding witches where there were none, Congress was finding Communists where there none.

Salem and its particular brand of condemnation seem to represent an American theme. Even though these trials happened over three hundred years ago, we can still feel their echo through the centuries.

NONFICTION

Boyer, Paul, and Nissenbaum, Stephen. *Salem Possessed: The Social Origins of Witchcraft*. Cambridge, Mass.: Harvard University Press, 1974.

Demos, John Putnam. *Entertaining Satan: Witchcraft and the Culture of Early New England*. New York: Oxford University Press, 1982.

Hill, Francis. *A Delusion of Satan: The Full Story of the Salem Witch Trials*. New York: Da Capo Press, 1997.

Hoffer, Peter Charles. *The Devil's Disciples: Makers of the Salem Witchcraft Trials*. Baltimore, Md.: The Johns Hopkins University Press, 1996.

Le Beau, Bryan F. *The Story of the Salem Witch Trials*. Upper Saddle River, N.J.: Prentice Hall, 1998.

FICTIONAL ACCOUNTS OF THE SALEM WITCH TRIALS

Hawthorne, Nathaniel. "Alice Doane's Appeal." 1835; in *Short Stories*, ed. Newton Arvin. New York: Vintage Books, 1980.

———. *House of the Seven Gables*. New York: Bantam Classics, 1987.

———. *The Scarlet Letter*. New York: Pocket Books, 1994.

———. "Young Goodman Brown." 1835; in *Short Stories*, ed. Newton Arvin. New York: Vintage Books, 1980.

Longfellow, Henry Wadsworth. *Giles Corey of Salem Farms*. 1868; in *Poems and Other Writings,* ed. J.D. McClatchy. New York: Library of America, 2000.

Miller, Arthur. *The Crucible*. New York: Penguin USA, 1970.